Return *to* DEADWOOD

PAUL HENRY JOHNSON

First Edition

Fulton Books, Inc.
Meadville, PA

First originally published by Fulton Books 2017

ISBN 978-1-63338-659-4 (Paperback)
ISBN 978-1-63338-660-0 (Digital)

Printed in the United States of America

PREFACE

In 1874 the War Department assigned General George Armstrong Custer to an expedition into the Black Hills, Lakota-Sioux Indian country in the Dakota Territory. He was sent there to confirm the rumors of a gold discovery. If those rumors were true, he was instructed to keep the discovery under hat. The United States government had entered into the Treaty of Fort Laramie, which acknowledged and confirmed that the Black Hills belonged to the Indians. Gold, indeed, had been discovered, and the chances of the government keeping the findings quiet were about as good as stopping flying sparks in a windy prairie fire. In 1875, the government met with the Indians to renegotiate the treaty. The Indians weren't at all pleased with the negotiations, and no agreement was reached. After that, the military made no effort to stop people from going into the territory, resulting in an avalanche of gold-seekers. These events birthed the lawless town of Deadwood in the Black Hills.

1

1876

The late afternoon sun glistened off the silver spurs of the tall, lanky stranger. His forearm struck the door of Nuttal and Mann's Saloon in the Black Hills mining town of Deadwood.

Across the street, Steel Madison leaned back against the barn-sided wood wall of the blacksmith's shop. The shop was no more than a small square building, with one side built as a double-flap door that was kept open during working hours. Steel, with a stoic stare, watched the swinging doors of the saloon come to a stop. "A gunfighter. Sometimes I wish I was a gunfighter... like, like that man with the silver spurs and the ivory gun handle," he mumbled.

A cockroach near his feet diverted his attention. Without thinking, he let a stream of tobacco fly from his lips, hitting his target square on. He'd only recently taken up chewing tobacco, a decision born out of frustration and anger. He knew his mother wouldn't approve; however, pretty much all the men in Deadwood were chewing and spitting. At first the taste hadn't been pleasant at all, but now he seemed okay with a chew. Blinded by the dark muck, his target turned wildly in circles. Within seconds it found its bearings and made its way toward a small knothole in the wood siding. Steel's dark, well-worn boot with a silver tip came crashing down. "I hate cockroaches," he grumbled, punctuating the act with another stream of tobacco. *I think I'll close up shop early and head up to the cemetery.*

Steel and his father, Blain, had first gotten wind of a gold discovery in the Black Hills from a young cowboy who was brimming with excitement. Early one July morning, he came by their blacksmith shop riding a good-looking chestnut horse. He reined in his mount and abruptly announced to Blain that he'd just arrived from Georgetown, Colorado. Upon dismounting, he said he was in town only momentarily to tend to some family business, which included getting new shoes on his pa's horse.

"Nice-looking sorrel," Blain said, giving a look at the cowboy's horse. "So you're in our fair city for only a short spell." Blain set down his hammer on a workbench and gave the cowboy his full attention.

"That's right. I'll be returnin' to Georgetown quicker than my ma's cat can lick up a bowl of fresh cream," he said with a grin. "I've been workin' for Charlie Utter, a good friend of Bill Hickok, Wild Bill Hickok. Mr. Utter is taking some thirty wagons, and maybe more, to the mining town of Deadwood in the territory of the Black Hills. Deadwood is in a gulch with a group of dead trees linin' the canyon. That's why they call the place Deadwood."

"Mining town…" Blain said with a thoughtful look.

"Gold! A prospector by the name of Pearson found gold near there on French Creek. Since his findin', the place has gone plum crazy. We're takin' all kinds of supplies, as well as a good bunch of ladies that want to provide services in Deadwood—painted ladies." The cowboy took out a pouch of tobacco and a thin piece of paper from his long-sleeved, plaid shirt pocket. With steady, practiced hands, he quickly had a cigarette rolled. He put the paper to his lips to seal it and then lit the end and inhaled.

"Panning for gold. I envy you. I've always had an itch to try something like that."

Steel, standing nearby, glanced at his father, catching the wishful look in his father's eyes. Not only that, most times his father kept working while he was talking. "A man can lose a lot of good working time if he stops to gab," his father had remarked more than once.

"Call me Red. They call me Red 'cause of my red hair," the cowboy said with a smile.

"I'm Blain Madison, and this is my son, Steel. Pleased to meet you, Red."

Steel gave Red a nod.

Red looked down for a moment, brushed his chin, and then looked up at Blain with a steady look. "You know, Mr. Madison, now that I'm thinkin' about it, I know Mr. Utter could use a good blacksmith or two. I recall he, in fact, mentioned as much while one of his men was working on a broken wagon hitch just a couple of weeks ago."

"Oh?" Blain asked, continuing to give Red his full attention.

Red exhaled and took a moment to watch the ringlets of smoke rise, and then he turned back to Blain with the same steady look. "Mr. Madison, you look as strong as an ox." Blain was an inch shorter than his son's six feet. He was clean-shaven with thinning brown hair that he combed straight back. His barrel chest and strong forearms made him look as if he could do the work of two or three men. Steel was much thinner than his father, but his broad shoulders and muscular arms, along with a handsome face, made him a good-looking specimen. Red turned to Steel. "You about twenty-one, twenty-two?"

"Twenty-two," Steel said, not knowing quite what to think of Red, except he was a fast talker and kind of entertaining.

"I'm only a couple of years your elder. You're a might taller than I am, and lookin' at your arms, I think you'd best me in an arm wrestle." Red turned to Blain. "I bet you've taught him pretty much all you know about being a blacksmith and all that. I can tell you with a certainty, you both would be mighty welcome in Deadwood. I'm downright sure of that, 'cause I know there's not a blacksmith in Deadwood. If you're interested, we're leavin' in three weeks, last week of July—you could do blacksmithin' and gold pannin'. Just get to Georgetown, Colorado, before then. We're settin' out from there. That's where Mr. Utter has his camp."

"Obliged for that invite," Blain said, "but I don't think the missus would take too kindly to Steel and me heading off to pan for gold." Blain hesitated for a moment as if his thoughts were elsewhere. "You're not going to ride that sorrel to Colorado are you?"

Red chuckled. "No, that's my pa's horse. I'll take the train to Kansas City and then switch trains to Denver. My horse, a nice little dapple-gray mare, is stabled in Denver, and I'll ride her to Georgetown."

"How close is Georgetown to Denver?" Blain asked.

"A good day's ride out of Denver. It's sittin' in a pretty little valley in the mountains west of Denver. It's pretty high up. Don't rightly know just how high, but I know some of them older miners have had a hard time breathin' at times. One old boy, Parley, had to just call it quits and get down out of them mountains. I can tell you, they took a whole lot of silver out of that area. They call her the Silver Queen of Colorado, but that's pretty much over now. The excitement is in the Black Hills. Mr. Utter knows what he's doin', I'm convinced of that."

Red tossed the cigarette on the ground and stamped out the burning with the toe of his well-worn black boot. He turned to his horse and gave her a pat on the neck. "My horse—my pa's horse, needs four new shoes. Can you help me out today?"

"We'll be pleased to. You'll have to wait a spell. Have you been to Deadwood?" Blain asked, approaching the sorrel and giving her several strokes on the neck.

"I haven't, but Mr. Utter has several times. For the last three years, I've lived in Denver. Seen a lot of changes there in that time. I'm looking forward to a change in scenery, but I know it don't get much prettier than Denver."

"Are you going to do any gold panning in Deadwood?" Steel asked, thinking he might as well join the conversation, and a little surprised his father was taking so much interest in Red.

"Oh, maybe a little, but I'm not going for the gold. It may sound funny, but I just enjoy workin' for Mr. Utter. He pays me a fair wage."

"Well, let me get started on that horse of yours," Blain said. "We wanna get you out of here so you can get back to Colorado, not that we don't enjoy your company."

2

Steel didn't give Red's words a second thought. It was just a friendly conversation at the blacksmith shop. Leaving his mother to go running off looking for gold in the Black Hills was out of the question. His father might have entertained a momentary wish, but that wish would soon fade.

Upon graduating from the College of Pennsylvania, Steel had gone to work full-time with his father. That was a little over four months ago. He had no intention of making blacksmithing his life's occupation. After a year of working with his father, it was understood that he'd apprentice with his grandfather. An only grandchild, he was well aware that his grandfather was counting on him to step into his shoes and manage the successful retail business his grandfather had built up over the years. Steel wasn't opposed to his grandfather's wishes, and he had, in fact, earned his degree in business with the intention of making the retail business his life's career.

Several days after Red came by the shop, Steel and his father were getting ready to close up for the day. Steel was sweeping up some metal filings while his father worked on a wrought-iron chair.

"I think I'm about finished cleaning up," Steel said. "I'm putting away the broom and hanging up my apron. Do you need any help?"

"No. I'm almost finished with this chair. I know Mr. Neader wants to pick it up first thing tomorrow morning. You know, Steel, I've been doing a might bit of thinking about what that fellow Red said."

Surprised by the comment, Steel turned and approached his father. "Oh? What kind of thinking?"

Blain stopped working and gave Steel a pensive look. "Well... I can see you and me kneeling by a mountain stream, working our pans, and finding yellow dust in the bottom of them pans and maybe even a nugget or two."

Steel chuckled. "That's some thinking. I think they call it wishful."

"If I were to go to Deadwood, would you be willing to come with me?"

"You're not going to Deadwood."

"If I were to go to Deadwood, would you come? I'm serious, would you come? I want an honest answer."

Steel shrugged, not knowing what to say. "I guess I'd go with you... yeah, I'd go, as long as we were back in a year so I could start working for grandfather."

"A year... That would be about right," Blain said thoughtfully. "Steel, I'm thinking of saying something to your mother tonight after dinner," Blain said matter-of-factly as he walked over to the sidewall and hung up his apron.

Steel stood speechless, staring at his father. He ran his fingers through his wavy brown hair. There was no mistaking the look in his father's tobacco-brown eyes. His father wasn't one to joke a lot, and Steel suddenly realized this was no joking matter. "About panning for gold near Deadwood?" he asked.

"That's what I'm thinkin'."

Trying to digest what he'd just heard, Steel took a deep breath and then exhaled, letting his father know that he wasn't jumping with excitement. "That would be something... that would be something. Well, don't get your hopes up. " Steel chuckled now that he thought about it. "I don't see Mother consenting in a raccoon's age." He shook his head, still trying to get the full import of what his father had just said.

Blain set the metal chair upright. "These chairs are ready for Mr. Neader. When I was gone yesterday afternoon and you asked where I was going, I told you I'd tell you later. Well, I took a few hours off to look up a fellow I shoed a horse for several weeks ago, a cowboy type, with a long beard, long black hair—wore an Indian feather in his hair. Looked like he could be part Indian."

"I remember him. He had a nice palomino mare."

"That's him. While I was shoeing his horse, he told me he'd been living in Colorado for the past three years and would be heading back after he'd made a dollar or two. He told me he was working at Marty's Feed Store. Well, I found him at Marty's and asked him if he'd heard of Charlie Utter. He said, 'Why sure!' Said Mr. Utter was a trapper, guide, and prospector around Colorado parts and was well known and thought of. Friend of Bill Hickok, he said. He also said Mr. Utter stood out in a crowd. Well groomed, which was most unusual for a mountain man. Said he had long blond hair and a mustache. Said he was a man of his word and you could give him a gold coin to hold for you and it'd be there when you needed it."

"Did you ask him if he'd heard about Mr. Utter leading a wagon train to the Black Hills?"

"I did. He said that he hadn't, but he hadn't been in touch with folks he knew in that area for some time. He did say that if he were going on a wagon train to the Black Hills, Mr. Utter would be the one he'd want to lead the train."

Steel gave his father a sober look. "You really are serious about approaching Mother tonight about going to look for gold."

Blain looked at Steel with a quick smile. "I am. Let's go home. Nothing ventured, nothing gained, as they say." He took off his apron and hung it up. "I've got to get to the shop a little earlier tomorrow. Mr. Neader is coming by early. Said he needs the chairs for a party he's throwing."

Steel didn't comment. He stood in a stupor, trying to imagine what might take place tonight. *If my father actually brings up the subject of gold panning in the Black Hills, it's not going to go well.* The more he thought about his father's proposal, the more he was convinced that his mother would never consent. *I think my father is setting himself up for a big disappointment.*

There was little said as they walked home, and nothing more was said about Red, Charlie Utter, or Deadwood. Steel continued to mull over in his mind the fact that his father, based on a cowboy's story and some additional information, had the intention of approaching his mother about going out west looking for gold. *Maybe I should have told him that I wouldn't be willing to go, and that would have ended his foolish idea... No, I couldn't tell him that. Well, we'll see what happens at dinner tonight.*

They lived in a nice colonial home, half an hour's walk from the blacksmith shop, not far from where the Schuylkill River runs into the Delaware River. They had lived there for fourteen years. For Steel, the best thing about their home was its location near prime fishing waters. He loved to fish.

While walking home, Steel couldn't help but ponder how his father might approach the subject with his mother. After doing some thinking, it wouldn't surprise him if his father came to his senses and abandoned the idea altogether. *Perhaps it's just my father's momentary would-be dream.* He kicked a small rock. "We'll see," he mumbled to himself.

His father gave him a sideward glance. "It's meant a lot to me to have you work by my side. I know you'll be working for your grandfather soon. I'm greatly appreciative of being able to share this time with you."

"I feel the same way. It's been a special time." Steel looked at his father and gave him a nod and a warm smile.

3

STEEL'S MOTHER, ELIZABETH, HAD a younger sister, Carole Ann, who had died at the age of five during a smallpox epidemic. Elizabeth had always been close to her parents, and with the death of her sister, they grew even closer. Whenever Steel's father brought up the subject of moving out of the Philadelphia area, his mother quickly shut down the conversation. "I love our home, and I'm not about to move away from my parents and Hanna. They're getting older, and I just like to be no more than a short buggy ride away," she'd say. Steel wasn't even sure why, from time to time, his father brought up the subject of moving. His father certainly knew the outcome was a foregone conclusion.

Steel's grandparents were seemingly in good health. His grandfather went to work daily, and his grandmother always seemed active in a number of social organizations. Hanna, the housekeeper, was considered a member of the family. Her parents were freed slaves. She had gained employment with his grandparents when she was seventeen and had been a second mother to Elizabeth. Everyone in the family loved Hanna.

Now, Hanna oversaw all the household activities. She had hired two girls to come in to do the weekly household chores and cleaning. She enjoyed cooking and kept that duty for herself, unless they were having a social event, at which time she'd bring in additional help as needed.

Elizabeth's father was the owner of successful department stores in Philadelphia, New York, and Boston. There was no question that because of Steel's grandparents, they were afforded social activities and events of the financial well-off. Steel knew his father had always wanted to move westward, but what trumped that longing was the fact that he didn't want to deprive his wife of some of the finer things—those social events primarily.

Dinner at the Madison home was meant to be the highlight of the day. The importance of the evening meal was a direct result of Hanna's influence. She had taught Elizabeth how to cook, primarily French cuisine; and like Hanna, Elizabeth enjoyed cooking. "Dinner is not to be something one rushes through simply to satisfy one's appetite," Hanna would say. "Easterners need to learn to eat more like folks in the South. I think they learned it from the French, who understand and appreciate the value of a well-planned meal."

At dinner that evening, the conversations were unusually short, which was a harbinger that something out of the norm was brewing. Steel caught his mother looking several times at his father with questioning glances. Steel had little doubt that she had an inkling that something was up, which only increased his unease.

Steel toyed with the remaining string beans on his plate, his anxiety increasing as the minutes passed. If his father were true to his word, he'd wait until the conclusion of dinner to bring up the subject of Deadwood, and that time was fast approaching. Steel set down his fork, feeling too nervous to eat. There was a long lull in the table conversation.

"Steel, are you feeling all right?" Giving him a direct look, his mother narrowed her eyes, as was her practice if she wasn't sure what was going on.

"I'm fine," said Steel with a quick response, trying to put on a better face. "I'm thinking I might go fishing after dinner. What are we having for dessert?"

Elizabeth got up from the table. "I forgot to tell you that I met our new neighbors this morning," she said. "They gave me some apples and I made an apple pie."

Steel's cheeks flared in a smile. "I knew I smelled something good, but I didn't see any pie when I got home," he said, for a brief moment shelving his unease.

"I kept it in the cupboard so you wouldn't be tempted to take off a piece of the crust," she answered with a motherly smile.

Steel returned the smile. "That was a wise move, and that was nice of them. I've been eying their apple tree for the last couple of weeks."

"They seem like real fine folks. They're younger than your father and me. They have two youngens, a boy eight and a girl four. It's kind of nice our neighborhood is expanding with a few new families moving in."

"What part of the country are they from?" Blain asked.

"Upstate New York, a town called Palmyra."

"Palmyra, I've heard of that place," Blain said. "I think that's where a man by the name of Joseph Smith, a good number of years ago, found a gold Bible, or such, and started a church. Mormons, I believe, and there was trouble, and most of their group ended up out west somewhere."

"I don't know. I don't ever recall hearing about a gold Bible or Mormons. Steel, you finish up your green beans. I'm not about to throw them away. And you sure aren't getting any pie until you finish."

"Yes, um," Steel said, picking up his fork.

"Speaking of gold..." Blain moved his chair back ever so slightly. "Liz, I need to talk to you about something." He cleared his throat. "A general in the United States Army, General Custer, has confirmed they've found gold in the Black Hills."

Steel set his fork back down and looked at his father. The moment had arrived.

"I don't know where the Black Hills are and don't rightly care. Blain, do you want some pie now or later? I know Steel wants his as soon as I'll givc it to him."

"Liz, sit back down, please. This is important," Blain said in a tone that commanded attention, a tone that he seldom employed.

Steel sucked in a breath and briefly held it.

His mother sat down slowly and rested her forearms on the table. Clasping her hands, she looked at Blain with a harden stare.

Steel had his mother's blue eyes. He wondered if his eyes looked so intense at times. *For a rather petite woman, my mother can look pretty threating if the occasion arises... and it looks like this is one of those occasions.*

"Well?" she asked, straightforwardly.

Steel felt as if his father were in a horse-drawn buggy driving off a steep cliff.

"The Black Hills are located in the northwest," Blain began. "I've been doing some thinking, and I think it'd be a right-down good opportunity for us—Steel and me—to go looking and panning for gold. As I said, General Custer has confirmed that gold is there. A cowboy, we shoed a horse for several days ago, said a wagon train will be leaving from Colorado in just a few weeks—end of July, for the Black Hills. He invited Steel and me to accompany the wagon train. He said they were in need of a blacksmith, and Steel and I would be more than welcome. We could do some gold panning on the side. We wouldn't be gone longer than a year, Liz. And Steel, he'd be back to start working for his grandfather like we talked about, years-end." Blain took in a quick breath. "I know you wouldn't be keen on goin'. I wouldn't want you to, too dangerous for a proper woman like yourself, but it'd be fine for Steel and me."

Steel couldn't believe his father had mustered the courage to do what he just did. He sat wide-eyed looking at his father, and then his eyes quickly shifted to his mother. He expected a torrential storm of words that would put a swift end to his father's dreams.

All was stone quiet for a long moment.

"What are you planning to do with your business?" his mother asked in a calm voice.

"I know I can sell the tools and such. When we get back, it won't be no trouble starting up again. My work will always be in demand, you know that."

"What about our house?"

"Liz, you can stay in the house. We've got enough saved so you don't need to worry none. Of course, you could live with your folks and rent the house or just keep it empty for a year. I'll leave that up to you."

She turned her head toward the window. Her expression was neither pleasant nor unpleasant… *Thoughtful,* Steel surmised.

"I've known for a long time you've wanted to move out west, and I do appreciate you staying here so I can be near my folks and Hanna," she said as she kept her gaze on the window. "You know I won't move away, so maybe this is the best way for you to satisfy some of that longing. I'm certainly not happy about Steel going." She turned and gave Steel a questioning look. "Steel, you do what you want. You're certainly old enough to make your own decisions, and you don't need my permission."

Steel thought that for the moment it was best to remain silent.

"You can both go. I won't try and stop you. A year goes by fast… I don't know how fast it'll go without you two not being here, though… I'll move in with my folks and Hanna. We can leave the house empty. I know my folks will be happy to have me live with them." She stood up. "I'm going to get Steel his piece of pie. Blain, do you want yours now or later?"

"Why… why, now will be just fine," Blain said. "And Liz, we, for sure, won't be longer than a year."

She made no response. She turned slowly, letting out a sigh and disappeared through the kitchen door.

As Steel and his father finished their pieces of apple pie, not one more word was said about the Black Hills. After Steel ate his last bite, he put down his fork and looked over at his father. "May I be excused? I'd like to get out to the river."

His father gave him a nod accompanied with a quick smile, communicating to Steel his contentment.

"The pie was excellent. Thanks Mother," he said loudly as she was in the kitchen cleaning up. "I'm going fishing. I'll be home a little after dark." Without saying anything else to his father, he went upstairs and grabbed his fishing gear. With questioning thoughts swirling in his head as to what might lie ahead, he left out the back door and headed for Schuylkill River.

That night, Steel got up from his bed and closed his bedroom window curtains. The moonlight was so intrusive it made sleeping all the more difficult. The warmth of his winter quilt wouldn't be needed… perhaps in the morning when the temperature cooled. He tossed the blanket to the side and lying on his back, stared up at the celling. *I never thought my mother would consent. She must think this will satisfy my father's longing to go out west, and when we return, he'll be happy to remain here. She can change her mind faster than lighting can strike, and I know father wouldn't go against her wishes if she did… She'll be well taken care of, living with my grandparents and Hanna. She spends a fair amount of time with them anyway. But… Savannah? What am I going to tell Savannah?*

Finally, Steel's churning thoughts gave way to emotional exhaustion and he slept.

4

Blain didn't let any grass grow under his feet. He started putting things in place for their departure the very next day. Early that morning, before leaving the house, he went into Steel's bedroom and tapped him on the shoulder.

Weary-eyed, Steel turned over and squinted at his father. "What time is it?" he asked.

"I told you I was going to the shop early this morning. After I finish things there, I've got a couple of matters I need to attend to. I won't be at work when you come in. Just wanted to let you know. Go back to sleep and dream of panning for gold."

"I was thinking last night. What if Mr. Utter won't let us join up with him? Red had no authority to speak for him."

"Don't give no mind to that. Like that fellow Red said, Mr. Utter will be happy to have us. And if he won't, we'll just figure out a way to get to Deadwood ourselves. We'll talk more later. You go back to sleep. Sorry I woke you up."

Steel turned over and buried his head in his pillow. His father's optimism didn't improve his mood; on the contrary, he wouldn't want to make a trip to Deadwood without someone like Mr. Utter leading the way, assuming he was all that Red said he was.

Steel's attempt to go back to sleep failed. He threw his legs over the side of the bed and was dressed in several minutes. Shuffling down the stairs, he found his mother sitting at the kitchen table having her morning cup of tea. He wasn't sure if she'd had words with his father, but by the look of the dark circles under her eyes, he could tell she hadn't had a good night's sleep.

"Mother, we'll be fine, and we'll be back before you know it."

"I hope you don't stay there for the entire year," she said, holding her cup of tea in two hands while she stared straight ahead in thought.

"To tell you the truth, I'm not that sold on going, but I think I need to go for father's sake."

"You're right. I've thought about it. I wouldn't want your Father going off without you. He's a mighty good man, but sometimes he's not level headed and this is one of those times. I've got all these emotions fighting each other. I'll be fine except for worrying. I can't help worrying, that's my nature. I know you want a piece of pie this morning. It's in the cupboard. Leave some for tonight. What are you going to tell Savannah?"

"I'll… I'll tell her that I'm going to be gone for a year or less, the truth. She's finishing up her schooling. There are no serious commitments between us."

"Well, you've been courting that girl for gonin' on four or five months, and it seems to me that you should be more than good friends. She's a lovely girl, and I suspect she's in love with you."

"I don't know about that," Steel said, telling a white lie.

"You can't do any better than Savannah. Even though I know you need to be with your father, I think you're foolish running off leaving her."

"I think she'll understand."

"I think she'll understand that you and your father will be heading off on a foolish adventure. I'll get you your pie. I know you need to get to work."

Steel had met Savannah while he was attending the College of Philadelphia. She, a Georgia girl, was attending a small private nursing school that was allowed to use some of its campus facilities. That's what brought her from her Georgia home to Philadelphia. He first saw her one fall afternoon, a pretty, blue-eyed, blond, sitting on a campus bench under a large, sugar maple tree. A light breeze scattered red, bright orange, and yellow leaves around her. Steel introduced himself with uncharacteristic boldness. Her beauty and soft Southern accent quickly won him over. They soon became good friends, seeing each other almost daily.

Steel stared at his piece of apple pie in thought. *I like Savannah. I like her a lot. Perhaps my mother is right. Perhaps I'm making a mistake, a monumental mistake.*

After eating the last bite of his pie, he said good-by to his mother, giving her a kiss on the cheek, and walked out the front door. For no conscious reason, he turned and looked at the house. He could see her standing at the front window watching him. He knew her heart was aching, and that only added to his discomfort and uncertainty.

Steel was glad to get to the shop that morning and start working, which helped take his mind off the trip and the pressing task of telling Savannah.

A little before noon, his father returned to the shop whistling a tune. "By jingles, the good Lord is looking after us," he said. "You know Peter Willingham, the owner of the blacksmith shop across town? Said he's looking to hire someone and expand. Said he'd buy anything we wanted to sell, and he'd give us a fair price. I told him a little of our plans, and he said he wished he was going with us. Steel, that'll give us some extra money we might need down the road."

Steel stopped filing the rough edges off the horseshoe and looked at his father. "Are you a hundred percent sure you want to go to the Black Hills? I know mother's going to worry about us from the day we leave until we return home."

"I'm sure—absolutely sure. Steel, it's something I need to do for myself," Blain said with sobriety. "If you're having second thoughts, I won't hold it against you for not going. I know your mother is unhappy about you leaving; and you're right, she is going to worry, and I know your grandfather is eager for you to start working for him, and there's your girl Savannah."

"I'm going with you," Steel said with reluctance in his tone. "I just want to make sure this is what you really want."

"Steel. It's in my bones. I hope that answers your question."

"It does." Steel picked up the horseshoe he was shaping and went back to work. "We're going to Deadwood," he said under his breath.

It wasn't long until the word was out about the planned trip. Neighbors, friends, and customers wanted to know all about it. Blain, generally a shy, quiet person blossomed like a rose. At the drop of a hat, he'd be more than willing to talk about their upcoming adventure. It pleased Steel to see his father getting so much enjoyment out of just planning and talking, which for the moment was the only positive in Steel's mind about the adventure.

Steel's grandparents were more than willing to have his mother move back in with them. For the time being, she decided to leave the home empty. During evening meals, nothing was said of Deadwood or panning for gold. Steel knew his father and mother preferred it that way. Discontent and arguing were demons that Steel's God-fearing father always preached against. Steel's father generally let his mother have her way, but if it was a matter that he felt strongly about, he'd hold firm, and in those rare situations he'd generally prevail.

5

Now that it was settled in Steel's mind that he and his father were going out west, he knew he had to break the news to Savannah. He had more than a suspicion that she wouldn't take the news well. After he'd wrestled with his thoughts in her regard, he decided there was no easy way of telling her. *I'll tell her that I'll be gone with my father for a year or less, and we should be returning about the time she completes her schooling.*

Steel looked over at his father working on a wagon hitch. "I'm hanging up my apron for the day. I'm going to try and meet Savannah at the end of her three o'clock class. I haven't as yet told her of our plans."

"You need to tell her before she hears the news from someone else."

"My thoughts exactly. I've got a feeling she's not going to be happy. I just wanted to make certain we were going."

"She's a special girl. She'll be fine. I'll see you tonight at dinner."

Steel walked out the shop door, thinking, *I don't share my father's optimism.*

That afternoon, he made his way to the school with a hurried step and an uncertain mind.

When he arrived at the campus, he looked at the clock on the face of the school's administration building. Seeing he was a few minutes early, he slowed his pace to an easy walk. A shade tree near Savannah's classroom provided a cool place to wait for her class to end. He stuffed his hands in his pockets and anxiously looked at the closed classroom door.

Chimes from a nearby church tolled the four o'clock hour and students began to file out of the reddish brick building. Steel wrinkled his brow, as he habitually did in unpleasant situations. "There she is," he said.

Savannah looked his way and gave him a warm smile.

As her steps quickened to greet him, so increased his uneasiness.

"What a most pleasant surprise," she said, beaming.

She wore a white summer dress with lacy, pink ribbons bordering the edge of her skirt. Her blond hair curled at her shoulders, and with her fair complexion she looked angelic. Her books were tucked under her arm.

"Do you have a few minutes so we can talk?" Steel asked.

"Of course. My next class doesn't start for another hour. I was planning on going to the library to study, but that can wait. Oh, it's so good to see you."

Steel swallowed hard. "Let's go sit on that bench." They walked over to a weathered wooden bench on a grassy area next to a building wrapped in English Ivy.

"Are you okay?" she asked, narrowing her eyes and lowering her tone.

"Yes… and no."

"You're wrinkling your forehead and hesitating, that's not a good sign."

"You know me only too well," Steel said as they sat down on the bench. Savannah held her books on her lap, pursed her lips and looked at Steel.

He quickly related the story of Red coming to their shop and his father's reaction." He paused, hoping for a comment. She said nothing. He proceeded to tell her what took place at dinner. "I was amazed my mother consented, truly amazed."

He hesitated for a moment. *I wish she'd say something,* he thought, and then continued, "As long as I can remember, my father has always had a yearning to go westward. I think Deadwood will help satisfy some of that desire. I've had reservations from the start about going, and I've expressed them to my father. He's absolutely determined to go and asked me to go with him. We'll be gone no longer than a year, and very likely less than a year, at least that's my hope."

"Steel, my word, I don't want you to go! A year is just too long of a time! It's hostile country! You could run into all kinds of trouble!" The words flew out of her mouth. "I'm sure your father can go by himself. I'm almost finished with my schooling. I was thinking about getting a nursing job here in Philadelphia."

"Walter will be coming back from Oxford in another month or two, didn't you say?" The minute he made the comment, he knew he should have kept his mouth shut.

"Walter! I'm sorry I ever mentioned his name. I don't want to marry Walter. I want to marry you!"

Her words stopped him cold. This was the first time marriage had come up.

"Savannah… I don't know what to say. My father is counting on me and I can't let him down, I just can't. I'll write. You've got your school to finish. The time will quickly pass and I'll be home."

"It's not that you can't. It's that you won't! Just know one thing, I love you and not Walter. The question is, do you love me? If you did, you wouldn't be going!" Savannah gave Steel a glare.

"Savannah…"

Her eyes moistened but her voice remained strong. "Steel, if you go, I may well be in Georgia when you return home. I'm not going to wait around for you while you're off on some silly escapade with your father. I need to get on with my life." She got up from the bench in a huff. "I'm going to the library. I need to study," she said firmly. Tears quickly filled her eyes. She sniffed, turned her head away from Steel, and briskly marched toward the library.

Steel remained seated, feeling that he'd handled things poorly. He watched her until she disappeared around the corner of a building. *I don't know what to think. I don't know if I'm in love with her. I like her a great deal. I can't deny that, and in time… I didn't intend on hurting her feelings but I have.* He got up from the bench. *Going to Deadwood could be a big mistake.* He stuck his hands in his pockets again, and with his head down walked slowly toward home.

6

A WEEK BEFORE DEPARTURE, Steel's father received a telegram: *Mr. Madison,* we *can use two good blacksmiths in Deadwood. Red and I hope to see you and your son shortly. Departing July 5 for the Black Hills. Charlie Utter, Wagon Train Boss.*

The telegram added fuel to Blain's exuberance, not that he needed it. Steel was experiencing firsthand how gold fever could take hold of a man, tie him into a knot, and make him forget just about everything else.

Steel saw Savannah one more time before they left for Deadwood. It was only for a few moments outside her apartment. He continued to try and convince her that if it weren't for his father he wouldn't be going. His words fell on deaf ears. Since their last meeting, he'd given considerable thought about her marriage comment and realized he wasn't in the same place she was in their relationship. Now with him leaving, he was acutely aware that his departure could mean the end of their relationship.

"I'll write," were his parting words.

She made no response but simply turned and shut the door.

He stood for several moments staring at her closed door. Finally, he turned and left for home, knowing that he may never see her again.

His mother and Savannah weren't the only ones Steel knew weren't happy with he and his father leaving for a year. His grandfather, a pragmatic businessman, strongly expressed his objections and concerns about them leaving to look for gold. His grandfather reaffirmed to Steel how he was counting on him to step into his shoes. "I'm getting older and I need you to start learning the retail business. College is fine, but it's no substitute for what I'll be teaching you. Steel, I hope you'll limit your stay to a year or less. I'll be awaiting your return, My Boy."

On the day of departure, after Steel and Blain finished getting Elizabeth settled in her folks' home, Blain hitched up his father-in-law's horse, Dolly, to a landau carriage. Dolly, a gentle coal black mare in color was a fine fit for the well-appointed transportation. Most of the time his grandfather hired a driver, but he had no qualms in taking the reins himself on occasion and today would be one of those occasions.

Blain loaded the carriage luggage compartment with a weathered leather satchel that had been sitting in storage for some time gathering dust. He had to polish up the metal fasteners to make them work properly. The satchel was packed with a couple of changes of clothes for both of them, a well-read Bible with frayed edges, a straight-edge razor, three bars of soap, a badger hair shaving brush, and a well-worn leather strap. It was Elizabeth who that morning had stood in the bedroom doorway with the shaving supplies. "I don't want the two of you coming back home with facial hair that the birds can nest in," she said.

In addition to the satchel, there was a rucksack that contained Steel's fishing gear and a tube that held a three-piece bamboo fly rod. These items, dear to Steel, he put in the inside seating area. He was counting on testing the Western streams whenever he found the opportunity to wet a line.

The Central Pacific train was scheduled to leave at two that afternoon. The station was no more than a twenty-minute buggy ride from Steel's grandparents' home.

"Giddyap," Blain said, giving the reins a healthy shake. Dolly tossed her head and then stepped smartly out of the carriage horse stall.

"Steel, latch the door and climb aboard. I'm sure your mother and grandparents are wondering where we're at."

Steel could hear the excitement in his father's voice and wished he could feel some of that positive emotion.

In less than a minute they were at the front entrance of the elegant, Tudor home. Elizabeth was standing on the porch behind her mother, who was seated in a white wicker chair absorbed in her needlework. Elizabeth's father stood on the side of the circular cobblestone driveway, examining the adjacent rose garden.

"Easy there, Dolly," Blain said. He gave the reins a tug. "Steel, you need to get down. Your grandfather is going to ride up with me. I think he has a hankering to take the reins."

Steel jumped down and stood by the carriage.

"That's right, Blain," Steel's grandfather said. He approached Dolly and looking into her eyes, gave her a couple of pats on the neck. "Good girl, Dolly," he said affectionately.

"Let me give you a hand," Blain said, extending his arm.

"Thank you, Blain."

"Steel, you need to get in. I think we're ready to go," Blain said. He looked at Elizabeth and her mother. "We'll be fine and be back before you know it."

Elizabeth nodded with a stoic expression.

Looking up from her needlework, Elizabeth's mother called out, "The both of you take care now."

"Wait," Steel said. Tears were streaming down his mother's face. For a moment, he wondered if she'd tell them not to go. She took a white lace handkerchief from her dress pocket and dabbed at her cheeks. Steel watched her force a smile. Without another word, he dashed up the steps to his mother's side and put his arms around her.

"You take good care of yourself, Steel," she choked out. "I've been putting up a good front. Truth be known, I'm hurting more than a might to see the two of you go. And take care of your father. I do love you both."

"I'll do that. You know I love you."

He knew his mother was aware of his hesitant feelings and even his downheartedness about leaving, but she made no effort to dissuade him. *My pa needs me. I'm sure that's why she hasn't said anything more about me going.*

Steel stepped into the carriage and looked out the window. He heard his grandfather click the reins. *Maybe, I'll feel better once we're on the train.*

7

After a long train ride, in which Steel continued to harbor questions about going, Blain and Steel spent the night at a shoddy Denver boarding house. The noise coming through the paper-thin walls didn't allow for much sleep. Even so, Blain remained in high spirits. Not wanting to dampen his father's excitement, Steel kept his uneasy feelings and discontentment to himself.

They rose early and grabbed a quick bite to eat at a hole in the wall café named Kathy's Kitchen. "We need to find a way to Georgetown," Blain said as he looked at Steel over a black cup of coffee. "I'm thinking we'll find a livery stable. I'll bet you dimes to dollars they can help us out and most likely someone there will know Charlie Utter."

"Livery stable… Sounds like a good idea," Steel said, still trying to get the sleep out of his eyes. He took a sip of coffee and continued, "I hope that tonight we won't have to stay in a place like we did last night. I think we both could use a good night's sleep."

"We'll deal with sleeping when we need to. After you finish your coffee and muffin, let's head out. I'm fine to go, as soon as I pay the lady and you're ready."

Their waitress, a short plump gal wearing a red-and-white-checkered dress that fell just below her knees, came their way. "Can I get you boys anything else this mornin'—more coffee?"

"We're fine. Can you tell us where the livery stable is?" Blain asked.

"You two look like city slickers. Don't see too many people wearing suits around here, and I can see you got your traveling bag. Where do you hail from?" She put her hands on her hips and waited for an answer.

"Philadelphia, we're from Philadelphia. Got in yesterday," Blain said.

"Hmm. That's a ways away. Never been back East, myself. To answer your question, you can find Ben Cather's livery stable about five blocks going north. Make a left on Pine Street, keep walkin' and you can't miss it or the smell. Just follow your nose. He sells horse manure there for planting things and such, so you'll most likely have some flies to greet you. Folks here have been trying to get him to move his business farther out of town but it hasn't happened yet. The town officials need to redo the zoning ordinances or something. Hope you don't get your suits smelled up too bad."

"Thanks for your food and your advice," Blain said.

After Blain paid the bill, they got up from the table and set out. It took them no time at all to find the livery stable. An unpleasant aroma greeted them when they were about a block away.

"The wind is blowing our way, and that waitress was right," Steel said, uncomfortable with the smell. The smell didn't seem to bother Blain or at least he didn't comment on it.

As they approached the stable, a young man in blue jeans and a short sleeve shirt was pitching hay to a half dozen corralled horses.

"We're looking for Mr. Cather," Blain called out.

The young man stopped working and leaned on his pitchfork. "He's in the office yonder, having a morning cup of coffee. Just give a good knock on the door."

"Much obliged," Blain said.

The office wasn't much more than a small shed.

Blain rapped his knuckles on the pine door. "Hello," he called out.

"Come on in," a gravelly voice answered.

An older man, a little frail looking, with a large clown-like nose and dark weathered skin, peeked up from a paper he was holding. "If you don't mind, I won't get up since my leg is hurting. I got kicked by a horse the other day. It was my own damn fault."

"Sorry to hear that," Blain said. "I've been kicked myself a time or two."

"From what you're carrying and wearin' I can see you boys are from out of town and traveling. What can I do for you?"

"My son and I are blacksmiths, and we're planning on joining up with Charlie Utter on his trip to the Black Hills."

"Where are you from?" Cather laid the paper down and sat back in his chair, eying them up and down.

"Philadelphia," Blain said.

"Philadelphia. So you're going with Charlie to Deadwood to look for gold." He nodded and gave them a thoughtful look.

"We'll be doing some blacksmithing too. That's the plan, anyway," Blain said.

"Charlie's as fine a man as they come. Can't say nothing bad about him." The man chuckled. "You know he's taken almost all our party ladies out of Denver—a hundred and fifty I heard tell. I don't know what Denver is going to do. I'm sure the prospectors are going to be throwing him a hoopin' party when he arrives in Deadwood. Only Charlie could pull something like that off. Of course, he hasn't done it yet."

"Our interest, as I said, is blacksmithing and panning for gold on the side, but we need to get to Georgetown. I understand it's about forty-five miles away."

"As the crow flies, that's right. It's higher up than Denver. He's got people going and coming between here and there all the time. I know some of his men are working on wagons here in Denver. I think that's your best bet." He took a sip of coffee. "I'll tell you how to get to where they are. Most likely, someone from there will be heading up to Georgetown today or tomorrow."

Cather spent half a minute giving them easy directions.

"We want to thank you for your time and help. We've found people in Denver to be a most friendly sort," Blain said.

"For the most part, we're a friendly sort. Happy to be of some help. You boys may want to think about getting you some new britches. Those clothes you're wearing, most likely, won't be the best thing for wagon travelin'. Again, hope you don't mind if I don't get up formal like."

"Don't mind at all and thanks again," Blain said. He and Steel backed out the doorway and closed the door.

They were glad for the information and happy to leave the stench.

"That waitress was right. And that fellow pitching hay, I don't know how he can work there. He's used to the smell, I guess," Steel said, shaking his head.

Blain and Steel welcomed the sight of a dozen covered wagons and the pounding of nails. They walked up to one of the young men fitting a canvas over the ribs of a wagon top.

"Howdy! Sorry to bother you," Blain called out.

The young man jumped down from the wagon. "What can I do for you two?"

"My name is Blain Madison and this is my son Steel. We need to get to Georgetown. We're planning on joining up with Mr. Utter's wagon train. We're both blacksmiths."

"My name is Josh Bolton. Pleased to meet you both. Mr. Utter told us to keep an eye out for you. From Philadelphia, I hear. Welcome to the West. No one's going to Georgetown today, but tomorrow morning Hank will be heading that way. He's taking some supplies in a buckboard. There'll be plenty of room for you and your gear."

"That's mighty good news," Blain said.

"That'll mean we'll need to stay here another night," Steel said with a frown. "We didn't get the best sleep last night. Any recommendations?"

"You're welcome to stay with me at my folks' place. We have plenty of room and Ma is one fine cook."

"Well, that's mighty neighborly of you," Blain said and glanced at Steel. "We won't turn down your invite. Are you sure it's going to sit okay with your folks?" Blain asked.

"They'll be welcome for the company. My pa may ask you about the political goings on in the East. You might be prepared for that."

"I don't know much, but I'll tell him what I do know," Blain said. "My son, Steel, knows a lot more than I do about those kinds of things. He'll be the one to answer your pa's questions."

Steel smiled and gave a nod, liking the prospects of a good night's sleep.

"I need to find Hank and let him know you'll be going with him. He generally don't head out for Georgetown until around nine-thirty or ten o'clock. You'll like Hank. He's an old prospector, likes to gab, works for Mr. Utter now. He knows mules about as well as anyone alive, I suspect. He'll be going on the wagon train and looking after twenty-five mules or more."

"We were planning on checking out the local blacksmith shop. We need to find out where we can buy some tools. I understand there's not much in Deadwood. And I'd like to send a telegram to the missus, letting her know we arrived in Denver. I take it there's no telegraph in Deadwood."

"You'd be right about that. Not a lot in Deadwood except saloons, and well, you'll find out. The blacksmith shop is not far from here. Just down that road there," he said, pointing his finger. "About two miles, I'd say. Why don't you do your business and see a little of Denver. It's a right pretty place. Meet me back here at six. I'll get a hold of Hank and let him know you'll be going with him tomorrow morning. Oh, you can leave your things here. I'll put them in the wagon and watch 'm for you. You might want to think about buying some different clothes. Those banker suits aren't going to be doin' you any good in Deadwood."

"We'll pick up some more suitable clothes this afternoon," Steel said, starting to feel that they stuck out like a couple of sore thumbs.

"Thanks, Josh we'll do that. We'll look forward to seeing you at six," Blain said. "And again, much obliged for the invite."

Just knowing they were going to get a good night's sleep went a long way in improving Steel's mood, and he could tell his father was much relieved knowing tomorrow they'd be in Georgetown and would be meeting Mr. Charlie Utter.

"I think the first thing we need to do is send that telegram, and I need to stop by the post office and send my letter to Savannah," Steel said.

"You haven't said a word to me about Savannah. I was going to ask you, how did she take things about us departing and all that?" Blain asked.

"Not good."

"Well, a year goes by fast. She'll be waiting for you when you get back."

"I'm not so sure about that. Let's go to the telegraph office," Steel said, not wanting to discuss his relationship with Savannah.

"Fine. After we send the telegram to your mother and get your letter off, we need to do some clothes shopping. I think Mr. Utter would be most amused if we showed up in these... What did Josh say? Banker's suits," Blain said. He shook his head and grinned.

"Agreed."

8

On their buckboard ride through pine-covered mountains leading up to Georgetown, Steel swept his gaze from the jagged snow-topped peaks to the gently sloping valleys below. "I don't ever recall seeing such spectacular country," he said.

Along the way, deer emerged from the forest to greet the travelers with curious looks before scampering off into the thicket. Hank pointed out a family of big horn sheep making their way along a high, rocky mountain ridge. Steel spotted a pair of eagles soaring at an altitude that made them barely visible to the eye. The ride was a pleasant prelude to Georgetown.

"Only thing that worries me some are bears and moose," Hank said. "That's why I keep old Betty Sue by my side. He threw a quick glance at his Winchester Rifle. Hank was an amiable old prospector like Josh had said. He talked a good part of the trip, relating mining stories, speaking to his two mules, and telling his companions about Charlie Utter who was somewhat of a legend in those parts of the country.

"Georgetown is a nice little mining town that has seen its glory days, at least for the time being. It sure as shootin' could come back to life in its full glory one of these days," Hank said with a hopeful tone.

When they arrived in Georgetown, Hank drove by the few small shops, a couple of eating places, and some business offices on the way to Charlie's camp, which was located in a large, open clearing on the northern outskirts of town. Hank never mentioned why Charlie chose Georgetown as his departure headquarters. Steel surmised that it could have been for financial reasons... and perhaps he preferred to be away from curious Denver onlookers.

Hank pointed out the bunkhouse and two corrals. "The Mules are in one corral and the horses in the other."

Not far from the bunkhouse was what appeared to be a four-man tent. "That large tent you see is Mr. Utter's living quarters," Hank said. "They call it a cabin tent. It's a might larger than most tents, and apparently it fits Charlie's needs. I'm not telling you anything out of school, but he goes into town every morning—ain't more than a hop, skip, and jump, as you can see, where religiously he gets a hair wash and a shave."

Reining in his mules Hank said, "There's Charlie now over by the mule corral." He took off his beaten-up, black hat with a drooping rim. He gave it a shake and the dust flew. "I suspect you'll be staying in the bunkhouse till we leave. Why don't the two of you go make Charlie's acquaintance, and I'll take your belongs over to the bunkhouse."

"Thanks, Hank," Blain said.

"I enjoyed the stories and the ride," Steel said.

Hank grinned. "Well, I enjoyed talking to you boys. You're a good addition to the company. There's one or two of Charlie's men that I don't rightly cotton to, but I don't do the hiring. Anyway, I'll catch you boys later."

Mr. Utter was looking at twenty-five to thirty corralled mules, all swishing their tails in the afternoon sun. Steel watched an unhappy mule take out its frustrations with a kick at one of its cohorts.

Mr. Utter turned when he heard Blain and Steel approaching. "I just bet you're my blacksmiths from Philadelphia," he said with a warm smile.

Mr. Utter was most impressive. *He' right off the cover of one of those Western magazines,* Steel thought. He was a few inches shorter than Steel's six feet and looked to be in his forties. He had a handsome face, almost boyish looking. His blond hair had a curl to it and fell just below his shoulders. He wore buckskins, hand-stitched leggings, beaded moccasins, and a deerskin vest with bear's claws for buttons. The pearl-handle pistols tucked into his belt, held Steel's attention for a long moment. He was truly something to behold.

"That would be right," Blain said. "Mr. Utter, I'm Blain Madison and this is my son, Steel."

Steel was sure glad they'd bought some suitable clothes yesterday. With what they'd brought from home and their new purchases of a couple of pairs each of tan denim paints, some long-sleeve cotton shirts, and two dark blue woolen coats, they should be set at least until they arrived in Deadwood. Hank had said that there was a mercantile store in Deadwood where they could purchase things if they had a need. They'd rolled up their sleeves that morning after it started to warm up, and Steel was now feeling comfortable as well as presentable.

"Pleased to meet you both," Mr. Utter said extending his hand. "Please call me Charlie."

Blain and Steel shook hands with Charlie. His handshake was firm but not a bone-crusher. Steel always felt that a handshake could tell a little bit about a person, and a firm one was good.

"This sure is a beautiful place. I could stay right here," Steel said, feeling genuinely excited for the first time since he'd left home.

"It is pretty, but when Mr. Winter Wind brings the snow in, you might be thinkin' a little differently. It gets cold enough to… I'll just say it gets mighty cold. Looking at you boys, I'm glad to have you for more reasons than one. If any of my hired hands get out of line with the working girls we're taking, I'm right certain I can count on your help. I always try and get good men to work for me, but I've got a couple on this trip that I'm not right sure of. I want you to know that I'm sincerely glad to have you both. Red told me you're both upstanding men."

Any lingering fatigue from the long trip melted away from Steel like butter on a hot summer's day. *Just seeing and hearing Charlie talk is something special,* Steel thought. By the look on his father's face, Steel was sure they shared the same feelings.

"We're excited to be here, and I sure did appreciate your encouraging wire," Blain said.

"Blain, you need to think about what tools you want to take. I'm going to leave that entirely up to the two of you. You'll need to go back to Denver to do your buying. If you need some money, I'll grubstake you," Charlie said with a serious tone.

"We're fine, money wise. We did have time in Denver to see where we could buy things. I just don't know if I can get an anvil."

"You can only do what you can do. I'll have Hank take you back with a buckboard to get what you need. I'm hoping to leave in three days. You didn't get here any too soon. The wagons should be finished tomorrow. We're working on some here. You can settle in at the bunkhouse. I'm planning on taking a fair amount of ladies, as you've probably heard. Working girls. It's up to about one hundred and eighty. And I'm taking some packing mules. So you're going to have to put up with the ladies and the mules. Don't know what's going to be the harder," he said smiling. "I'd like to get the ladies settled in as soon as possible. They'll be coming in the night before we leave. I'll tell you more about that later."

Blain shook his head. "You're a mighty ambitious man," he said.

"I think foolish is a better word than ambitious. That reminds me, I'll need you boys to drive wagons. I suspect you haven't ever driven one, but you can learn fast. Some of the women will be driving too."

"We can do that," Blain said quickly.

"Yes, sir, we can," Steel added.

"Steel, you're a good-looking young man. Those broad shoulders and blue eyes are going to dazzle some of the ladies we're taking. You best be a might careful."

Steel felt his cheeks warm. He knew he and his father weren't going to get into any trouble, but he was thinking he was glad his mother didn't know the particulars of the trip.

Oh, my good friend Bill Hickok will be joining us to help keep everyone in line. He's run into some hard luck lately, and is going to try and improve his fortunes in Deadwood."

"Wild Bill Hickok, going with us! I've read stories about him in our local papers," Blain said.

"Probably most of them stories are true," Charlie said with a wink and a smile.

"Is he going to pan for gold?" Blain asked.

"Gambling. Bill will be spending most of his time with cards in his hand. There are two main types of places in Deadwood right now, saloons for drinking and gambling and boarding houses for working girls. The houses have been built, but they're pretty much empty and waiting to be filled. That reminds me, I suspect you've heard of Calamity Jane in your news articles, the best dag gum girl I've ever seen with a pistol or rifle. Well, she'll be going with us, too. I'd put her against any man, except Bill Hickok. So we're going to be traveling with some pretty reputable company."

"I can't believe we'll be going on the same wagon train with them," Blain said.

"Blain, it sounds like you're as happy as a pig in mud," Charlie said with a grin.

"I am."

"Well, you'll be even happier when you see that yellow dust looking up at you."

Steel could tell that for his father life didn't get much better than right now. Like Charlie, he could hear the excitement in his father's voice and see it in his face. He hoped that excitement would continue, but Steel had a strange foreboding that the future didn't hold all that his father had hoped for.

"Red is over at the bunkhouse fiddling with his gun. Why don't you boys go say hello. He'll be right glad to see you. We'll be eating around six this evening. You'll meet my brother Steve and most of the rest of the hired hands then. Steve is going to be leaving tomorrow. He'll be in Deadwood to greet us when we arrive."

"We'll look forward to that," Blain said.

From the corner of his eye, Steel spotted a grey cat perched on the corral fence railing. A lizard's tail dangled from its mouth and then it was gone. The cat swished its tail back and forth and gave Steel a lazy look.

"Hold on just a minute," Charlie said. "I'm thinking… some good friends of mine, Lucy Winthrop and her daughter Cattie, are comin' with us." Mr. Utter tightened his lips and, for a quick moment, gazed out at the horizon in thought. "I won't tell you their story now. Deadwood isn't the place for them, but they're set on getting out of Denver. Cattie is about as pretty a thing as you've ever seen. She's about your age, Steel, a few years younger maybe. I'm going to put one of you drivin' their wagon, and I'd appreciate it if both of you would keep a watchful eye on them. They're not working ladies so to speak. They'll be helping with the cooking at one of the Deadwood saloons. I still would like to talk them into not coming. I'm going to try one more time, but I don't think I'm gonna be successful." Shaking his head and frowning, Charlie paused and looked down at the ground.

"We'll be more than happy to keep an eye on them," Blain said.

"You two go get settled in now."

"Let us know how we can help you get ready," Blain said.

"Plan on going back with Hank to Denver tomorrow morning, and get what you think is best in the way of blacksmith items. I'm taking some older wagons. When you get back, if you could check them and if you think something needs fixing, let me know. I'd prefer to do it now than after we get underway."

"We'd be much obliged to do that, and if there's anything else you can think of, just let us know," Blain said.

Steel and Blain walked toward the bunkhouse, feeling that they couldn't have received a better welcome. Steel could understand now why Red was so high on Mr. Utter. He was about as personable a person as Steel had ever met.

9

THE DAY BEFORE DEPARTURE was quite an event. Throughout the day, working girls were being ferried up to Georgetown in buckboards. Charlie, mounted on a handsome dark palomino, directed traffic and barked out instructions. Steel could tell he was in his element. The ladies giggled and smiled as the hired hands helped them settle into their assigned wagons. Everyone seemed to be enjoying the moment.

Blain and Steel helped Hank pack the mules. Most of the food they needed for the trip was being loaded on Hank's mules. Charlie planned for two chuck wagons, but they'd be limited to carrying coffee, sugar, cooking oil, and cooking and eating utensils.

"My mules are acting real fine today, which I'm grateful for," Hank said, patting one of his mules on the rump. "I gave them a little extra feed last night. We'll see how they fare come tomorrow morning. Steel, bring that sack of flour here. Ol' Jack can handle another sack."

Steel, with a sack of flour on his shoulder, walked over to where Hank was standing.

"Just hoist that sack up, and I'll secure it," Hank said. "A mule is the most temperamental animal I know. I don't know what they're going to be feeling like from one day to the next. Sometimes it's one hour to the next."

"You handle them well," Steel said as he steadied the sack.

"I learned most of what I need to know in handling mules from my second wife. I never knew what to expect from Gladys. Learned to be patient. That's what it takes, patience, and to talk sweetly to them. I don't say harsh words to my mules. Strange as it may sound, they know I love 'em. Mules are damn smart, unlike sheep the most unintelligent animals I know. You get one sheep to walk over a cliff to its death the rest will follow. Blain we're gonna put that sack on another mule. Ol' Jack has got all he can carry. He's not really that old, but I call him Ol Jack anyway. Guess you can tell I got names for all my mules."

Around three o'clock, Charlie motioned to Blain and Steel to come over to where he was standing. He held the reins of his horse in his hand, looking over the activities, making certain everything was going as planned. "How you boys doin'?"

"Fine and dandy," Blain said.

"I appreciate you helping Hank. He doesn't let just anyone work with him when dealing with his mules. I know he likes the both of you."

"We like him," Steel said.

"As you can see, the working girls are coming in. They're a happy lot right now. We'll see how things progress once we get underway. A lot of these gals I'm taking have lost husbands or their fathers and have really no one to provide for them. Being a working girl is about the only way of surviving for some of them. Don't judge 'm too harshly, and maybe like the good book says, it's best we don't judge 'em at all."

"I've got to hand it to you, Charlie," Blain said, shaking his head. "I don't know anyone who'd take on a venture like you're taking on, and as you said, it all seems to be going real well."

"For the time being anyway, for the time being. I've got two madams that will help keep things in hand. You'll meet 'em, Dirty Em and Madam Mustachio. They're both savvy business gals, I can tell you that. Take those girls over to wagon eight!" Charlie shouted to one of the buckboard drivers.

Steel looked on with admiration. If he hadn't watched with his own eyes the orchestration of settling in of all these ladies, he wouldn't have believed it. It crossed his mind more than once what his mother would be thinking if she had an inkling of what was going on. He couldn't help but smile to himself.

"The reason I called you over here is that I mentioned the other day Lucy Winthrop and her daughter Cattie will be accompanying us," Charlie said.

"Right, I remember," Blain said. "And you'd like us to help lookout for them, making sure no one causes them any trouble or harm."

"That's right. I did try one more time to convince Lucy that she and Cattie should remain in Denver. As I expected, she's not takin' my advice. I wanted to talk to you before they got here and now will have to do. I'll tell you a little of their background. I was a good friend of Lucy's pa. He saved my bacon a long time ago. Let me just say, I owe him my life. His only daughter, Lucy, married a no-good varmint from back east. Lucy's folks were killed in a questionable buggy accident and her husband went through her substantial inheritance drinking, gambling, and womanizing in about three years. He started beating her and she left him to protect herself and Cattie. By the way, Cattie was educated in some fancy school, I believe in Virginia. Her grandfather set up a trust for her schooling so her no-good pa couldn't touch it. He was in the process of doing the same thing for Lucy when her grandparents got killed. I heard tell the so called accident happened the day before the trust papers were to be signed."

"Do you think it wasn't an accident?" Blain asked.

"I do. Nothing that could be proved. Lucy told me one night her husband came home drunk and told her he'd killed her folks and he was gonna kill her if she gave him any trouble. Cattie had just come home from school. Lucy came to see me, and I moved them out to a little cabin I own in Denver. I told her husband I'd shoot him dead if he ever came near them. With me leaving for Deadwood, Lucy said she wasn't about to stay in Denver or the surrounding area."

"I can't blame her none," Blain said.

"I can't either," Charlie said. "Her husband got caught breaking into a saloon, probably for cash and liquor. He's in jail right now, supposedly for two years, but you never know about that, sometimes they get out early. Anyway, I don't think Deadwood is the best place for them, but if things don't work out there… Well, we'll just wait and see."

"As we said, we'll be pleased to help you lookout for them and thanks for telling us about their situation," Blain said.

"I meant to ask you, were you able to find an anvil?"

"We did. It's an old one, but it'll do the job and we got the basic tools we'll need."

"Glad to hear that. You're working with Hank, so let's pack those things on one of his mules. And thanks for looking at those wagon hitches."

"Happy to help out," Blain said.

"Steel, your pa and I have been doin' all the jawing. How are you doin'?"

"Fine. Everyone has been friendly, and I love the country."

"Steel's a fly fisherman. I know he's eager to try out some of the western streams," Blain said.

"Son, you'll have plenty of chances to fish. You can fish while your pa pans for gold."

"That's the idea," Steel said with a grin.

"At dinner tonight, I'll introduce you to Lucy and Cattie. I'm assigning them to wagon twelve. Blain, I'm going to have you drive that wagon, and, Steel, I'll have you drive wagon eleven with some of the working girls."

"We'll be happy to Mr. Utter," Blain said.

"Now I insist, the both of you call me Charlie."

"Thanks, Charlie," Steel said with a nod.

"I'm gonna get back on my horse. It looks like they need some direction over yonder. I'll catch you boys a little later, and again, I'm sure glad to have you along."

10

It was late afternoon, and dinnertime was the next event of the day. In an open area, bordered by a forest of lofty pine trees, Charlie's hired hands had set up tables and benches. In two barbeque pits, four cooks were busy roasting chunks of beef on makeshift spits. The aroma floated through the camp, whetting everyone's appetite. The working ladies stood in small groups visiting, laughing, and getting their personal things squared away at their assigned wagons. Charlie had his men too busy getting ready for tomorrow's departure to pay much attention to the ladies other than answering a question or two. It was a right-orderly operation.

Blain and Steel stood by the mule corral, just finishing up with helping Hank.

"I'm getting hungry. Things sure smell mighty appetizing," Blain said as he glanced back over his shoulder at Hank who was having a friendly conversation with one of his mules. "Are you sure Hank doesn't need us anymore today?" he asked, dusting off his pants.

"He told me the mules were ready to go for tomorrow morning and we were fine to call it a day. I wasn't about to argue with him. I'm definitely ready to take a break," Steel said, wiping his brow."

"I am too. I must admit, I'm not used to this altitude."

Steel looked over at Hank who looked as fresh as a daisy. "Hank is still talking to his mules. Josh was right. One thing's for certain, Hank sure knows mules," he said.

"Yeah, he does. I'm thinking we're an hour or so away from eating. Charlie said dinner is around six. Let's go back to the bunkhouse and get cleaned up. I might even catch a few minutes of shut-eye," Blain said. "To be honest, I've been so excited, I haven't slept much these last few nights; and with this altitude, I'm finally feeling a little tuckered out. Steel, take a peek at those thunderclouds yonder."

Steel looked north and saw a collection of dark, imposing clouds.

"They don't look threating, just sitting there behind that far mountain range, but they do give me some concern. We didn't give any mind to rainy weather," Blain said.

"You're right. I'm sure we're going to run into some summer thunderstorms along the way. I'm guessing they can be pretty severe at times. We should have bought a couple of slickers when we bought our other things."

"I've an idea," Blain said. "We packed a fair number of canvas tents on the mules today along with the food. Hank said Charlie intends on selling them to prospectors. Said there's quite a tent village just outside Deadwood. I'm sure he'd sell us one. I'll bet one of the ladies going with us brought some scissors and sewing things. It wouldn't be that hard to make a couple of slickers."

"Hm... That should work. Good thinking. We're going to need something, that's for sure."

"Once we get under way I'll talk to Charlie," Blain said. "Certainly, don't want to ask him today about rain gear."

"I'll leave it up to you, but don't wait too long," Steel took another look at the distant clouds. *I wonder what kind of dark clouds lie up ahead?* Steel wondered, unhappy with the pessimism that kept creeping into his thoughts.

When they entered the bunkhouse, Steel left the door open, hoping the outside breeze would cool things down some. Blain immediately plopped down on one of the bottom bunks, and was sawing logs in no time at all. Thinking good thoughts about fishing, Steel got out his fishing gear and started rummaging through his fly collection.

It was almost an hour later when Steel heard the ringing of the dinner bell. He put his fishing tackle away in a satchel, slipped it under his bunk with his fly rod and walked over to Blain who was sleeping soundly. "Time for chow," Steel said, giving his father a good shake on the shoulder.

"Seems I just went to sleep," was the drowsy reply.

"You slept nearly an hour."

They finished readying themselves for dinner, along with some of the working hands that had returned to the bunkhouse to cleanup, and then they made a beeline toward the enticing aroma. Two lines had already formed with people holding plates and eying the food. Blain and Steel got in line and kept an eye open for Red who said he'd join them at dinnertime.

The menu consisted of barbequed beef, fresh corn on the cob brought in from Denver, oven baked beans, sourdough rolls from Georgetown, and the *piece de resistance*: Dutch oven peach cobbler for dessert.

Blain and Steel found seats at a long table with a couple of Charlie's working hands and some painted ladies.

"This is as good a tasting a meal as I've eaten," Steel said to the others. He knew the mountain air and afternoon's hard work were major contributors to his enjoyment of the feast. "There's Red now," he said, raising his hand to motion for Red to join them. It always put a smile on his face when he saw Red, such a good-natured and upbeat fellow.

Across the table were three working girls. One of them, a cute, little blonde, who looked about nineteen, gave Steel a smile and a wink. Steel returned a polite smile and then turned his attention to Red. "A long day. Good to see you, Red."

"It's been a hell of a long day, and I'm hungry enough to eat a bear."

"Charlie sure knows how to do things up right," Blain said, putting down his spoon and looking at an empty dish of peach cobbler.

"Sorry I'm late, Blain, Steel, ladies." Red sat down with a plate stacked high with food. "Took me longer than I thought with the horses but I think I got them squared away."

"I wonder, who's going to be doing the cleaning up and all that?" Blain asked.

"Oh, Mr. Utter's taking care of that," one of the ladies spoke up. "We volunteered, but Mr. Utter said we'd be havin' plenty of work on the trail and he's hired some of the local folks here in Georgetown to do the cleanup work."

"That's right," Red said. "He's had this all planned out for some time."

"Charlie continues to impress me," Steel said.

"Me too," Red said.

Their heads turned in the direction of guitar music. It was coming from one of Charlie's boys sitting on the corner of a table strumming away. Everyone soon gathered around him. One of the painted ladies put in a song request and joined the cowboy, impressing everyone with her vocal skills.

There were two things Charlie insisted on: There was to be no liquor and everyone was to be in their sleeping quarters by nine o'clock that night. They'd be setting out soon after they could see the sun come up over the mountains. The men were to sleep in the bunkhouse and tents, and the women would sleep in the wagons.

After an hour of impromptu entertainment, enjoyed by all, Charlie stepped up onto one of the tables. "We've had a right fine evening, and tomorrow we'll be leaving a little after sunrise, so it's time to hit the hay. We've got a long journey ahead of us, but I'm anticipating we'll all arrive in Deadwood in a couple of weeks fine and dandy. I know there's many a prospector in Deadwood dreaming tonight about you ladies."

A chorus of laughter followed his words. "We're dreaming too," one of the ladies called out, "of some of that Deadwood gold falling into our petticoats."

"Yes!" went up a unison cry.

"I do want you to know that we'll be going through Cheyenne, Wyoming, to pick up approximately a hundred gold-seekers. They're paying for passage, and I need to make a little money on this trip. We'll pick up additional supplies there, which will take us through the last leg of our trip. You all should know what wagon you're sleeping in, and I'll see you tomorrow mornin'. Good night ladies," Charlie said and stepped down.

Everyone joined in giving Charlie a healthy round of applause.

Charlie quickly maneuvered over to where Blain and Steel stood. "Come with me. There's Lucy and Cattie heading for their wagon. I want to introduce you to 'em."

"I haven't seen Mr. Hickok or Calamity Jane yet," Blain said.

Steel smiled. He knew his father was excited about meeting them, so those words came as no surprise.

"They'll join up with us tomorrow morning bright and early—Lucy!" Charlie called out.

Lucy and her daughter stopped and turned around. Seeing Charlie, they smiled and walked toward him.

"Lucy, Cattie, I'd like to introduce you to Blain and his son Steel. Blain will drive your wagon. Steel will drive the wagon right in front of you with working ladies."

"We're pleased to meet you," Lucy said. "Charlie told us a little about you. You're from Philadelphia and are blacksmiths going to Deadwood to do some gold panning. My daughter Cattie went to law school in Virginia. She, not long ago, graduated with a law degree from Williams and Mary, and returned home to Denver last month," she said with a mother's pride.

"I'm impressed," Blain said.

"That is impressive. Law school graduate," Steel said.

"She's a smart young lady," Charlie chimed in.

Looking down with a shy expression, Cattie made no response.

"I'm sure this is a whole new experience for both of you, as well as for us," Blain said. "We're pleased to make your acquaintance."

"You'll get to know each other better on the trip," Charlie said. "Lucy, Cattie, these two gentlemen, and they are gentlemen, will help you out if you need something. To put it right out there, I don't want any of my men unduly bothering you."

"Charlie, I appreciate that," Lucy said. We'll be fine, and I'm just grateful you're willing to take us with you."

"We'll say good-night," Charlie said, "and I hope you get a good night's sleep. It might take you a few nights to get used to sleepin' in a wagon."

"I'm sure we'll make out just fine," Lucy said.

"Good night, ma'am and Cattie," Blain said.

"Both of you, please, call me Lucy," she said in pleasant voice with a parting smile.

"Good night, Lucy, Cattie. We'll see you tomorrow morning," Steel said.

"Good night," Cattie said with a quick uncertain smile.

Steel could tell by Cattie's tentative look that she was unsure of everything that was going on; and mostly, it hadn't been in her plans to be going to Deadwood. One thing for certain—Charlie was right—she was certainly attractive. Her long, black hair in ringlets cascaded down with the ends resting well below her shoulders. She had a slender, attractive figure, and her blue-green eyes under long, dark lashes held his attention for a long moment.

Steel had to commend her for her loyalty to her mother. With her education, she could secure a job most anywhere, yet she's here going to Deadwood to help her mother work in a saloon kitchen. *Amazing. It'll be interesting to see how she handles things.* Seeing Cattie brought Savannah to mind: *I wonder how Savannah's doing?* He let out a long breath, thinking of the last time he saw her and how poorly that went. *Perhaps it would be the best for her if she returned to Georgia.*

"I'll say goodnight to you boys," Charlie said. "I'll see you tomorrow mornin'. I'm going to check things with Em and Mustachio, making sure they're getting their girls settled in." Charlie turned and walked toward another group of wagons.

Blain and Steel headed toward the bunkhouse. "Mrs. Winthrop… Lucy and her daughter Cattie seem to be right fine people," Blain said. "Charlie was right, Cattie is a mighty pretty young lady, and her mother is a nice looking woman, too. You can tell she's her mother's daughter. The girl's got her mother's pretty looks."

"Coming from a Southern school and with her father in jail, a possible murderer, and really the unknown they're facing now, it can't be too easy for her," Steel said.

"You're right about that. We'll keep a good eye on 'em."

"I wonder how Mother is doing and Savannah? I hope my letter makes Savannah feel better. She wasn't happy with me going," Steel said, talking to himself more than his father.

"I suspect they're doing just fine. I'm sure your mother had a nice dinner tonight with her folks that Hanna cooked up. I've got to hand it to Charlie. All these ladies, there's not too many people that could pull off what he's doin'."

"Agreed," Steel said, thinking his father's way of dealing with being away from home was to talk or think about home as little as possible.

11

On the morning of departure, water droplets covered the canvas tops of the wagons. With the sun's warmth, clouds of mist rose from the morning dew, only to fade quickly into the air. Hustle and bustle abounded as the travelers readied for the journey northward.

A little over an hour after sunrise, the wagon train rolled out in an orderly fashion. The wagons with accompanying horsemen led the way followed by a string of Hank's mules. Blain and Steel gripped the reins and moved their wagons into line. Charlie rode back and forth on his palomino, making certain everything was going as planned. Bill Hickok and Calamity Jane rode in early that morning. Both had pistols that were visible and rifles in their scabbards. In awe, Blain and Steel watched Charlie give them a warm welcome. Riding side by side, the three of them made what could be an historic portrait. Although the rest of the wagon folks went about their business without any fanfare, there was an air of excitement that couldn't be denied.

Things went well that first day except for a couple of Hank's mules that decided to be disagreeable a little before noon. They bolted and broke the rope they were tethered to, running off like delinquent children. Red and a couple of the boys had their horses on them pronto. Several minutes later the critters were back in line behaving.

Steel could see that Hank was rankled by the incident, but it didn't upset Charlie. For the rest of the day, no more mishaps occurred. Some of the ladies sang as the wagons rolled along, and their songs were a pleasant addition to the day's scenic journey.

The weather couldn't have been more cooperative. It had been a sunny day without intrusive thundershowers that could appear out of seemingly nowhere bringing wind, rain, and at times hail the size of marbles. Charlie rode by Blain's wagon and commented on their good fortune. "I hope the weather continues nice for the rest of our trip. I saw dark thunderclouds hanging on them hills last evening. I've got a feeling in my bones we're going to meet up with their kinfolk sooner or later."

"I hate to admit it," Blain said, "but Steel and I forgot about buying any rain gear."

"I brought at least four dozen extra slickers, and you're welcome to help yourself. They're packed in one of the chuck wagons. Go ask one of the biscuit rollers and they'll fix you and Steel up. Always need extra slickers on a trip like this. What I don't use, I'll sell in Deadwood. Better get a couple for Lucy and Cattie while you're at it."

"Mighty obliged," Blain said, feeling a little embarrassed about his lack of foresight.

"I'll catch you later," Charlie said and rode on to the next wagon.

Right before nightfall, an inquisitive bobcat made an unwelcomed appearance and unnerved the mules. Hank relied on Steel to help settle them down. As soon as the mules quieted down, Steel headed for Lucy and Cattie's cooking fire. He hadn't eaten much all day and had been thinking about dinner for the past two hours.

A large orange moon peeked over the horizon. *The moon with the cooking fires, good smelling food, and circled wagons make for a nice, homey evening,* Steel thought. "Smells awfully good," he said, eying the iron pot. "Charlie said my father and I were to rely on you for dinner and breakfast."

"It's our privilege to be able to cook for you and your father. I just hope it's to your liking," Lucy said.

"I'm sure it will be. Sorry I'm late. I was helping Hank with his mules."

"Cattie and I have eaten, but we've been looking for you. We heard the mules making a commotion and thought you might be helping Hank out. I made plenty of stew, so help yourself. There's a bowl and a spoon by the kettle and some biscuits. Oh, there's a small jar of honey next to you."

Steel took the ladle, filled his bowl to the brim, and then sat down next to Cattie. She had her hands in her lap and her gaze on the fire.

"Cattie, how'd your first day on the trail go?" Steel asked.

"I enjoyed my day. The scenery coming out of the mountains was breathtaking. I rode up front with your father for a good part of the day. He told me a lot about you." She looked at him out of the corner of her eye and gave him a coquettish smile.

Steel almost choked on his spoonful of stew. "Oh, what did he tell you?" he asked, feeling a little amused.

"You like to fish and you have a girl back home. Savannah, I believe, is her name."

"Savannah and I are good friends. She's from Georgia, and she's studying to be a nurse," Steel was quick to reply.

"Cattie, let the poor boy eat," Lucy said.

Cattie laughed, and Steel joined her in light laughter. "I'm going to have a serious talk with my father."

Steel couldn't believe his father was so forthcoming with his personal information. *For a quiet man, somewhat of a social recluse, my father has completely changed into an outgoing, friendly, talkative person,* Steel thought, knowing he couldn't get upset with his father.

"Do you know when your father is coming to dinner?" Lucy asked. "I want to be sure to keep the food warm for him."

"He's over with Charlie checking on a wagon hitch they were having some trouble with. He should be here shortly. I'm surprised he's not here now."

"You're a blacksmith," Cattie said. She hesitated for a moment and then said, "Steel, you're well named."

"I've been told that once or twice. Lucy, this stew is really good, and I'm not just saying that to be nice."

"Steel, I'm glad you like it. Being hungry does help… I appreciate the compliment."

"Do you mind telling me why they call you a blacksmith?" Cattie asked.

Steel raised his brows.

"Cattie, let the poor man finish his dinner," Lucy said with a scowl.

"I'm fine." Steel said. "No one's ever asked me that." He stopped eating and thought for a moment. "The term *black* is a reference to metals that we work with. These metals develop a layer of dark or black oxides as we work on them. *Smith* is from the word *smit*, or to hit. So a blacksmith is one who hits black metal." He smiled before continuing. "We have a forge for heating the metal to malleability, along with an anvil, a hard surface to work the metal against. We use hammers and other tools for beating and refining the metal."

"Thank you. I do find that interesting, truly I do."

"We don't work with a great deal of light in our shop. That's so we can better judge the temperature of the metal by its color while we're working or shaping it. My father and I are also farriers. A farrier is a person who specializes in making horseshoes and fitting them properly. That's probably more information than you wanted to know."

"No, not at all, but now I'll let you finish your stew."

It didn't take long for Steel to empty the bowl. He got up again and got a biscuit and layered it with honey.

"So do you plan on making blacksmithing your life's work?" Cattie asked.

"Cattie, I think you've found out enough from his father about his personal affairs," Lucy said.

"Lucy, it's the lawyer in her," Steel said with a grin. "No. I graduated last year from the College of Philadelphia. I enjoy business and plan on working for my grandfather. He's a businessman and owns three retail stores. I wanted to work with my father for a spell—not more than a year, and then settle into a carrier with my grandfather. This adventure, I call it, is something my father wanted to do, and he asked me to join him. Frankly, I'm not interested in gold panning. Kind of a detour to my plans, I guess you could say, but it'll all work out."

"I'm sure things will work out for you," Cattie said with sincerity.

"Cattie, now that you know pretty much everything about me, tell me about yourself. I think you'd call it *quid pro quo*." He gave a quick smile. "You graduated from law school..."

"William & Mary Law School. My grandfather was a businessman. He wanted me, the only grandchild, to go to law school. He felt that no matter what I did in life, a legal education would be advantageous."

"I'm impressed. I don't know any lady lawyers."

"I have a law degree. I haven't applied to practice in any state."

"From what I've been told, I understand there's no law and order in Deadwood, so your law degree isn't going to do you a lot of good there," Steel said. "I'm sure you could find a high-quality job in Denver or just about anywhere."

"I wanted to stay in Denver and had a good job offer at one of the local banks, but Mother wanted to leave the area for a little while. I suspect Charlie told you about my father."

Steel gave a nod.

"I don't think we'll be in Deadwood longer than six or seven months, if that." Cattie gave her mother a quick look.

She didn't respond to Cattie's comment. She stood by the dwindling fire and gazed at the night sky, seemingly deep in thought. Steel had the feeling that as attractive as the rising moon was, she had her mind on other things. He suspected he'd opened up a tender spot in their relationship and now regretted making the comment about a job in Denver.

"I notice you were carrying a long tube that you put in our wagon along with your other things. I'm curious," Cattie said.

"Do you need to know all my secrets?" Steel teased. "That's my fly fishing rod. It's a three-piece bamboo rod. I make my own flies out of different kinds of materials, mostly feathers and furs of different types. The idea is to make a fly that matches as closely as possible what a fish might be looking to eat at that particular moment. The bamboo rod loads the line, enabling me to cast the line out a fair distance over the water. There's a lot to it. Dedicated fly fishermen spend a lifetime learning and trying to improve their fishing techniques and abilities."

"I think I'd like to learn how to fly fish!"

Steel leaned back and almost fell off the log he was sitting on. "You're joking, or as my father would say, you're joshing me."

"No, really I would. Will you teach me?"

Her face and serious tone firmed up Steel's surprise.

"Okay… yes. I'm hoping to do some fishing along the way to Deadwood. Hank asked me tonight if I'd help him with his mules at the end of the day's travels. I'm not sure now if I'm going to get a chance to fish on the trip; and of course, we'd need to be fairly close to a stream when we settle in for the night." He thought for a moment, still surprised by her request. "When I go out, I'll take you, but it might not be until after we get to Deadwood."

"I'm looking forward to going with you, and I'm not just saying that to be joshing you." Cattie gave Steel a quick smile and then she looked over at her mother. "I've finally got something to look forward to," she said, politely, obviously sending a message to her mother.

"There's my father coming now. I'm sure he'll enjoy your cooking as much as I have."

"Thank you, Steel."

Steel kept his eyes on his father. "I need to have a serious talk with you," Steel said as his father approached them. Steel turned and looked at Cattie. They exchanged smiles.

"Oh?" his father questioned. He gave Steel a cursory glance and then focused on the pot of stew.

12

THE WAGONS ROLLED ALONG without any major mishaps the first few days. It seemed that after the third day everyone had adjusted to a suitable routine. The most enjoyable times were in the evenings around the campfires with guitar playing, singing, and some dancing with the working girls. Charlie kept a tight herd on things, and reminded everyone more than once that there was no liquor. "If I catch anyone of you—man or woman—liquored up, you'll be going to Deadwood on your own. And that's a promise."

During the daytime, as they moved along, an occasional spring, thunder-and-lighting storm came whipping in and quickly moved out. During these times, slickers were appreciated. The mules and the horses were the most riled by the inclement weather. Charlie always had an eye out for an early snowstorm, but so far, Lady Luck was a welcomed companion.

The nights were lit with stars so close, it seemed as if a body could reach up, gather them in, and put them in a basket. An occasional coyote yelped and howled, breaking up the stillness of the night. With a Winchester rifle at his side, Hank slept next to his mules making sure no unwanted critter would disturb them. For the most part, the men slept out in the open. They could take cover under a wagon if need be. A few of them slept in pup tents.

To date, Steel had thoroughly enjoyed the trip. He liked driving the wagon. He knew he might get tired of driving before the end of their journey, but for now, he had no complaints. Cattie started riding beside him for a good part of the day. He enjoyed her quick wit and sense of humor. Thoughts of his mother and Savannah hadn't subsided, but admittedly those thoughts had taken a back seat to the daily routine.

On the morning sunrise, the fourth day on the trail, a scream rent the air followed by a gunshot. One of the younger, working girls had found a large diamondback rattler coiled up behind the wagon she was staying in. When Steel got there, Calamity Jane had a rifle resting on her arm, and Hank was holding up a dead snake by its tail.

"Fine lookin' rattler. It'll make a good headband," Hank said. "I'm going to skin him up and cook him for dinner. Rattler tastes a lot like chicken."

Steel arrived just in time to hear Hank's comment and gave him a questioning look.

"Missy, you all right?" Calamity said. "That snake would have scared me, too."

When Charlie arrived, all was well to his relief. "Just a friendly rattler. Thanks, Calamity. Let's get packed up folks. We need to move out," he said.

"Hank, are you really going to eat that snake?" Steel asked.

"Dang tootin', I am. Come over tonight at suppertime and I'll give you a couple of bites. It's more tender than young sage hen."

"I think I'll stick to Lucy's cooking and sage hens, but thanks anyway," Steel said, giving Hank a look of wonderment.

"Thanks again, Calamity," Charlie said.

"It weren't nothin'. Not the first snake I ever shot. Course most of the snakes I've shot had two legs."

Charlie smiled and gave her a nod.

The party broke up, and in a little more than an hour the wagon wheels were rolling.

Steel and Cattie's relationship developed quickly. They spent the evenings together around the campfire, and during the day she was by his side on the wagon seat. Even though they'd camped near some streams, the work was such that Steel hadn't had a chance to take her out fly fishing. Every now and then she'd remind him of his promise to take her fishing.

"As soon as I get the chance, we'll go."

They stopped in Cheyenne and picked up a good number of people, wagon ready, who were looking forward to making their fortunes in the region of Deadwood. Steel continued to be amazed at how the hopes of finding gold excited people. They quickly loaded up the supplies they needed to complete the last leg of the trip, and Charlie had the wagon train moving out with only a day's delay.

Several days out of Deadwood, while most everyone was sitting around the cooking fires finishing dinner and enjoying the evening hour, Hank came marching up to Lucy's fire.

"Hello, Hank. We've extra. Come and join us," Lucy said.

"Thanks, Lucy, maybe another time," Hank said. He put his hands on his hip and looked at Blain. "I could use a little help with one of the mules. Blain, I need to repack that anvil on Butter Cup. It's shifted over to one side and she's not happy with that. I was wonderin' if you could you give me a hand."

"Hank, I think I'll have Steel go with you, if you don't mind. My back is bothering me a bit and I'd just like to sit here by the fire a little longer," Blain said.

"I'd be pleased to have Steel's help," Hank said. "I just didn't want to take him away from Cattie."

Steel and Cattie looked at each other. For the first time, Steel realized that people were thinking of them as an item. "Happy to help you, Hank," Steel said, and was quickly on his feet.

Steel didn't miss Lucy and his father's smiles.

"When I'm finished helping Hank, I'll bring back some more brushwood for the fire."

"I won't keep him long, Cattie," Hank said.

"Cattie, I think I'll go to the wagon and get us a couple of shawls," Lucy said. "It's cooling down real fast this evening." She got up and wrapped her arms around herself.

Steel admired Lucy. He could tell by her manners that she'd been raised in a well-to-do family. It was funny how some good women picked the wrong men to marry and vice versa. He knew his mother and father loved each other, but what each wanted out of life was quite different. His father always wanted a large family and his mother was happy with just one child. His father had an adventurous heart, wanting to move out West, whereas his mother was a city girl and enjoyed the social life a city could offer. The blind love of youth had brought them together, and after a fashion they made it work.

Steel and Hank set off toward the mules.

"Things have been going real well," Hank said. "Got to hand it to Charlie, he keeps things movin' in good order, and the people we picked up in Laramie have been behaving themselves."

"What's that?" Steel asked."

"Sounds like a slap!"

"Oh! You hurt me! Get away from me you big ox!"

"I bet one of the workin' gals is in trouble," Hank said. "I spoke too soon about things going real well."

They rushed to the back of the wagon and found Rusty, one of the hired hands, holding Lilia, a pretty, sporting girl, by her shoulders. He was trying to press his lips on hers. She swished her head from side to side, while pressing her hands against him in an effort to free herself from his strong grip.

"Leave her be!" Steel shouted.

"Get out of here, Steel! She's been teasing me with her looks the last three days! She's just a damn sportin' girl, and I'm gonna give her some sport!"

"I said, leave her be!" Steel stepped forward, grabbed Rusty's shoulder and yanked him away.

Rusty turned on Steel with venom in his eyes. His hand moved toward his revolver. Steel's fist flew, landing square on Rusty's jaw with a loud crack.

Rusty did a stutter step back and fell backward, landing with a thud on his backside. He looked up at Steel standing over him. His hand reached for his gun. His revolver cleared the holster.

A shot rang out and the gun flew out of Rusty's hand. Steel turned. Behind him, Bill Hickok stood about ten feet away with a drawn pistol.

"You're damn lucky I didn't kill you. Trying to shoot an unarmed man," Hickok said coolly.

Charlie ran up with several other men and ladies.

Rusty remained on the ground, looking up like a wounded coyote.

"What's going on, Bill?" Charlie asked.

Lilia spoke up. "I was fighting off Rusty and yelled. Steel pulled him away from me and knocked him on his back. Rusty pulled his gun and was gonna shoot Steel when Mr. Hickok shot the gun out of his hand."

Mr. Hickok nodded and holstered his gun. "That's right, Charlie," he said.

"Rusty, I'm going to give you a horse and enough grub to get you to Deadwood. When you get there, see my brother Steve and he'll give you some pay. I want the horse back when we get to Deadwood. Get your things. I want you out of here tonight. You've got almost a full moon, so you got some light. If you're not out of here in half an hour, you can walk to Deadwood." Charlie turned to Lilia. "Lilia, I don't want any more trouble or you'll be walkin' to Deadwood too. Things are going well and I sure don't want any flirtin' hussy causing trouble with my men. Do you understand?"

"Yes," she said, looking down sheepishly.

Steel could tell Charlie was hopping mad at Lilia. He always referred to the working women as "lady" or "ladies."

Rusty got up slowly, dusting off his pants. When he was upright, he ran his hand along his jaw. "I think my jaw is broke." He looked around for his gun.

"Your gun landed under that wagon wheel. Be real careful how you put it back in your holster," Hickok said.

It took Rusty a moment to find it. He holstered his gun and turned to Steel, saying under his breath, "When you get to Deadwood, I'm gonna get you good, Kid."

Hickok heard Rusty's threat. "You cause him any trouble, I'll personally come after you, and put a bullet between your eyes."

Rusty gave Steel a last hard stare and then sauntered off, stroking his jaw.

"Thanks, Mr. Hickok. Good thing you were passing by," Steel said. "I thought I was a dead man."

"Happy to help you."

"Thank you, Steel," Lilia said, attempting to brush her hair back in place.

"I almost didn't hire Rusty," Charlie said. "I just had a feeling. Should have gone with my instincts. Get a good night's sleep. We're up early tomorrow. Bill, I need to talk to you about something on the way back to your tent."

"Steel, again I thank you," Lilia said, batting her eyes at Steel and putting her hand on his arm for a moment.

"Good night, Lilia," Steel said. She had made eyes at him more than once, so he suspected Rusty was telling the truth, though it still was no cause for him to force himself on her.

As they were parting, Dirty Em came marching in like a mad, wet ma hen. "Charlie, Lilia's one of my girls. Sorry about the problem. It won't happen again. Lilia, get back to the wagon!"

Em took Lila by the arm and turned her toward their wagon. Lilia walked away with her nose high and a swing to her hips.

Charlie smiled. "Em 'll handle the matter real fine, that I'm certain of," he said.

Charlie and Mr. Hickok walked away and the small crowd dispersed.

"That girl is walkin' trouble," Hank said, "but that was some shooting by Mr. Hickok."

"I wish I could shoot like that," Steel said, thoughtfully.

"Shooting like that can be both heaven and hell. More times than not it's going to land you in hell," Hank said. "Let's go look at Butter Cup."

13

The wagons rolled into Deadwood on a Saturday afternoon causing more excitement than a Fourth of July parade. A couple of prospectors had seen a dust cloud about five miles out of town and had whipped their mules back to town as fast as they could get them to run. "The wagon train is comin'! The wagon train is comin'!" they cried.

Rusty had arrived in Deadwood two days earlier, so most of the menfolk were waiting with money jingling in their pockets for the sporting ladies to arrive. Before they reached town, Charlie had his men tack the wagons' canvas covers up, displaying the working ladies for the onlookers. The ladies smiled and waved, and the men clapped and hollered.

Cattie sat next to Steel as he handled the reins of his wagon. He wasn't sure what she and Lucy thought of the display, but he suspected Lucy might be having some serious second thoughts about her decision to go to Deadwood.

An upstart miners' town, Deadwood wasn't much of a town to look at. A few saloons, houses for the working girls, a livery stable, mercantile store, a couple of small eating places, a barbershop, a Chinese laundry, and that was pretty much the extent of it. Just outside of town they had passed a sizable tent village where most of the prospectors parked their bedrolls.

Charlie took the wagons and mules through the middle of town, making a real show of the whole event. He rode his handsome palomino and led the parade smiling and waving to the crowd—a crowd that reciprocated with applause and enthusiastic yells of, "Good man Charlie! You did it Charlie! We're beholden to you Charlie!"

He tipped his hat to the appreciative onlookers, which consisted of mainly full-bearded prospectors and a few fancy gamblers. If one looked hard enough, one could find a few women's faces hidden in the throng. Bill Hickok and Calamity Jane were at Charlie's side. It was a sight for the patrons of Deadwood to see and write about in their journals.

Steel noticed Rusty standing in front of one of the saloons with a cigarette hanging on his lip. He glared at Steel as the wagons rolled by. Steel had the feeling that he and Rusty would be meeting again, and it wouldn't be a friendly get-together.

Steel was quick to notice that every man was carrying a sidearm. He knew his father's strong opposition to guns. *We're going to each need to carry a gun. Maybe Charlie can help me convince my father that we should buy a couple of revolvers. I'll give it few of days... Charlie might mention something without me saying anything,* he thought, hoping it would be sooner rather than later.

Charlie rode up to Steel's wagon. "Steel, Cattie, welcome to Deadwood. Not much of a looking town right now. Give it a year and there'll be a lot of changes. I'll see you at my camp." He rode off smiling and waving to the crowd.

Steel turned to Cattie, "Charlie's happy. What do you think?"

"I wish my mother and I had never left Denver. It was a big mistake."

Steel couldn't slight her for her feelings. Truth be told, Deadwood looked like a pretty dismal place.

Hoping to put a little light in her spirit, Steel said, "I need to take you fishing."

"I did meet you, and I'm glad for that," she said, resting her hand on his arm.

He looked over at her. "I'm glad I met you, too. I have the feeling, most people aren't going to get a lot of sleep tonight," he said with a frown.

"I saw Rusty giving you the stare. You need to be careful."

"Rusty doesn't concern me, but I'll keep an eye out."

As expected, Charlie had things set up at his camp: a good-size corral, a small bunkhouse, and an area where most of his men would be living in tents. Charlie's personal residence would be a nice-size tent. It was common knowledge that he enjoyed a daily bath and hair-wash. Deadwood would at least provide him with those luxuries. Blain and Steel decided to purchase a tent from Charlie for their living quarters, which was really their only option.

"I'm not takin' any of your money," Charley said. "I'm just glad to have you boys here. There are a couple of sizes. Make sure you pick out the larger size. Hank 'll help you out."

The covered wagons circled when they arrived at the camp. Charlie rode into the center and dismounted. Em, Mustachio, and Red were quickly by his side.

"Ladies, Em and Mustachio will get you organized. I suspect they've already laid out the plans. The town, as you can see, is a short walk from my camp. Some of you will be going into town tonight or maybe all of you." The crowd started clapping. Charlie put up his hands for quiet. "Be patient cause it's not gonna happen all at once. I do want to say, I'm proud of you ladies. Except for a couple of incidents, you've all been very well behaved, especially after we picked up additional menfolk in Cheyenne, which did cause me some concern. I laid the rules down and you followed them."

Charlie took off his hat and held it in two hands and then continued, "That brings me to you gold-seekers we picked up in Cheyenne. I got plenty of tents if you're interested in buying one and I'll charge you a fair price. I don't believe in giving anyone the little end of the horn. I hope you all strike it rich in the business of your choice. Red is going to coordinate things with you Cheyenne people. Coming in, you saw the tent city, and I suspect that's where most of you wantin' to prospect will be settin' down your stakes. You can stay at my camp for a night or two but after that I may get one of Hank's nastiest mules to kick you out."

Laughter broke out.

"Speaking of mules, we'll be selling some of them. If you want a mule to help you with your prospecting, you can take that up with

Hank. Again, I wish you all good luck. We'll do our best to help you get settled in. And I thank you."

Everyone applauded for a long minute. Steel looked at their faces, and saw excitement and hope in their eyes. Everybody would be beginning a new life. *Optimism is a good thing,* he thought. There would be discouragements, but for the moment there was a shining light in their faces.

"Red, we need to get those tents off the mules," Charlie said, "so we can get them to those who are fixing to buy 'em. Hank will coordinate the unpacking, but you need to get some of the Cheyenne men to give him a hand. Then I want you and the boys to work with Em and Mustachio, getting the working gals settled or whatever the two madams want you to help them with."

"Understood," Red said. He tipped his hat, turned in the direction of the mules and was off.

Lucy and Cattie would be sleeping in the wagon that first night. Blain and Steel would move them into a small cabin in the morning. During an earlier visit to Deadwood, Charlie had purchased a cabin from a prospector and his wife with the intent of possibly using it as his residence. The prospector had a streak of good luck right after the cabin was finished. His wife had had enough of Deadwood and insisted they move back to Laramie where most of their kinfolk resided. With the addition of Lucy and Cattie, Charlie had no problem giving up the cabin. He was used to living in a tent and was content as long as he had fine blankets, a mirror, combs, brushes to keep his long blond hair looking proper, and a straightedge razor.

Sunday was a settling-in day. Steel and Blain moved Lucy and Cattie into Charlie's cabin. It was pleasantly accommodating with an iron-cast cooking stove, a river rock fireplace, and two bedrooms with burlap curtains hanging on the windows. Charlie had bought the furniture from the owners, and other than a need of dusting and a good sweeping out, it was quite livable.

Blain and Steel's tent was a quick set-up at Charlie's compound. They needed to find or make some cots to put their bedrolls on. *The weather is manageable now, but fall will soon be looking us in the face. Building a small wooden shelter might be a prudent idea,* Steel thought.

"As nice as Charlie's tent is, I'd be surprised if he plans on staying in it for the winter," he remarked to his father.

"Let's get settled in and then we can think about the next step," Blain said.

14

Early Monday morning, Blain and Steel met with Charlie and several of his men out in front of Nuttal and Mann's Saloon. "I think that empty lot across the way is going to work just fine for your blacksmith shop," Charlie said. "I bought the lot the last time I was in Deadwood. In fact, I bought several lots. I'd have to pay a might more for them now. The first order of business is putting up some kind of a structure that'll serve as a blacksmith shop for the two of you," he said, surveying the lot. "Blain, you've been honest with me and said your time here will run out in about a year or less. I'll need to bring in a new blacksmith or two, hopefully people on a permanent basis. That's why I need to own the land and building for the shop, so I'm picking up all the costs. I hope you're agreeable?"

"That couldn't work out better for us. I've been wondering how we were going to handle that. Takes a load off my mind. We're appreciative," Blain said.

"I do believe we can have something suitable in three or four days. My man, Dusty, knows where to get the lumber and such. They'll get that picked up this morning, and I suspect they'll start hammering by noon. Blain, you came here to look for that yellow dust, so I'm thinking you and Steel should head out to French or Cherry Creek and do a little panning today. Steel, I recollect now you like to fish. Go get your fishing pole and head out to one of the streams."

"I think we can do that," Blain said with an approving nod.

"Yes, we can," Steel said.

Steel knew his father had been eager to try his panning skills, the minute they arrived, and he'd been giving more than a thought or two about going fishing with Cattie.

"When you're ready, go over to the livery stable and old man Marks will fix you up with a couple of horses and give you directions. There are a number of creeks in the area. I'd suggest you start out on the most noteworthy one and that's French Creek. That's where gold was first discovered in this area. It's a nice little stream and I know Steel can find some fish waitin' for him there."

"That sounds good to me. Where would you suggest we get dinner tonight?" Blain asked.

"I've been meaning to tell you, you can get dinner at Nuttal's. You don't have to play cards or drink their whiskey. I'm going to arrange today for you boys to dine there in the back kitchen, that is, if you'd like."

Blain and Steel looked at each other and gave a grateful nod.

"I'll have Lucy keep your tab and you can settle up weekly."

"That works better than fine for us," Blain said.

"I'm glad to hear Lucy and Cattie like the cabin. Thanks for settling them in."

"We were happy to do it," Blain said.

"It's not a bad place at all," Charlie said. "Right now, I need to go over to the livery stable and then I'm heading back to camp for a meeting. I'll catch you boys later. Blain, you find some of that Black Hills gold, you hear? And I'll tell Mr. Marks to set you up with horses."

"I'm taking Cattie if she can go. If you could tell Mr. Marks three horses," Steel said.

"That'll do Cattie good. I'll let him know. Three horses."

"Thanks, Charlie," Steel said.

Steel glanced at Blain. "I'm heading over to Nuttal's. I don't want to hold you up. I'll see you this evening. Good luck panning." Steel turned and started walking toward the saloon.

"Sure you don't want me to wait for you?"

"I'm sure," Steel said with a glance back at his father.

"I'll see you this evening then, if not before. I just thought of something: I've got to go to the mercantile and buy me a pan! "

"That might be a good idea," Steel called out and then chuckled, thinking his father was so excited he could have ridden out to French Creek without a gold mining pan.

Steel, happy about the day's newly hatched prospects, pushed the kitchen door open at Nuttal's.

Tending some eggs and sizzling bacon slices, Lucy stood over one of the cast iron stoves with a spatula in her hand. She glanced over at Steel and gave him a warm smile.

A tall man, thin as a rail with sunken cheeks and a baldhead, wearing a cook's apron, greeted Steel with a friendly smile. He stood next to a large, square, chopping block. "Just cutting up a few venison steaks for dinner. What can we do you for Son?" he said in a deep, raspy voice.

"Sam this is Steel," Lucy said. "He and his father, Blain, helped us on the wagon trip. I suspect he's looking for Cattie," she said as she turned an egg over.

"Nice to meet you, Sam."

"Likewise."

"You're right, Lucy. I'm heading out to French Creek and was hoping she'd be able to join me."

"Fishing?" Lucy asked, continuing to focus on her cooking.

"Yes, fishing. I know she might be busy, but I did promise I'd ask her—does she know how to sit in a saddle?"

"She's an excellent rider. I'm sure we can let her break away. Can't we Sam?"

"I reckon so."

"Steel it would do her a world of good to go with you. I sent her out back a few minutes ago to empty a bucket of water. She should have been back by now. I don't know what's keeping her. I'm almost finished with this breakfast order. You're welcome to go out back and find her."

"I'll do that." Steel pushed the back door open and scanned the back area. Cattie was nowhere in sight. An empty, turned-over water bucket by a back storage shed caught his eye.

"Cattie!" Steel called out, hearing sounds coming from behind the shed. His heart raced. He ran toward the back of the shed.

Cattie was twisting and struggling on the ground, trying to free herself from the clutches of a huge, bearded man on top of her. The man's large hand covered her mouth, muffling the cries for help.

Her attacker turned and looked up at Steel like a wild beast protecting its kill. "Get the hell out of here, or I'll kill you!" he roared.

Steel's emotions at a fever's pitch, ran over, grasped the attacker's shoulders and threw him off Cattie as if the man were a rag doll.

The assailant's private parts, under a flopping potbelly, were exposed due to his unbutton trousers. He gave a quick glance down at his nakedness, which few seconds gave Steel the chance to deliver a punishing blow.

Steel, with an anger he'd never before experienced, drew his foot back and with all the force his adrenaline could muster, he buried the silver-tip toe of his boot directly into the attacker's private parts.

The man screamed as blood flowed down his exposed legs.

Steel turned to Cattie. "Are you okay?"

"I'm okay, I'm okay," she said, trying to catch her breath.

"He didn't—"

"Y-you came just in time," she stammered. Tears streamed down her flushed face.

"Go into your mother. I'm not finished here." Steel stared at the man lying on his back, moaning like a wounded animal. Steel was just about to issue a blow to his head when he checked his emotions.

The man continued to whimper and moan. "Don't kick me again. I need the doc. He's playing cards at the table next to the kitchen. Please, please, go get the doc. I'm hurting! Oh I'm hurting! I'm bleeding all over! Please get the doc, please."

Steel could see he'd cause the man some serious damage. Under his potbelly, his private parts were a bloody mess.

"I'll go fetch him," Steel said reluctantly.

Steel turned and made no rush to get to the back door. When he entered the kitchen, he paused. Lucy was holding Cattie and stroking her hair. Her head rested on her mother's shoulder.

"Steel, anything I can do? Sam asked raising his Bowie knife.

"No, he's not going anywhere. He's calling for the doctor."

"Doc's playing cards at the first table you see going out the kitchen," Sam said.

Steel nodded, turned and went out into the gambling hall. "I need a doctor."

The four men at the nearest card table looked over at Steel. One motioned his head to the right in the direction of an older man, clean-shaven, with grey hair and wearing spectacles.

"If you could come out back," Steel said calmly. "There's a man calling for you. He tried to attack the young lady working in the kitchen—Cattie. I believe she's all right. She's with her mother. The man does look like he needs your help. He's hurting, hurting pretty bad."

"Did you do the hurtin'?"

"I did, and I'd do it again."

"Good." Doc laid his cards on the table, took a drink of whiskey and got up slowly. "Tried to harm that young lady working in the kitchen. Pretty little gal. Let's look at the varmint. I think I'm going to let him hurt awhile."

Doc and the three other men got up from the card table and followed Steel into the kitchen. The doc stopped for a moment and checked on Cattie. He looked over at Steel, "She's okay," he said. Then the five of them went through the back door. Carrying his Bowie knife, Sam brought up the rear.

The large potbelly man lay on the ground still crying and moaning. "Doc, he, he kicked me. What's he done to me?"

"Let me take a look. Sam, hand me that dishtowel. Um… Well, you're not going to be bothering the ladies anymore, and you're most likely going to hell. Somehow that boot-kick almost ripped off your lizard. Never seen anything like it. Best I can do right now is to try and stop the bleeding. I'll get you over to my office, and then I'm going to have to cut the rest of your lizard off. You can see it's just hanging there by a piece of skin. Serves you right. Don't feel a bit sorry for you. I've seen you around town. What's your name?"

"Jake 's my name. Please, please, Doc, put me back together."

"Jake, I can't do that, and the women will be better off."

"Damdest thing I ever did see, Doc," Sam said. "I can finish cutting his lizard off right now. I keep my Bowie real sharp for cutting venison steaks."

Jake's jaw dropped. "Don't let him touch me with that knife, Doc!"

"Sam, I'd let you do it except for the fact that I like a good venison steak now and then, and the thought of using the same knife for the steaks as for his lizard removal don't sound too appetizing. I'll do it at my office, but thanks for the offer."

"I'm just hurting so much, Doc, you gotta help me."

"You're going to be hurting for a spell, I suspect, and it serves your damn hide right. Ain't got the least bit of sympathy for you." The doc turned to the other men. "If you men would help me lift him up. Let's walk him over to my office. We're not going to take him through the saloon. Don't want to get that bloodied up. I ain't happy, Jake, I had the best darn hand of cards I've had all week, and I'm leaving half a glass of good whiskey."

Doc turned to Steel and nodded. He looked down at Steel's boots. "By golly, you've got a metal toe covering on that right boot."

"I'd wear the toe out on my right boot faster than my left in my work. My father and I fashioned a metal plate to cover the tip of the boot. It works well."

"That piece of metal on your boot. I'm sure is what sliced Jake up good. Come on boys, let's get him out of here."

Within minutes, the news of what happened in the back of Nuttal's spread like a wildfire. People were laughing and snickering at Big Jake's fate.

A prospector ran up to Charlie and Mr. Marks who were standing in front of the livery stable visiting. "Did you hear what just went down at Nuttal's?" The excitement in his voice didn't escape Charlie.

"No. Calm down Old Timer. I was just heading over there. What happened?" Charlie asked, thinking some gambling killing might have gotten him excited.

"Big Jake was trying to have his way with a young lady in the back of Nuttal's. Don't know if she was a painted lady. Anyway, someone yanked Jake off her and kicked 'im with the toe of his boot that almost tore off his snake. They said his snake was hanging by a piece of his skin and Doc has to cut it all the way off. Said Jake was moaning and crying like a baby all the way to Doc's office."

With an inkling that Steel and Cattie might be involved, Charlie said to Mr. Marks, "I'll see you later." Walking at a brisk pace, he arrived at Nuttal's in no more than a couple of minutes. He found Steel, Cattie, and Lucy sitting at the kitchen table. Sam was manning the grill.

"I just got word. How are you doing, Cattie?" Charlie asked with concern in his voice and a questioning look.

"I'm fine. If Steel hadn't come—I don't know where he got his strength. He grabbed that big man by the shoulders and threw him off me like the man was a skinny little kid," Cattie said with an uneasy voice.

Charlie turned to Steel, gave him a nod, and then addressed Lucy. "Lucy, what happened is the type of thing I've been worrying about all along. I know what happened could have happened anywhere, but I think you can see now there are more unsavory gents around Deadwood than most places."

"You're right, Charlie. I should have listened to you. We never should have come. Charlie, when you can work things out, I think it's best we return to Denver. I feel awful about coming, putting you out and everything, and my daughter, Cattie…"

"Don't you fret none about that. You and Cattie haven't been any trouble at all. Staying here in Deadwood is more about your safety than anything," Charlie said. "But that's the right decision, getting out of here."

"I honestly don't know what I was thinking about, Charlie. I just didn't want to be in the same town with John. But you've been right all along, Deadwood is not the place for us."

"It may take me three or four weeks, but I'll get you back to Denver as soon as I can. Meantime, I'm going to let this town know that I'm watching out for you and Cattie, and anyone causes you trouble, they'll be dealing with me."

"Thanks, Charlie. I know I'm always thanking you," Lucy said as a semblance of a smile appeared on her face.

"Cattie, I'm glad you're okay. Steel, good thing you were around. I need to leave. I've an appointment to meet someone at my place," Charlie said. "I'll catch you a little later. Again, Lucy, four weeks at the longest, I promise." Charlie gave them an encouraging look and then left through the back door of the kitchen.

Charlie's words took Steel by surprise. He was glad Cattie would be in a safer place, have a good job—a place where she wanted to be. He realized that he was going to miss her immensely, and that gave him pause to acknowledge that he'd fallen in love with her. This was a different feeling than he'd ever felt for Savannah. It was a revelation that he knew was real, but it brought him no joy, only concern as to what the future would hold.

"Steel, are you all right?" Lucy asked.

"Yes... Yes, I'm fine." He turned to Cattie, "Cattie, the reason I happened to come over so early is, I thought we might go fishing out at French Creek. I don't know if you feel up to going..."

"Oh yes, I'd love to go."

Steel looked at Lucy, and she gave Steel an approving nod.

"I need to pick up the fishing gear. You'll need a jacket. I'll get us a couple of horses at the livery stable."

"I'll be ready. I'll bring something for us to eat."

"Good idea. Lucy, I'm not sure what time we'll return. I like to fish the caddis hatch, which will most likely happen toward evening."

"Steel, I never worry about Cattie when she's with you."

Steel appreciated Lucy's confidence in him and returned a warm smile.

"Cattie, I'll meet you at your place with the horses, say in about half-an-hour. "Lucy, my father left a little earlier for French Creek to pan for gold. My guess is that he won't be back for dinner until later than usual."

"If he's panning for gold, he'll be out there until the last dog is hung," Sam said. "We'll save something for him."

"You're right, Sam. He might not even come by Nuttal's tonight, now that I think about it," Steel said.

"We'll be looking for him anyway," Lucy said. "You two have a good time."

"Lucy, Sam, thanks," Steel said. He gave Cattie a quick look, turned and walked out of the kitchen as he was starting to relax a little. His eagerness to get to French Creek and get his fishing line in the water was helpful in cooling down his emotions.

As he headed back to his tent, he realized he could have delivered a lethal blow to Jake without any qualms.

15

The early afternoon ride out to French Creek seemed to have a calming effect on Cattie. She commented on the beauty of the day and was quick to point out several deer feeding in a small, grassy meadow, a bobcat that eyed them from a rocky ledge, and a lonely coyote looking for a late afternoon meal. Steel was sure her emotions were still tender and would likely continue as such until she and Lucy permanently left Deadwood.

Steel found a pleasant location near the stream to tie up the horses and set up his fly rod. He spotted several quiet pools with riffles running into them.

It didn't take him long to string his rod and select a fly. He spent twenty minutes or so showing Cattie how to shoot the line out in the desired direction. "Try not to take the rod back past one o'clock," he repeated several times.

When he thought she was ready, he moved her into a position above the nearest pool.

"Now, we're going to cast our line into the riffle and let it float with the current into that nice lazy pool. Give it a try."

After several attempts, Cattie made a manageable presentation. The brown-feathered fly entered the pool and glided on top of the water without any disturbance.

Suddenly the fly vanished!

"Set the hook, Cattie! Lift the rod tip! He's on your line! Keep your rod tip high… Let him run… Nice fish. Try and keep a firm line. Rod tip up, you don't want him to throw the hook… Good… Reel in a little, he may take off… Be careful… There he goes! Patience… Reel him in again… He's starting to tire… Easy… Lift the rode tip higher, keep his head out of the moss… Guide him over to me… That's it… That's it…"

Steel knelt down at the edge of the stream "Got 'im. I think he's about eighteen inches. Look at the red coloring on the sides." Steel cradled the fish in his hands. "Gorgeous fish. Let me get the hook out, and we'll turn him loose." Steel removed the hook and gently slid the fish back into the cold water. With a swish of its tail, it was gone.

Steel looked up at Cattie and smiled. "Nice job," he said.

She beamed.

When Steel stood up he pulled Cattie to him.

Their lips met.

The softness of her lips sent his emotions soaring.

Slowly she drew her head back. "That was awfully nice," she whispered.

"Catching the rainbow or the kiss?" Steel asked with a glow in his eye.

"Both."

A nice ending for a harrowing day, Steel thought.

When Steel returned to Charlie's camp that evening after dropping Cattie off, Red was at the bunkhouse door to greet him.

"Steel, you're out late. Bet you were with Cattie. How's she doin'?"

"I was with Cattie, she's fine. Did a little fishing on French Creek."

"I'm right glad to hear she's okay. Glad you came upon things when you did. Catch anything?"

"We did."

"The talk of the town is about you and your silver-toe boot doing Big Jake in. He's got two brothers. All three of them are mean hombres. You best get yourself a gun and learn how to use it. The whole damn town is getting a real hoot out of it. I guess you heard about Doc and his jar?"

"I heard. Mr. Marks told me," Steel said not amused.

"Come on, Steel. You've gotta find that mighty funny. I think it's the funniest thing to happen in this damn town. I understand Doc even labeled it *Lizard in a Jar*."

"I'm going to call it a night, Red. I've got to get over to the shop early in the morning."

"Do you have any tobacco?"

"I don't chew."

"That's right. I thought just about every one chewed some. Men that is."

"I don't, and my father doesn't either."

"You're right, Charlie don't chew, and there are others I know now that I think about it."

"It's kind of a dirty habit," Steel said.

"You're right about it being dirty, and once it gets a hold on you it's damn hard to quit. I'll go get some from Jack. I know he's always got extra. I know your pa don't like my cussin'. Mr. Utter don't like it either and won't tolerate it around the ladies, even the workin' ladies. Another one of my bad habits."

"Red, better a good man that cusses some than a bad man that doesn't cuss at all. And you're a good man."

"I appreciate your wisdom and your friendship, Steel. Hope you get a good night's sleep. There's Jack now, coming our way."

"Red, Steel," Jack said as he approached, "I'm getting ready to turn in, but wanted to talk to Steel about Big Jake."

"I told him he could be in for a storm," Red said.

"At Nuttal's this evening all the table talk was about you and Big Jake. They're no longer referring to him as Big Jake. They're calling him Jacqueline. I think the whole town is getting a pile of enjoyment out of what happened. Did you hear that Doc put his lizard in one of those canning jars filled with some preserving liquid? He has it on his shelf for people to see. People are going in his office to take a look, if you can believe that. Just never know what interests people."

"Mr. Marks told me all about it," Steel said, sluffing off the remark.

"The main thing I wanted to tell you, there's a gent who said he heard Jake swear on his ma's grave that he's gonna kill you. Steel, you need to be totin' a talkin' iron."

"Yeah, he's right, Steel. I told you the same thing. We don't want to lose our blacksmith."

"Thanks for the advice, but I don't know. My father is opposed to guns in a big way."

"I like your pa, but he'd better savvy up fast for your health. You both need lead pushers."

Steel nodded, thinking they were preaching to the choir. He'd been thinking he needed a gun ever since they arrived in Deadwood... and even before. He planned to mention it to Charlie and ask him to try and persuade his father to purchase a couple of guns. His father had always been a man set in his ways, a hard man to change his thinking once he had a firm opinion of something, and guns were one of those things he'd always been opposed to ever since Steel could remember.

16

From sunrise to sundown, the next three days, Blain and Steel helped Charlie's men complete the blacksmith shop. By the end of the fourth day it was finished, allowing them to move in the anvil and working tools. After that, for the next two days, they worked morning till night blacksmithing and then took Sunday off. "Thank the good Lord for the Sabbath," Blain said. It wasn't to their liking or their intent to be tied down to blacksmithing like they were, but it was more out of a self-imposed commitment to Charlie.

Moving into the second week, Madam Mollie Johnson, the successful proprietor of one of Deadwood's brothels, brought over a couple of horses for Blain to take a look and see if he was interested in buying them. Mollie was known as the "Queen of the Blondes." An attractive blonde by any man's standards, and one of the main beneficiaries of Charlie's efforts in bringing the working ladies to Deadwood. A cowboy had lost big to Mollie in a Faro game at the Bella Union Saloon the night before. He'd put up two horses on a final losing bet. Charlie recommended that Mollie take the horses she'd won over to the blacksmith shop as Mr. Madison had mentioned that he and his son had been looking to buy a couple of horses.

Blain and Steel took a shine to the two mares the minute they laid eyes on them. Their heads were white as a first winter's snow, their manes and chests chestnut brown with white continuing over their hindquarters. It looked as if someone had taken a paintbrush, stood back, and sprinkled black and brown spots of various shapes and sizes on the white portion of their coats.

Blain looked to Steel and said, "I've never seen horses marked so pretty."

There wasn't any wrangling over the price. Blain felt Mollie's asking price was fair and the purchase was quickly concluded.

"Steel, you take the horses over to the livery stable. Tell Mr. Marks I'll be over later to make boarding arrangements." Blain turned to Mollie. "I want to thank you kindly for coming over here first. My boy and I are mighty pleased. I'll bring the money over in about an hour if that's fine with you."

"That'll work fine. I know Charlie thinks a lot of the both of you boys. I know you don't come to my place, but I'm glad you bought the horses."

"We need some saddles, bridles and a couple of good horse blankets," Steel said.

"I'd give you bridles if I had 'em. The cowboy I won the horses from gave them to me with hackamores, which you're welcome to have. Don't have any use for hackamores."

"Thank you," Bain said. "We're much appreciative."

"I need to get back. Things start getting busy at my place in an hour or so. Steel, I wanted to tell you one of Jake's brothers roughed up one of my girls and none of them are welcome at my place anymore. I put the word out, and they're not going to get past the front door of any of the lady establishments. Anyway, you watch your back." She gave a wink, turned on her heel, causing the white ruffles of her petticoat to show, and marched down the middle of the street with a light swing of her hips.

"I can't believe we got these horses," Steel said.

"We need to thank the good Lord and Charlie. When you get back from the livery stable, we'll go over to the mercantile store and buy two saddles, bridles, and a couple of horse blankets. That should do us up just fine. By the way, I heard today, they're getting twenty dollars an ounce for gold. I need to get my pan working."

"I'm thinking we should buy a couple of guns too, holsters and such," Steel said. "Most everyone in Deadwood is packing a gun."

"You know I don't believe in guns. I think we'll just trust the Lord. I know this Jake thing might be bothering you. If he shot you in the back a gun wouldn't do you no good anyway."

"I think the Lord expects us to use some common sense. David was armed with a sling."

"I just don't think guns is the Christian way."

Steel wasn't happy with his father's response, but it wasn't unexpected. He did have his own money and could well afford to buy a gun… but he didn't want to go against his father's wishes, not just yet anyway.

The day after they bought the horses, the cowboy who had lost them to Miss Mollie came by the blacksmith shop. "You won't find finer horses than them two. Broke my heart to lose 'em. Hell, little too much whiskey, I shoulda known better. I still have a horse left. I got three horses from the Nez Perce tribe. They're Indian tribes that live west of the Rockies. I learned they use to be a fishing tribe, but come into some horses from the Spanish and Pueblo Revolt. They bred 'em to be strong and good at going hunt'n'—no problem catching up with the buffalo, and they're might pretty too. Anyways, I traded one of my best Spencer Rifles for three horses. Just wanted you boys to know you got something special with them horses."

"We're sorry about your bad luck," Blain said, "but we'll see they're taken good care of. That was mighty nice of you to come by. You might want to watch your drinking. You don't want to lose that third horse."

"I appreciate the advice and I know you're right, 'cause I don't hold my liquor well. After one Brigham Young cocktail, I'm done for."

17

Blain and Steel soon found out what it was like to live in a lawless town. The saloons and brothels did a thriving business, and along with that there was a daily fight or killing. It seemed as if the cemetery saw as much action as the local saloons. Other than that, there wasn't much going on. There were gamblers aplenty, and Nuttal's was where Charlie would generally spend his afternoons and evenings. Bill Hickok was hoping to recover his prior financial losses at the gaming table and that's where he could be found. Calamity Jane had made friends with Dora DuFran, Deadwood's most prosperous madam. Charlie said he wasn't sure what that friendship would lead to. "Everyone needs to find work to support oneself, one way or another," he said.

Tuesday morning, Blain's excitement was high as he readied himself for the day. He hung up the towel that he'd used to wipe the last bit of shaving cream from his face. "Steel, I've got to get out to French Creek today and do some panning. That's the reason I came to Deadwood. We put in a hard day yesterday. Come noon, I'm heading out."

"You go ahead. I'll hold things down here. I know there are a lot of people wanting work done, but we can only do what we can do. And you're right, you came here to pan for gold. Go and enjoy the day."

Blain left for French Creek a little after the noon hour, riding before one of the Indian ponies. He didn't pay much attention to the ride there. His thoughts were on getting his pan in the water and finding some of that yellow dust. He found a nice little spot to settle at and reined in his horse. In no time, he was kneeling by the stream scooping up gravel and working his pan.

That afternoon, he picked up a little yellow color while working his way downstream. *At twenty dollars an ounce, I know I'm making more than blacksmith pay.* At the end of the day his knees were getting sore and his back ached. A good meal started to sound more appealing than kneeling by the stream. He'd really never considered physically just how hard panning for gold was on the limbs and back.

He glanced over his shoulder at the sinking sun and felt the air's chill starting to wrap around him. He put his cold reddish hands in the water for a last scoop of gravel in his pan. In the diminished light, his eyes searched hard in the swirling gravel and sand.

Suddenly, his eyes widened and he blinked several times not quite believing what he saw. Amongst the gravel, two gold nuggets stood out, shinning up at him. His heart raced and with shaking hands, he plucked the nuggets out. He felt the weight of them in his cold fingers as he stared at them for a long moment. Almost magically, the soreness in his body melted away. With care, he placed his two prizes in his red and white handkerchief and carefully wrapped them up. He put the handkerchief into his pant's pocket beside a small bottle that contained flakes of gold that he'd panned that day.

Blain's Indian pony couldn't get him to town fast enough. He tied the pony to the hitching rail in front of Nuttal's, jumped onto the boardwalk and went through the saloon's doors, thinking he'd find Charlie there. "I just panned the prettiest gold nuggets in French Creek," he announced.

Most eyes turned his way.

He took out his handkerchief and went to the closest table with outstretched hands.

"You're a mighty lucky man," one of the card players said, peering down at the two nuggets. They're two beauties, all right."

Blain went to the next table.

Charlie was playing cards with Bill Hickok and two other gents at a table in the far corner. When Charlie saw Blain and the commotion, he put his cards face down on the table and got up from his chair. "Excuse me boys," he said, and quickly worked his way around the tables toward Blain.

Blain saw Charlie coming his way. "Charlie, look what I panned in French Creek just when I was ready to call it a day."

"You did good, Blain." Charlie put his hand on Blain's shoulder and in a quiet, calm voice said, "Blain, don't ever tell anyone what you've found, let alone show them. Take a good look at the people in here. Do they look like your Sunday-go-to-meeting folks? Announcing your gold find in a town like this is a little like saying you don't want to live much longer. I don't want to lose my blacksmith. Wrap them nuggets back up, and I strongly suggest, since you mentioned French Creek, that you take a French leave and head straight back to camp tonight. Do you get what I mean?"

Blain looked around, deflated. Most everyone was staring at him, knowing Charlie was giving him a talking to.

"I don't know what I was thinking... The excitement of finding two gold nuggets... You're right. How could I have been so foolish?" He folded the side of his handkerchief over the nuggets and put them back into his pocket.

"Let me see them nuggets," someone called out.

"Not tonight," Charlie said.

Blain looked out at the onlookers, feeling he'd like to hide in a hole.

"Don't pay no mind to Leroy, he's a dunderhead," Charlie said. "Blain, you don't carry a gun so watch yourself. I'd wait at least four or five days before going back out to French Creek. Try another stream for a spell." Charlie looked Blain square in the eye. "Again, go straight back to camp tonight. Now, I need to get back to my card game. You be careful."

Blain turned and walked out of the saloon like a puppy with its tail between his legs. The wind clearly had gone out of his sails.

That night, before turning in, Blain meekly confessed to Steel what took place in the saloon that night. Steel was excited about his father's funding but was concerned about him heeding Charlie's advice.

"Cherry Creek would be a good place to try your luck," Steel said.

"From what I've heard, most of the findings are on French Creek... That's where I'm going to pan... French Creek is where I'll make my fortune!"

Steel watched his father turn his back to him in his bunk, and within minutes he was sawing logs.

The next morning, to Steel's chagrin, Blain was chomping at the bit to get back out on French Creek. Steel had hoped Charlie's talk would at least have detoured his father from wanting to go out there again so soon. That didn't appear to be the case. Sure enough, after lunch, the desire for gold outweighed Charlie's advice and good common sense.

"I've got to get back to that spot, Steel! I've just got an overwhelming feeling there are more nuggets waiting for me there."

"You need to listen to Charlie. He knows what he's talking about."

"I'll be fine. Charlie worries too much. I'll be back a little after sundown. Don't you worry none about me." Blain turned and marched off at a fast pace in the direction of the livery stable.

Steel stood there for a moment dumfounded by his father's actions.

It wasn't more than fifteen minutes when his father returned riding one of the Indian ponies. Steel walked out of the shop and looked up at him with no intention of hiding his scowl.

"Steel, I won't go panning tomorrow, that's a promise. You can take a little time off and go fishing with Cattie."

"Too much work. I won't have time," Steel said disgustedly. Again, I don't understand why you won't listen to Charlie. He wouldn't tell you not to go out panning unless he knew what he was talking about!"

"I don't like you takin' that tone with me. I told you, I'll be fine. Charlie worries too much and you're sounding like Charlie. I'll most likely pan while there's enough light to see the glitter. See you tonight." Blain turned his horse in the direction of French Creek and dug in his heels.

Listening to the horse's hooves pound the ground and watching his father gallop off into the midday sunshine, produced a foreboding feeling. Dejectedly, Steel turned and walked back into the shop. *I've got a lot of work to do.*

Awaiting his father's return, Steel's ominous feelings lingered with him for the remainder of the daylight hours. Charlie had come by mid-afternoon to check up on Blain. When Steel told him he'd gone back out to French Creek, Charlie shook his head in disbelief.

"Charlie, do you think I should go out and look for him?"

"No. I don't think you'd find him. He wouldn't come anyway, and I don't want you gettin' kilt. I'm glad you had the common sense not to go. He's gonna get his damn self kilt." Charlie again shook his head, kicked at the dirt, turned and walked toward Nuttal's.

Charlie's foretelling only added to Steel's concern. He'd never seen Charlie so distressed, and that was the first time he'd heard him swear.

Steel locked the shop door, as the light was quickly fading now that the sun had dipped below the hills. He turned and took a long look in the direction of French Creek. He didn't expect his father to come riding in until well after dark. He thought he'd continue with his plans and go see Cattie and get something to eat.

As he was turning to leave the shop for Nuttal's, his eye caught Chatan, an Indian friend of Charlie's, whom Steel had met earlier that week. He was riding into town with another pony alongside.

Steel's heart turned cold as he watched Chatan's horse slow from a trot to a walk. He could make out a man draped facedown over the pony's saddle. He knew without looking at the face that the form was the body of his father. He stood there for an instant in a trance, watching the head and dangling arms move up and down with the rhythm of the pony's gait. The cloud of darkness that he'd been feeling all day now consumed him. He felt an emotion of anger because of his father's disobedience. *If he'd only listened to Charlie*… His eyes watered. He loved his father and would greatly miss him. *What will I tell my mother?*

18

THE LIGHT WIND WHISTLED through the pines. The late afternoon sun cast shadows across the small gathering. Steel, Charlie, Red, Hank, Lucy, and Cattie stood silently, as two of Charlie's men lowered Blain's casket into the ground.

Charlie said a few words and then they watched in silence as shovels of dirt began to hit the pine box. Steel thought about placing his father's Bible in the grave but decided that his father would rather have him keep the Good Book. Lucy and Cattie tossed some wildflowers they'd gathered into the grave.

Steel's thoughts turned to his mother as he watched the grave fill with dirt. He wondered what she was doing that very moment. He still wasn't sure how or when he'd tell her. He felt he needed to let his emotions settle before he'd be able to make that decision. There had been six killings since the wagon train arrived in Deadwood, his father's death being the seventh. *That's the Deadwood way... people getting killed, buried, and then the living taking up where they left off, seemingly without an afterthought. One thing I know, I'm going to do what I can to find out who killed my father. Chatan, I need to talk to Chatan... and I need to buy a gun!*

The short time Steel had been in Deadwood, he'd seen an eclectic group of men, some good and some bad. One thing they all had in common was carrying pistols. Some men like Charlie and Mr. Hickok had two pistols. Gunfighters walked with a swagger all their own. It seemed that their firearms were apart of them. Some had holsters leathered down on their leg and some didn't. He noticed the way folks turned their eyes downward and moved out of the way when a gunfighter's jangling spurs headed in their direction.

At first sunlight, the day after interring his father, Steel was up, dressed, and walking with a purposeful stride over to Marks' Livery Stable. He found Mr. Marks with a pitchfork in his hand, standing next to a small stack of hay. In his mid-fifties, Mr. Marks had a slight built and not much hair. He always greeted people with a pleasant smile. He'd talk your ear off if he wasn't working, and even when he was working if you were standing nearby you'd get an earful. He'd told Steel and his father that gold panning didn't interest him.

"I can make a good living for myself with my livery stable. Gold can do strange things to a man. I do like the excitement of a mining town though. That's why I let Charlie talk me into coming to Deadwood. So far, I've no regrets. However, in this town, I should have been an undertaker—easy work and never a lack of business. You just need someone to build pine boxes and a couple of boys to work the shovels." Two days ago, Steel and Blain had gone to check on their horses and had that conversation.

"Morning to you, Steel," Mr. Marks said. He leaned his pitchfork up against a stall. "Sure sorry about your pa being killed, and I take back my remark about wanting to be an undertaker. I wouldn't want the job."

"I wouldn't want the job either," Steel said.

"How are you holding up, Son?"

"It'll take time. My father and I were close."

"Don't mean to overstep myself at a time like this, but if you would have a mind to be selling one of those Indian ponies, I would sure enough be interested."

"Matter of fact, that's why I came to see you this morning."

"Well, now if that don't mean something… I don't know what price your pa paid for them mares you bought from Mollie, but I suspect it was fair price, and I'd be willing to pay you a like price."

Steel told him the price and asked, "I was wondering if I could get free boarding for the mare I'm keeping. Maybe a month of boarding?"

"Well now..." Mr. Marks rubbed his chin. "Let's say two months." He smiled and held out his hand.

Steel nodded as the men shook hands.

"Oh, and my father's saddle? It's new."

"Don't need another saddle, but I'd be obliged to sell it for you. I get prospectors, from time to time, comin' wanting to buy a horse or saddle. I don't think it'll take long for me to sell it."

"That'd be fine."

"You wait here and I'll be right back with your money. Oh, which mare are you wanting to keep?"

"The one with the black spot on her face. I call her Paint, because she looks like an artist painted her up with spots."

"Yeah, that's a right fine name. I was kind of partial to that mare myself. But that's fine with me. They're both real, good-looking Indian ponies."

"I'm heading over to the mercantile. I should be back in about twenty minutes. I'm planning on going out to the Lakota Village. I understand it's about a forty-five minute horseback ride east of town."

"Forty-five minutes give or take how fast you want to push your horse. I know Charlie and a few other gents were out there last week, trading some things for buffalo hides. Fine sleeping blankets those hides make. I'll have Paint saddled and ready to go for you when you get back."

"You don't have to do that, I can saddle her."

"Happy to do it. Let me get that money for you."

Steel, with more money in his pocket than needed, headed straight for the mercantile store.

If I'm going to stay here for a spell, like I know Charlie wants, I'm buying a gun, and I'm doing it this morning!

19

Steel wrapped the gun belt around his waist while the store clerk, Mr. Nance, eyed him closely. Steel's heartbeat beat a little faster as he fastened the buckle and then adjusted the holster down on his right hip so that his fingertips fell in the middle of the holster. A five and one-half inch barrel Colt pistol with an ivory handle laid on the counter in front of him. He picked up the gun and eased it into the holster. For a moment, his fingers undulated against the cold ivory handle. He let out a deep breath. *I'm going out each morning at first sunrise to practice.*

"That's a mighty fine gun, Steel. None finer. Have you ever shot a Colt pistol, or any pistol?"

For a split moment, Steel thought about lying but it just wasn't in his nature. He glanced down at the wood-plank floor. "No, sir."

Mr. Nance nodded and looked hard at Steel. "I wouldn't be wearing that gun in Deadwood until you've done a little practicing. Let me tell you about the gun you're buying. You're buying the same gun as Mr. Hickok has tucked into his belt. He's got two of them. Showed 'em to me. They're engraved J. B. Hickok 1869. They're both .36 caliber Colt Army Richards Mason conversion. It was called the Navy Revolver and designed by Samuel Colt. At first, it was a cap and ball revolver. It was converted to a metallic cartridge revolver later on… I suspect in the early fifties. Hand me the gun for a minute." Mr. Nance took the gun from Steel. "See, it's front-loaded." He placed the gun on the counter. "You'll need some cartridges like those in this box. I'll open it up and take one out and show you. These cartridges are slightly tapered to fit the chambers of the cylinder. Well, there you have it. As I said, the same as Mr. Hickok."

"I just hope I get half as good as Mr. Hickok."

"That can be good and bad."

"I'll need a good supply of cartridges. I plan on going out in the mornings and practicing."

"Best you stay away from French Creek. I recommend you go south of town near Cherry Creek. There's a stand of pines about five miles out that should suit you fine. I don't think you'll run into anybody out there."

"I'll do that. Thanks for the advice."

"I got a real nice box that I'll put your Colt in. Again, as much as you'd like, best not go wearing that pistol around town until you know how to use it. I'm just telling you what your pa would say, rest his soul."

Mr. Nance took the Colt pistol and placed it into a wooden box with carvings on the side. The box was lined with a soft velvet cloth. Steel looked admiringly at his Colt pistol and then unbuckled the holster and laid it on the counter next to the box. Mr. Nance reached under the counter and produced two more boxes of cartridges, which he placed with the other items.

I can't believe the gun is mine.

"Steel, I've never seen you wearing a hat. You need a good-looking hat—the kind cowhand drovers have."

"I've been thinking about buying a hat, now that you mention it."

"Buying a hat is a little like buying a gun, but not so much so. Buying and wearing a hat gives you a different feeling. I don't know if it's a more important feeling, but it's a different feeling when you've got a good-looking hat on, that's for plum sure. I just got some new ones in several days ago, some bowlers with brims; but no, you're the Stetson type." Mr. Nance studied Steel for a moment. "Yes, you're the Stetson type. Stetson would do you right fine."

Mr. Nance came out from behind the counter and walked over to a shelf about eye level. "This is a Stetson," he said, taking a dark brown hat off the shelf. "A man by the name of John Stetson, a hat maker, I believe from New Jersey, developed this hat. It's in fact got a name, called Boss of the Plains. You can see it's flat-brimmed with a straight-sided crown on top. This hat is made of a variety of materials: felt, beaver and rabbit fur. It's the one most cowboys are now wearing. They became popular during the cattle drives over the northern and southern plains. It'll last you a lifetime. Around Deadwood that might not be very long if you aren't careful. I know you know what I mean," he said soberly.

Steel eyed the hats on the shelf not sure what he liked.

"Here, try this one on," Mr. Nance said, handing Steel the Stetson.

Steel had never had what could be called a real hat. In the winter he wore knitted caps that his grandma had crafted. He took the Stetson gingerly in his hands and put it on. "Fits fine. I like it. Yes, I like it," Steel said. *Mr. Nance is right, I do have a different feeling,* he thought and stood up a little straighter.

"That looks right fine on you. The ladies are going to be looking your way."

"I don't know about that but I'll take it. If you could total up my bill. Oh, I'll take a can of chewing tobacco too." Buying chewing tobacco was a spur of the moment thought. Maybe it was out of anger against his father for going against Charlie's strong advice and getting himself killed. Anyway, he'd give it a try.

Mr. Nance handed Steel a small round can with a picture of a cowboy riding a bucking bronco on the label. He quickly tucked the can in his back pocket.

"Almost forgot, a mail rider came in yesterday. I've got a letter for you."

"A letter for me?" He raised his brows. "From my mother I suspect..." His heart saddened at the thought of her. He still wrestled with how to tell her of his father's death.

"It's not from your ma unless her name is Miss Savannah Mayfield. And the letter smells real nice. Hate to give it up."

"Savannah? Savannah, you say?" His jaw dropped.

"While you're standing there with your mouth open, I'll go fetch the letter."

Savannah, Savannah wrote me. I guess I shouldn't be that surprised since I did write her.

Mr. Nance returned holding the letter near his face and handed it to Steel. "Here's your letter. Put it up to your nose. Smells real nice, don't it?"

"Yes, it does." Steel's emotions of surprise turned to wondering what Savannah had written.

"Right nice-looking stamp of George Washington, too," Mr. Nance said. "You wouldn't be receiving any letters if Charlie hadn't set up a mail-rider service. For the time being, riders are only going back and forth between Cheyenne and Deadwood. If a letter to a Deadwood resident ends up somewhere else, it has to be rerouted to Cheyenne to finally make its way here. That Charlie has his hands in more pies than a pie-maker on Christmas."

"I won't argue that one," Steel said. "I need to be on my way, but I want to thank you for the information and advice on the gun. Oh, and the hat suggestion, and the letter."

"You take care now and don't forget what I told you. You're looking mighty good wearing that Stetson; and again, I'm sure sorry about your pa."

Steel folded the letter and put it in his shirt pocket. "Do you mind if I leave my purchases with you? I'll pick them up before you close."

"I'll be happy to keep 'em for you. I'm closing around seven. If you don't make it by then, they'll be here for you tomorrow."

"Thanks, Mr. Nance."

20

Having gotten directions to the Lakota Village from Mr. Marks at the livery stable, Steel rode out of town at an easy gait. The enjoyment of the ride was lost in his thoughts about finding his father's killer, his mother, and more than once about Savannah's letter, which he'd wait until night to read.

Before long, he saw several pillars of smoke rising in the eastern sky. *They must be from the Indian village cooking fires,* he thought, thinking now would be a good time to direct his attention on finding Chatan.

Out of seemingly nowhere, the sound of horses' hooves pounded through the air. He jerked his head to the side and saw two young Indian braves riding toward him at a full gallop. Their heels dug into their horses' sides as they slapped the animals' hindquarters and let out some war whoops.

Paint held her ground, veering neither to the left or the right, even as one of the ponies bore down on her.

At the last moment, the rider turned his mount to the side, and with a whoop, rode off with his cohort in the direction of the village. The incident unnerved Steel. He leaned forward and patted Paint on her neck with a gratitude he knew he couldn't adequately convey.

Paint was a buffalo horse. Steel had the feeling she'd faced greater threats than the two Indian braves.

It wasn't long before teepees came into view. Steel had been right thinking the smoke he'd seen earlier came from the Indian cooking fires. The village was busy with the day's activities. The women wore attractive, full-length beaded dresses. Several women were working on stretched-out hides, while others were working around the fires. Children played out in the open. A dog slept in front of a tent and another chased laughing children.

Steel admired the artwork on their lodgings. Colorful drawings of deer, buffalo, rabbits, and foxes spanned the covers of the teepees. The villagers looked cheerful and contented.

A well-worn trail led down into a wide, grassy gully where twenty-five to thirty horses grazed. Six young boys kicked a leather ball back and forth among the unnerved horses. When they saw Steel approaching, one of the boys picked up the ball and two of them ran up the gully toward the village. The horses went back to feeding contentedly but the boys stood, seemingly, watching Steel's every movement.

A horseman appeared on the other side of the gully.

"Chatan," Steel said to himself, breathing an immediate sigh of relief. He reined in his horse and waited.

Chatan raised his hand as he approached Steel. Steel responded in kind. Two eagle feathers dangled from the Indian's long black hair. His legs hung below his horse's belly. His back was straight and his chin held high. *He looks proud, even majestic,* Steel thought.

"Steel."

"Chatan."

"You want me to take you where I saw the man who killed your father."

"Yes. It's been two days now. I'm hoping to find him working the section of the stream where my father was killed."

"You want to kill him?"

"I want justice."

"Justice is to kill him," Chatan said. "Follow me. I take you to the place."

Chatan nudged his horse forward and Steel followed. In a little more than half an hour, Chatan reined in his horse on the top of a small knoll overlooking French Creek. A lone man with a soiled grey hat knelt by the side of the stream. He was so fixated on panning, and with the light rustle of the afternoon breeze, he didn't notice the onlookers.

He'd set up a small campsite not far from the stream. A vestige of smoke rose from smoldering ambers, and a dark brown army horse was tethered to an old, nearby log. The horse looked content munching the ends of the creek-side grass. Should the man turn around, Steel and Chatan would be easily visible.

"I've seen him in Nuttal's," Steel said.

"He is the one who shot your father. The horse, I know the horse. Use my rifle to shoot him."

"No, I'm not going to shoot him in the back like he shot my father. He'll be coming to town. I'm not ready yet to avenge my father's death, but I will avenge it."

"This is bad man. He shot your father in the back. You should kill him now." Chatan started to unsheathe his rifle. "I will kill him for you," Chatan said.

"No. He's mine to deal with. Please, Chatan."

Chatan took his hand off his rifle and let it fall back into the leather casing.

The intent to take a man's life and actually doing it were two different things. Steel had never killed anyone. He wouldn't even shoot a rabbit and he released the fish that he caught. He recalled his emotions against Jake... At the time he was near dealing him a fatal blow but held back... Could he pull the trigger and send a deadly bullet on its way? He wouldn't know for certain until that moment presented itself, but now was not the time. In any confrontation with guns, either man could be killed. *In the end, the only real benefactor will be the Ingleside Cemetery,* he thought.

Steel's horse whinnied, interrupting his thoughts.

The man in the grey hat dropped his pan, spun around and crouched low. He drew his pistol and stared up at Steel and Chatan like a cornered fox.

"Let's go. I know who he is now," Steel said.

"He has only pistol and no cover, an easy target."

"No, no."

The man's head turned from side to side, searching for cover. There wasn't even a grouping of stream-side willows to take refuge behind.

"He'll be coming to Deadwood. This will give him something to cause him concern—great concern," Steel said.

"Hmm," Chatan mumbled.

Steel hoped that Chatan could see that there might be some merit in not killing him now, but from the look on his face, Steel had the impression that Chatan saw his hesitation as a failure... perhaps even cowardice.

They turned their horses and were soon out of sight. After riding half-a-mile, Chatan reined in his horse. Steel followed him, pulling up abruptly on the reins.

"We need to take different paths," Chatan said. "I return to my village. I not go to Deadwood. My village no longer trade with the white man. There is much bad between government and my people. They no keep treaty."

"I have a little understanding of that. I am sorry for your people. I know more white people are coming. It will not be easy. Thank you for your help, Chatan."

Chatan turned his horse, lightly brushed its sides with the heels of his moccasins and soon disappeared over a small bluff.

21

There were still a few hours of sunlight in the day when Steel rode back into town. He took Paint to the livery stable and unsaddled her. "Give her a good rubdown and feed her well tonight," he said to the stable boy and handed him a silver dollar.

"I'll do that," the stable boy said, looking down at the silver coin, astonished at his good fortune.

Trying to convey his thanks, Steel patted Paint on the neck and looked into her large, hazel eyes. Paint tossed her head, seeming to acknowledge his appreciation. *I need to go by the mercantile and pick up my purchases before the store closes, and then I'll go to the tent and read Savannah's letter.*

He reached into his back pocket and took out his can of chewing tobacco. Opening the lid, he took out a small pinch and tucked it between his back teeth and his cheek as he'd seen Red do a number of times. *I'll give it a try for a week or two and see if I like it.*

"Just closing up for the day. You made it just in time," Mr. Nance said with his work apron in his hand. I'll get your things. That hat looks mighty good on you."

"Thanks. I appreciate you holding things."

"Have you read that perfumed letter yet?" he asked with a broad smile.

"Tonight." Steel said as he walked out of the door of the mercantile store with a box tucked under his arm and carrying a bag with his holster and ammunition. There was excitement in his breast, knowing tomorrow morning he'd be pulling the trigger of his Colt for the first time.

"Steel, you take care and don't forget what I told you,'" Mr. Nance hollered out.

"Will do." Steel looked down the street at the blacksmith shop. Work started to press on his mind. *I think I need to go to the shop. I can get a couple of hours in before dark. Savannah's letter can wait until later.* Steel changed direction and had started walking toward the shop when he saw Charlie coming his way.

They met in the middle of the street.

"I saw Mr. Marks at the livery stable," Charlie said. "He told me you were headed over to the mercantile before closing. I wanted to catch up with you."

"I picked up some things I bought this morning, now I'm going over to the shop to get in a couple of hours work. I hope I didn't make too many people unhappy."

"Don't give no mind if anyone says something. You just lost your pa. No one expects you to get back in the saddle right away. I just wanted to check up on you and see how you're doing. Like your hat."

"One of the items that I bought this morning. I want to thank you again for the kind words you said about my father."

"It's not hard to say nice words about a good man. Well, that Stetson looks mighty fine on you. I wear a Stetson myself. Anyway, I got two horses I was hoping to get shoed when you could get around to it."

"Bring them by around ten tomorrow morning. It shouldn't be a problem." Steel well knew there would be others waiting at his door, but he'd always move Charlie to the front of the line unless someone else had a true emergency.

"I can do that."

"From that box, it looks like you bought yourself a gun."

Steel nodded. "A five-and-a-half inch barrel Colt with an ivory handle. Mr. Nance said that it was the finest gun he had for sale, and a good-looking holster," Steel said, exuberance in his voice.

Charlie stood there for a moment blank-faced.

"Steel, I think that's a right fine idea. If your pa—rest his soul, had had a gun, he might just be alive today."

"He sure was against having a gun," Steel said, feeling an emotion of unpleasantness.

"I tried to talk him into taking a pistol or a rifle when he went panning as you well know," Charlie said. "Steel, I do want to stress that having a gun can be an invite for trouble. You're going to need to be careful."

"I know that. And I know I need to practice. I'm planning on going out early every morning."

"I've been thinking about you… your pa." His words came like a slow moving locomotive. "I need to get you some help. You know, Bill Hickok and I are best of friends. How'd you like it if I were to ask him to take you out and have him learn you how to use that Colt?"

Steel blinked hard. "Well… well, that would be more than I could ask for… Taught by Mr. Hickok… You'd ask him to help me?" Steel stammered, trying to find words to express his surprise at the proposal.

"Bill knows about your pa's killing. He liked your pa. He said if he could help you out he'd be obliged to."

"He did save my life on the trip here."

"That's right, he did save your bacon. You knocked the cow-dung out of Rusty that was bothering the sporting gal. Coward-like, Rusty pulled his gun and Bill shot the gun out of his hand. I remember that as clear as day. I know Rusty is still around town. He stays out of my way, gambles over at the Bella Union Saloon."

"I've seen Rusty around a few times. He spoke to me once. Said if Hickok leaves town he's coming looking for me. I'm not paying him any mind though, I think he's all mouth."

"He for darn shootin' doesn't want to tangle with Bill, and I suspect he doesn't want to tangle with you unless he's got the drop on you. That's the way those coward-like are, but don't take 'em too lightly. Let me ask you something that's been on my mind. With your pa getting killed, and Cattie and Lucy leaving in a few weeks, have you given any thought about how long you might be staying in Deadwood?"

"I wanted to talk to you about that. I'm thinking maybe three or four months. I don't want to leave you high and dry. If you'd bring another blacksmith in as soon as you reasonably could, I'd appreciate it. You know, I'm still trying to figure out how and when to tell my mother of my father's death."

Charlie stared at the ground for a moment and then looked up at Steel with compassion.

"Steel, I don't have an easy answer to that. I think you best just have to write your ma and tell her outright."

"I don't know."

"I'll see if I can get you some help right away. I know the work is piling up."

"I'd greatly appreciate that. If you could find someone that's willing to work and isn't interested in gold panning... that's probably an impossibility here in Deadwood—I can certainly pay a reasonable wage."

"There are a few of those sorts in town. Not many though. I'll see what I can do, that's a promise. I'll see you tomorrow around ten. I'll let you know then about Bill Hickok. I'm playing cards with him tonight."

"Thanks, Charlie." Steel was glad Charlie hadn't asked him about his afternoon activities. He was concerned that Mr. Marks, knowing that he'd ventured out to the Lakota village, might have said something. Mr. Marks always seemed more than willing to spread the local news. Steel had no intention of involving Charlie in his personal affairs unless doing so was absolutely necessary.

The prospect of being taught to shoot by a legend like Mr. Hickok was almost too much to fathom. Steel had observed Mr. Hickok closely for brief moments. A few inches over six feet in height made him taller than most men. He had a thin face, postured with a black drooping mustache. His strong grey eyes, shielded by a wide-brim black hat, telegraphed that he wasn't a man to be pushed around, yet he wasn't harsh looking. Curly blond hair fell loose onto his shoulders. He had an enviable build with broad shoulders and a thin waist. His everyday attire consisted of top boots, riding breeches, and a dark shirt with a handkerchief around his neck. Like Charlie, he carried two Colt pistols secured by a red sash around his waist. It seemed to Steel that Mr. Hickok rarely changed his expression. Steel could tell that playing cards was not an amusing game to him like it was to Charlie. To Mr. Hickok playing cards was a serious business.

Steel worked a good two hours at the shop that day. Tiredness was an unwelcome fellow but there he was looking Steel in the face. Steel intended to catch a quick bite at Nuttal's, walk Cattie home, and then read Savannah's letter before turning off the lantern. *I hope Cattie doesn't need to stay late tonight. I could use a good night's sleep.*

The smell of fried sage hen met Steel when he walked through the kitchen door. He'd planned on eating a light dinner but immediately changed his mind.

"I like your hat," Lucy said. There's a hook behind the door to hang it on.

Cattie and Sam turned and looked at Steel.

"Mighty becoming," Sam said.

"I do like your hat," Cattie said. "You're turning into a cowboy." She smiled.

"Could be," Steel said. He took his hat off and placed it on the hook alongside of Sam's cap.

Steel took his time eating and finally started to relax though the image of his father's killer haunted his thoughts.

By the time he finished dinner, Cattie was ready to go home. Lucy had left a little earlier, knowing Steel would be there to walk her home. On their way to the cabin, Cattie again expressed her relief and excitement about returning to Denver. "I'm hoping I can find employment at the bank where I interviewed. It'll be good to leave Deadwood," she said with a faraway look.

On the doorstep, she approached him. He took her into his arms for a lingering kiss.

"I love you," she said.

"And I love you." Her reassuring words warmed Steel's heart, providing an encouraging note to a long and another emotional day.

Steel walked quickly through town trying not to pay attention to the cacophony of sounds that emanated from Deadwood's nighttime activities. *It'll be good to be back in my tent... Savannah's letter, I need to read her letter.*

Steel tossed his hat and purchases on the end of his cot and lit one of the two kerosene lanterns. Taking the letter out of his pocket, he opened it, edged close to the light, sat down on the corner of his cot, and started to read.

Dear Steel,

I received your letter sent from Denver. I can't express how excited I was to hear from you. I assume that by the time my letter reaches you, you'll have completed the wagon train trip to Deadwood. I'm certain you and your father have had many adventures along the way, all of which I'm most interested in hearing about. I apologize that I acted so harshly with you before you left. I hope you understand my feelings were crushed.

I want you to know that I met your mother yesterday at a tea social. She's a very pretty lady and most charming. We're planning on getting together from time to time, which I look forward to. I know she lives across town with your grandparents. She has invited me over for a visit, and I'm planning on doing that in the near future.

I've decided to take a nursing job here in Philadelphia. My mother asked me if my decision was partially due to the young man that I met. I told her that was possibly so.

Oh, we went shopping downtown the other day, and went into your grandfather's store. I was so very much impressed. It was one of the finest stores in the area. I purchased a lovely purse.

You know the Centennial Exposition is still going on. I believe it is scheduled to close in November. My mother and I went to the fairgrounds yesterday and took in some of the art exhibits. It was a most exhilarating experience.

I have been riding almost every day. There's a lovely trail down by the river. I always think of you when I'm near the river. I remember your mother mentioning how much you loved fly fishing. I went fishing once with my father when I was eight or nine. I must admit it wasn't a pleasant experience. I felt so sorry for the fish.

The weather here has been hot and a little humid, but nothing like the humidity in the South. I'm so looking forward to the fall and all the fall colors. It'll be my first fall in Philadelphia, and I understand the colors of the leaves are truly something to behold.

I know we've had very little time to really get to know each other, but I want you to know I had a special feeling about you when we first met, and I think you had a special feeling toward me.

I'm looking forward to receiving your letters, so please write. I'll keep you in my thoughts, and certainly hope no harm comes to you or your father.

Affectionately,
Savannah

PS, I hope, and your mother hopes, that you and your father won't stay for the full year.

Now that Steel had fallen in love with Cattie, this letter presented a new problem. "What am I going to do? I need to be honest with Savannah. I don't want to hurt her feelings," he said out loud. He put the letter with his father's Bible and placed them beside his cot. *I'll just have to think on things... I'll write her or maybe just wait until I return home. I don't know.*

Steel's desires for a good night's sleep were not to be. He tossed and turned all night, trying to resolve some of the questions that had plagued him. Savannah's letter only added to his woes. He arose early, dressed quickly, and decided to get a jump on his work.

Steel arrived at the blacksmith shop just as the sun's rays broke over the town's scanty buildings. The morning chill was still in the air. He went right to work and was able to complete a couple of work requests before Charlie arrived at ten that morning with his two horses to be shoed.

"Mr. Hickok will meet you at one o'clock today at the livery stable," Charlie said in an affirmative tone. "I've got to run, but I'll see you at noon to get the horses."

"I'll have them ready for you. Thanks, Charlie."

"No, I thank you," Charlie said.

In a few hours I'll be going out shooting with Mr. Hickok—can't believe it!

Steel went right to work shoeing Charlie's horses, while he tried to imagine what it was going to be like to be taught by Mr. Hickok. Savannah's letter and informing his mother of his father's death continued to badger his thoughts. For the moment, knowing that in a few hours Mr. Hickok would be teaching him how to shoot, gave him a partial respite from those concerns. *I hope I'm a quick learner. I don't want to disappoint Mr. Hickok or Charlie for that matter.*

He had Charlie's horses shoed in no time at all and left them tethered on the hitching rail for him to pick up at twelve o'clock. Charlie wasn't one to be late, and as the twelve o'clock hour drew closer, Steel kept a close eye on his father's pocket watch.

There's Charlie coming my way! Steel hung up his work apron and got things ready to close up shop.

"Thanks for shoeing my horses," Charlie said, as he approached the open siding to the shop. "I'm selling them to a couple of tender-footers that we picked up in Laramie. They said they were tired of dealing with the two mules I sold them. When I sold them the mules, I told them if they weren't happy, I'd buy 'm back at a small discount. They didn't look like mule people, and I had a strong feeling they'd be bringing 'em back."

"I'm going over to Nuttal's now and grab lunch and then to the livery stable. I want to be a little early for Mr. Hickok," Steel said.

"Good. You don't want to keep him waiting, that's for sure. It's a big afternoon for you. Learned how to shoot by Bill Hickok, now that's something to tell your grandchildren about."

"I'm looking forward to this afternoon."

"I can see that in your face and hear it in your voice. I know it'll be an afternoon you'll never forget. I'll catch you a little later."

"See you this evening, Charlie."

Steel closed up the shop and hurried over to Nuttal's even though he knew he had time to spare.

"Lucy, Sam, Cattie, good morning, or I should say good afternoon since it's a little after twelve," Steel said with an upbeat tone as he entered the kitchen.

"Steel, you're here early," Cattie said, raising her brows. "I generally don't expect you until one o'clock or after. You sound cheerful—exuberant."

"I have to tend to something at one this afternoon. I hope coming early won't cause you any trouble," he said, as he hung up his hat.

"Not a question of trouble, just a question of if we've got something to eat right now that's to your likin'," Sam said. "We've made up some beef barley soup. Used moose meat, mighty good to the taste, if I should say so, and some fresh baked rolls. Will that suit you?"

"Sounds better than good," Steel said. "I'm grateful for whatever you have."

"I'll get you a bowl," Cattie said.

"Cattie, I'll tell you tonight about this afternoon. Charlie only confirmed things a little earlier today."

Lucy looked over at him. "You bought yourself a gun and you're going out to practice shooting," she said.

Steel gave a light chuckle and shook his head. "What makes you think that?"

"It's true!" Cattie said and smiled.

"That's right, I did buy a gun, and that's what I'll be doing."

"Whom are you going out with?" Cattie asked.

"Mr. Hickok," Steel said under his breath.

Lucy and Sam turned and stared at Steel.

"Mr. Hickok is going to teach you how to shoot?" Sam asked with a disbelieving look.

"Charlie arranged it."

"Well, I'll be," Sam said. "That Charlie can pretty much arrange anything. I just bet he could arrange snow on a hot summer's day."

"I thought your father didn't believe in guns," Lucy said.

"He didn't, but I think a man living in Deadwood needs to carry a gun."

"Lucy, he's right," Sam said.

"Maybe so," Lucy said, "but I'm not a lover of guns." She hesitated for a moment and then continued, "Living in a place like Deadwood, I can see why a man would consider having a gun as a necessity."

"I'd appreciate it if you didn't tell anyone that Mr. Hickok is the one who is teaching me."

"We won't say a word," Sam said. "Mr. Hickok himself teaching you how to shoot. Something to tell your grandchildren about."

"That's what Charlie said," Steel replied. He sat down at the small table, while Cattie placed a bowl of soup and roll in in front of him. In a few minutes, he was looking at an empty bowl and the roll had disappeared.

"You certainly ate that fast. I've a piece of berry pie for you if you have time," Lucy said.

"Thanks Lucy, if you could save that for supper. I'll see you all tonight," Steel said, getting up from the table.

All three stopped what they were doing and gave Steel smiles.

"Good luck," Cattie said.

Steel put on his hat and quickly exited out the back door.

22

Steel and Mr. Hickok stood side by side under a large pine tree. Their horses were tethered to the trunk of a fallen pine tree a few hundred feet behind them. They looked out over a clearing of short prairie grass that extended about hundred yards. To the right side of the clearing was a small ravine. Except for some chattering squirrels, and several searching vultures overhead, they were alone. Steel had strapped on his holster and loaded his gun.

Mr. Hickok had tacked up an old wanted poster on a large seasoned pine tree that stood alone in the clearing. "Old wanted posters make good targets. I found a couple I was hoping to collect on but never did. We'll make good use of them now. Let's see, we're about twenty paces away. It's a good distance to start learning from. How are you feeling?"

"I'm fine. Looking forward to learning all I can."

Mr. Hickok nodded. "Good. Let's get started. To be fast with a gun, it's important not to tighten up. When you tighten up your muscles slow down, they don't cooperate like they should. So remember to keep your shooting arm and shoulder relaxed. If you can learn that simple trick, you're going to be a might faster than most men. Now, the other thing you need to work on is always aiming at a small spot on your target. That old wanted poster that I nailed to the pine, I want you to aim at the man's nose on the poster. Get your mind to think that way. Faster is a relaxed arm and shoulder, and hitting your target is aiming smaller. Now without going for your Colt, take that right arm and shake it a little, move your fingers some, try to feel that arm and hand relaxing. Fine. Now, I want you to draw your Colt nice and easy and from the hip aim it at your target. Nothing fast. Don't pull the trigger and keep that arm relaxed."

Mr. Hickok made Steel relax and practice drawing his gun for a good half-hour without firing a bullet. "Now, I'm going to have you aim from the hip and pull the trigger. Don't tighten up. I want you to shoot from the hip. I don't expect you to hit the target. Give it a try."

A shot rang out. The poster fluttered but remained tacked on the tree.

"Dern, boy! You hit it first crack. Lucky shot, maybe. Holster your Peacemaker and try it again."

Steel put the gun back into his holster and gave a light shake of his arm and shoulder.

"Good. Now draw!"

Again, a shot rang out and again the poster fluttered.

"Do it again."

Steel repeated his actions a third time with the same results.

Mr. Hickok stood there silent for a moment.

Steel wasn't sure what to think. He was hoping for some words of encouragement.

"Do it again."

A shot rang out and the poster moved.

"You've never shot no gun before?"

"No, sir. Not even a rifle. That's the honest truth."

"I have to tell you, Steel, you're going to be fast and a dern good shot. You're picking up what I'm telling you faster than I ever thought you would. I've learned a few people how to shoot, but I've never seen anyone like you. I've been told I'm gifted with a gun. I'm telling you, Son, you have a natural ability—a gift. What you just did, if I hadn't witnessed it with my own eyes, I wouldn't have believed it."

"I've always wanted to shoot a revolver since I can remember, but my father never wanted me to have anything to do with guns. I've always kept my feelings about guns to myself. I've practiced shooting in my mind more than once."

"Well, whatever you did it sure seems to be working, and you dern well need a shootin' iron in Deadwood. I want you to not only practice in the mornings, like you said you were planning to, but I want you to practice in your tent every night for at least a half-hour. You do it over and over again. From what I've seen today, in just the little time I've been with you, it's not going to take you long to get real good, and I mean real good."

"Mr. Hickok, I've got question. You don't use a holster, and you tuck your guns into your belt, butts-forward?"

"I've tried several different ways and you might well want to change your style someday, but I use what's called a reverse or a twist. It's a cavalry draw, and I picked it up there. For right now, you stick with one gun and the holster you bought. There's more than one good gunfighter that uses that setup."

"I'll do that. Thanks."

"I wasn't planning on teaching you this right off, but you're showing such an ability, I'm going to teach you a little trick that just might save your life."

"Sounds good to me."

"Let's say you have someone call you out. Their goal is to kill you in front of as many people as possible to enhance their reputation; so most likely, it's going to take place on the main street of town. He'll call your name when you've got your back to him and say he's planning on killing you. You'll turn and he'll have a split-second jump on you while you're trying to get your gun out. You're going to drop to one knee while spinning around, making you a smaller target and flustering the hombre who's trying to kill you. You're going to hope that he misses, or hesitates. You're going to draw at the same time, and then when you're facing him, you're going to raise your gun to eyelevel and fire. This is not a hip shoot. Let's give it a try. Turn your back to the target. When I say go, spin, drop to one knee, draw your gun and aim from eyelevel and fire."

"I'll give it a go." Steel turned his back to the target and shook out his arm.

"Go!"

Steel spun, drew his gun, dropped to his left knee, aimed and fired.

The poster fluttered.

"Damn! Well done! Steel, you're one fast learner. It took me a month of practicing to do what you just did. I want to see you do that again. Might have been a lucky shot but from what I've seen so far, I don't think so. I just can't believe you haven't used a gun before. Do it again."

Steel got up and turned his back to the target.

"Go!" Mr. Hickok said, watching Steel and then turning his head to look at the target.

"That target is getting plum full of holes. Mighty good Steel, mighty good. So practice that. It just might save your life someday. And dropping to your knee is not a bad idea if you're facing more than one person, and that could happen. I'll be honest. My knees aren't as young as yours. Takes young knees to do what you just did."

"Did you teach yourself that move?"

"An old gunfighter by the name of Pete Walker. Yeah, good old Pete taught me that move. I reckon I was about your age. I think Pete's still alive," Mr. Hickok said thoughtfully. "Married a pretty, painted lady and took her to San Francisco." Mr. Hickok hesitated for a minute and then continued, "As far as I know, he's still kicking around. I got several friends like Pete that married painted ladies and made them respectable again." He took off his hat, looked at it for a moment and then put it back on.

"I'll work on that move, Mr. Hickok. I like to fly fish. I'd drop to my knee quite often and cast my fishing rod when I'm looking at a quiet pool of water. I don't want the fish to see me."

"Fly fishing? I've used worms to fish for catfish and perch but that's about it. Haven't done a whole lot of fishing. I heard about what happened the other day with that Jake fellow. I know it's all over town. You watch yourself 'cause he's going to be looking for you. And there's that fellow you walloped on the wagon train. You've got a couple of scalawags that would like to cut you down. I know my friend Charlie warned you to be careful and watch your back and I'm telling you the same thing. That's why I always play cards with my back to the wall."

Steel nodded.

"Steel, you just keep practicing. You're going to be mighty good. I need to get back to Nuttal's. The cards were right good to me last night and I'm hoping on keeping that winning streak alive. We'll do this again next week the same time, if that works for you."

"Yes, sir, that sure would be fine."

"Oh, I got something for you."

Mr. Hickok went over to his horse and untied a brown leather scabbard. He brought the scabbard back to Steel. He untied a leather string and opened up a covering flap, then pulled out a rifle. "This is a Winchester rifle. I want you to have it."

"I can't accept that—no."

"Well, I insist, and that's that and you don't argue with Bill Hickok. Every man needs a rifle. It's loaded for bear and you can find some more bullets in the pouch pocket. With a rifle you just aim using the sight and shoot. I want you to give it a try. Shooting a rifle is a whole lot easier than shooting a pistol from the hip. I've got another rifle. Don't really need two. I'm giving you the carrycase too."

"I sure want to thank you, Mr. Hickok, and I'll keep practicing. You can rest assured of that." Steel took the rifle in his hands and studied it for a long moment.

"Practicing, that's what it takes," Mr. Hickok reaffirmed. "I'm still shaking my head on just how good a shot you are right now."

The compliment couldn't have pleased Steel more. "I'm going to stay for a short spell" he said, "but I need to get back before too long. I've got a lot of work waiting for me at the shop. I'm hoping Charlie can find someone to give me a hand."

"You talk to him. He'll find you some help. Charlie does about anything he puts his mind to. I consider it a privilege to be his friend. I ran into some bad financial luck, and he kinda takes people like you and me under his wing. He's a good man that Charlie. I have a hard time beating him in cards though. Got to watch my bets when I'm playing with him."

"I know he thinks a lot of you," Steel said. "You're both good men."

"I thank you, Steel. I'm going to get my horse and mosey back to town. I meant to tell you, that's a fine-looking horse—Indian pony. I know Mollie won them horses in a poker game and sold them to your pa. I wish I'd been as lucky. That Miss Mollie is more than a pretty, painted lady, she's a right good business gal."

"Do you mind if I ask you one last thing?"

"Go right ahead."

"I know you've killed men... I just—"

Mr. Hickok strolled over to the fallen tree and untied the reins of his horse. He turned to Steel. "I've been a stagecoach driver, lawman in the territories of Kansas and Nebraska, spy and scout for the Union Army, and a gambler. I've killed some men, but I never killed anyone that didn't deserve killing or I've killed in self-defense. There are those that I consider coldblooded killers, and I ain't no coldblooded killer. Now, I'm going to pick up stakes and get out of here. I enjoyed teaching you, Steel. See you in town, and we're on for next week."

Mr. Hickok put his foot in the stirrup and swung his leg over the saddle.

"Again, I want to thank you, Mr. Hickok. And good luck with your poker game."

Mr. Hickok tipped his hat, turned his horse toward town, and was soon out of sight.

Steel looked at the rifle in his hand, eying it up and down. *I can't believe my good fortune. A Winchester rifle given to me by none other than Mr. Hickok, himself.*

His gaze shifted to the wanted poster. Raising the rifle to eye level, he sighted in on the nose of the man on the poster. His finger slowly tightened on the trigger. With a loud crack the bullet sped on its way. The poster fluttered as his bullet found its mark. He squeezed off another shot and then another. *Mr. Hickok is right: it's a lot easier hitting the target with the rifle than my Colt, shooting from the hip. I'll practice both, but shooting from the hip is what I need to get good at.*

"Sorry, Mr. Squirrel for shooting up your pine tree. You'd better get used to it because I'm going to be back here most every morning for a little while."

Steel stayed for another half-hour practicing and then headed back to town with a new sense of self-confidence. He liked the feel of a gun in his hand and even the sudden crack of a bullet. The reward was watching the target flutter, knowing his bullet had found its mark. Of course, he'd only been shooting at a wanted poster hanging on an old pine tree. *How will I react if I have to face a man in a real life-and-death situation? Hopefully that won't happen,* he thought, not wanting to answer his own question. He'd been giving more than a little thought to his father's murderer. If he could somehow get the drop on him, Charlie had said he and his boys would hang him. *That's the plan!*

23

CHARLIE STOPPED BY THE blacksmith shop later that afternoon. Steel suspected that the visit was to learn how things went that afternoon with Mr. Hickok.

"Steel, I've got some welcome news for you. But before I tell you, how did your learning go with Mr. Hickok?"

"It couldn't have gone better. I'm getting the hang of using a Peacemaker," Steel said with a grin. "Oh, and Mr. Hickok gave me his Winchester rifle—I said no, I couldn't accept it, but he insisted."

Charlie smiled. "You don't say no to Mr. Hickok. To give you one of his rifles is a real indication that he thinks a lot of you. I'm real pleased to hear that. I knew your time with him would go well. I've a feeling you're a fast learner."

"I've got a lot of practicing to do. He's going out with me again next week. Did you get your new mail riders going?"

"Not yet. The good news. I've got someone coming over to your shop tomorrow morning to see if you like him. I think you will. He's looking forward to working with you and said he isn't much interested in gold panning. You tell me the time you want him to come by the shop."

"That is good news. I'm thinking about nine. I'll be doing some shooting practice most every morning, early."

"I'll let him know. He's a Swede and a tenderfoot. Name is Lucas, Lucas Johansson. He's about your age, little taller, strong. He said his relatives are still in Sweden. He came to America by himself three years ago. He hasn't found a lot of gold, feels a little discouraged, and is looking for work. He needs to eat."

"How did you meet him?"

"Mr. Nance, at the mercantile, told me about him. Said he came into his store looking for a job. Right now he's living in a tent north of town. I tracked him down, and as I said he's excited about you giving him a try. I made it right clear that you're the boss and if you weren't happy he'd have to find something else. He does speak pretty fair English. I think you'll like him."

"I'm much obliged. I can sure use his help. I look forward to meeting him."

"I'll stop by tomorrow toward the end of the day to see how things went. If you decide not to use Lucas, I think I'll give him a try. Right now, I'm trying to line up mail riders. I'd like to get that going as soon as I can. I need to cut and run. A card game is waiting for me. Bill gave you his Winchester, how about that," Charlie said with a shake of his head as he walked off smiling.

"See you later, Charlie."

24

STEEL HUNG UP HIS apron a little after six that evening. He felt Mr. Hickok had been sincere in his praise. Steel had seen the holes in the target. He stopped for a minute. A thought gave him pause to reflect: *With Cattie and her mom returning to Denver, if this Lucas fellow works out, I could teach him enough in three or four weeks to get by until Charlie finds an experienced blacksmith, or two… I could possibly get out of Deadwood about the same time they leave for Denver.*

Excited to share his experience about his afternoon with Mr. Hickok, Steel closed up the shop and headed over to Nuttal's. While walking across the street, he thought of the sliver-spurred gunfighter he'd watched enter the saloon shortly after his father's killing, an image he'd catalogued in his mind. Steel didn't have silver spurs, and he wasn't a gunfighter, but he did have an ivory-handled gun on his hip.

When Steel entered the kitchen, Sam was standing over the grill, and Cattie was leaning against the sink with a knife in one hand and a half-peeled potato in the other.

"Cattie, Sam," Steel said.

"Howdy, Steel. Hang up your hat, and tell us how things went with Mr. Hickok." Sam said, putting down a large two-prong fork.

"I don't think it could have gone any better. Mr. Hickok is a real gentleman. He gave me one of his Winchester rifles."

"Bill Hickok gave you a Winchester rifle! If that ain't something," Sam said, slapping his knee.

"You must have impressed him," Cattie said. "But that doesn't surprise me. I see you're wearing your gun. I'm glad. You've made some enemies. Hopefully, they'll leave you alone."

"Now that I'm lookin' at you," Sam said, "you look like a gunfighter, especially when you're wearing your Stetson."

"I'm not a gunfighter, and I'm not trying to become one. I would like to see the man who killed my father with a noose around his neck. I don't intend on getting into a gunfight with him, but I do realize that pretty much everything in Deadwood of that nature is more likely to be settled with a lead bullet than a hanging noose."

"There's Big Jake that you may have to reckon with," Sam said. "I'm sure he'd like to send you to Boot Hill."

"Let's talk about more pleasant things," Cattie said.

"You're right. Sorry, Miss Cattie, my apology," Sam said.

"Cattie, I know it's getting late, but I thought I'd see if you were interested in taking a ride out to French Creek. There's a hunter's moon tonight, and the trout will be feeding into the late hours."

"I'm going to need her here," Sam said with a serious face and then cracked a smile. "Just joshing you. Lucy's going to be back in a few minutes, and we can hold down the fort. Finish peeling that spud, and the two of you skedaddle out of here and enjoy yourselves."

"Are you sure you don't need me, Sam?"

"I'm sure."

"Let's do what we did last time. I'll pack something to eat, you get the horses and fishing things, and we'll meet at my place," Cattie said.

"That works for me. See you later, Sam. Cattie, I should be at your place… twenty, twenty-five minutes."

"Have a good time, and bring back a few fish this time to fry up."

Steel grabbed his hat and went out the kitchen door.

When Steel and Cattie arrived at their fishing spot, a full moon was creeping up over the horizon. It was a picture-perfect evening. The afternoon breeze had settled down, and all that could be heard was the soft sound of the stream meandering its way through the grassy meadow.

Steel gathered some wood for a small fire while Cattie laid out a blanket on a patch of grass near the stream. An old pine loomed overhead. After Steel had a fire started, he walked over to the edge of the stream and studied the pool. Every now and then, the nose of a rising trout broke the silent surface as it slurped a fluttering caddis. Steel turned and looked at Cattie. "Cattie, the caddis hatch is starting to happen. There are a few risers, and I can see some caddis landing on the water."

She looked at him. "Come and sit down by me. I know you're hungry. Let's eat, and then we can fish."

"No argument. I smelled that fried chicken all the way here. We'll have plenty of time to fish."

They took their time eating. For some unspoken reason, neither seemed excited to start fishing. Cattie packed up the food and utensils and put them in a pack she'd brought. She placed the pack at the stump of the tree, leaving the blanket spread out on the ground. "Steel, you go ahead and start fishing. I'll watch you fish. It's so peaceful… I can see the moon rising higher and higher… Did you hear the owl?"

"A great horned owl," Steel was quick to respond. "I'll sit down with you, and we can watch the moon rise together."

"I'd like that."

Steel lowered himself to the blanket next to her. He turned and looked into her deep-blue green eyes.

Slowly she lifted her face. Their lips touched, and she was in his arms. She backed away for a moment and turned onto her back, gazing up at him as she lay on the blanket. Reaching up to put her arms around his neck, she drew him down on her. Again their lips met.

The moon was high in the nighttime sky when Steel placed the blanket into his saddlebags. "I don't think your mother is going to be happy."

Cattie took a deep breath and looked up into Steel's eyes. Again they were in each other's arms.

"My mother will be just fine."

"We didn't catch one fish," Steel said.

"You're right. I can't imagine why."

Smiling, Steel said, "Sam is going to ask us why we didn't bring any fish back."

Again their lips met. The softness was gone. He felt her whole body press into his. He backed away, taking a deep breath. "I've got to get you back. Your mother is going to be worried. I suspect she's worrying right now—I don't want to get on her bad side."

"That's not going to happen, but I suppose you're right," she said, gazing into his eyes.

They readied things for their ride back to town and reluctantly rode off under a bright moon and starlit sky.

25

"BILL HICKOK HAS BEEN shot and kilt! He's been shot and kilt!" an old prospector yelled as he rushed out of Nuttal's.

People walking down the street stopped in their tracks. A man on a horse reined in the animal with a jolt. Others looked back and forth as if they weren't sure they'd heard correctly. Could it be true that Bill Hickok was dead, or was it just a prospector who had too much booze making a wild claim?

"Bill Hickok dead? I don't believe it!" another man shouted.

"I saw it! I saw the whole thing," the prospector said to a group of men that headed his way. "I was having a whiskey, watching Mr. Hickok play cards with Captain Massey and two other gents. The man came through the saloon doors, went up behind Mr. Hickok, and shot him square in the back of the head. It weren't pretty. Most cowardly thing I've ever seen."

"I've seen Hickok play cards. He always sits in a chair where his back is to the wall," one of the men said.

"His back wasn't to the wall today. His killer ran out the back door of the saloon," the prospector said.

"Step aside, old man, we want to see," one of the men said, pushing the prospector to the side of the door. "Maybe you've had too much scamper juice."

The men crowded though the saloon doors. At a corner table, close to the back of the main room, eight or nine men stood huddled around the table.

One of the men turned to the approaching onlookers. "Hickok is dead. It ain't pretty. Someone needs to get the undertaker and his good friend Charlie. Charlie needs to know," the man said. "Someone get Charlie! I saw him over at the livery stable not long ago."

The prospector continued down the street shouting, "Bill Hickok, he's been shot and kilt!"

Hearing the commotion, Steel stopped his work and went outside to see what was going on. A man standing outside Nuttal's looked over at Steel and hollered, "Mr. Hickok has been shot in the back of the head while playing cards at Nuttal's!"

Steel stood blank-faced for a long moment. His heart plunged like it had when he saw his father's body draped over the Indian pony. *Yesterday, Mr. Hickok was well and alive, teaching me how to shoot. How can it be? Deadwood! People need to pay. The man who killed my father needs to pay! Whoever killed Mr. Hickok needs to pay!* A need for revenge and justice coursed through his emotions.

Steel learned later that day that the man who had shot Mr. Hickok was a man named Jack McCall. McCall had played cards with Mr. Hickok the night before, and apparently, Mr. Hickok had won a fair amount of money from him. Those who were at the gaming table said Mr. Hickok returned some of the money but received no thanks, and McCall left a disgruntled loser.

The word was out from people who played cards with Mr. Hickok that it was the only time they'd known him to play when his back wasn't against the wall. It was said when he arrived at the gaming table, he'd asked a man named Charlie Rich, who was already seated, to let him have his chair, but Mr. Rich adamantly refused.

A gambler who was at the same table added, "We were playing five-card stud. Bill's hand—I'm going to call it *a dead man's hand,* consisted of two black aces, two black eights, and a card in the hole. I don't think I ever want to see those cards in my hand. I know Charlie Rich is feeling mighty low right now. He said if he'd switched places with Bill, he might just be alive today and McCall would be dead. McCall hightailed it out of the saloon before anyone realized what happened. Several men went after him, but he was gone like a bat out of hell."

Steel watched Charlie and Calamity Jane rush into the saloon together. The undertaker followed a few minutes later. This wasn't your normal Deadwood shooting: Bill Hickok, being the legend he was, commanded everyone's attention and regrets. The whole town was instantly in a frenzy, mourning his loss.

Steel closed up shop and went over to Nuttal's, entering through the back kitchen door. Cattie's and Lucy's eyes were swollen with tearstains on their cheeks. Somber-faced, they sat around the kitchen table with Sam.

Steel pulled up a chair and joined them.

"The saloon is closed for the rest of the day, and it looks like we're going to be closed tomorrow," Sam said. "I know Charlie's planning the funeral and things right now. He's gonna miss his good friend something terrible."

"I think I'll go back to the cabin," Cattie said. "Steel, your father and now Mr. Hickok, it's so upsetting." She turned to Steel. "Steel, I worry for your safety. You know, Rusty said if Mr. Hickok ever left town, he would come after you."

"I'll be fine. Lucy, Cattie, I'll walk you both home," Steel said.

"I think I'll stay with Sam a little longer and see if anyone needs me to do something," said Lucy. "They've been planning now for quite a while. They may want something to eat when they're finished."

Steel got up from his chair. He knew Cattie was right about Rusty. Rusty wasn't the type to make idle threats, and Steel had the feeling that Rusty wasn't afraid of Charlie. He might even go after Charlie, except Charlie's men would be after him fast.

Steel opened the door to the saloon area and let Cattie precede him. The room was empty except for Charlie and four others seated at the table with him.

Thcy walkcd quietly not wanting to disturb their planning efforts.

Charlie raised his hand and motioned Steel and Cattie over to his table.

"How are you holding up, Charlie?" Steel asked in a concerned tone.

"Losing your pa, you can understand some of my feelings. A man couldn't have had a better friend than Bill Hickok. Now my good friend is dead and that dirty, cowardly McCall has left Deadwood to who knows where. They'll find him and justice will be served. He'll be hung by the neck for what he did, mark my words. Steel, Cattie, I don't know if you know everyone at the table: Jane, Billy, Maw, and Tom Nutall the part owner of Nutall and Mann's. They're all friends of Bill Hickok."

"We were all sorry to hear about your pa's killing," Jane said.

"Too much killing going on. This town needs a good sheriff," Mr. Nutall said. "And it's going to happen sooner now that the government isn't trying to protect the Indian rights."

"You can't blame the Indians. The government makes a treaty and then wants to change the rules every few years," Charlie said.

"That's right, but you got all these people heading out west, you've got to accommodate them too. There ain't no easy solution," Mr. Nutall said.

"Steel was out with my dear deceased friend yesterday afternoon. Bill was teaching him how to use a new Colt pistol he just bought at the mercantile. The town knows what Steel did to Big Jake." There was momentary chuckle from Mr. Nutall. "And he beat up a cowboy—who deserved it—on the wagon trip here. Well, he's made a couple of enemies, and Bill was helping him out so he could, hopefully, protect himself. He's good with his fists but no match against flying lead." Charlie hesitated for a moment. "Steel, Cattie, we're planning Wild Bill's funeral. It'll be tomorrow afternoon at three o'clock at my place. I was getting ready to read what I wrote. The reason I called you over is I'd like you to hear what I wrote, you being educated like you are."

Steel nodded.

"Before I start, I want you all to know," he said with a quiver in his voice, "I'm taking care of things the best I can, the funeral arrangements and all that. For the time being, Bill will be buried right here in Deadwood at the Ingleside Cemetery. I might have the body moved at a later date, depending on the circumstances." Charlie picked up a piece of paper lying on the table. With a slight tremor in his hands and a sniffle, he stretched his arms and squinted his eyes.

He began to read:

Died in Deadwood, Black Hills, August 2, 1876, from the effects of a pistol shot. J. B. Hickok (Wild Bill) formerly of Cheyenne, Wyoming. Funeral services will be held at Charlie Utter's Camp, on Thursday afternoon, August 3, 1876, at three o'clock. All are respectfully invited to attend.

Charlie looked up for a moment and then his eyes turned back to his paper.

"Oh, and I'm having old Mike Mckine make up a grave marker that reads: *Wild Bill Hickok killed by the assassin Jack McCall in Deadwood, Black Hills, August 2, 1876. Pard, we will meet again in the happy hunting ground to part no more. Goodbye, Colorado Charlie, C. Utter.*" Charlie set down the paper and wiped his eyes.

"I think that's mighty fine, Charlie. Wild Bill would be pleased," said Mr. Nuttal.

"Sounds real good, Charlie," Jane said, tears running down her cheeks.

Maw nodded.

"How does it sound to you, Cattie, Steel?"

"Mr. Hickok would be pleased. I wouldn't change a thing," Cattie said.

"Agreed," Steel said and gave an approving nod.

"Good. Then that does it. Thank you, thank you all."

26

MOST EVERYONE IN TOWN turned out for Mr. Hickok's funeral at Charlie's camp. If there was to be a fitting time for a funeral, the afternoon presented itself fine: Lazy, white, puffy clouds with grey under bellies drifted orderly across an azure sky, a comfortable breeze was blowing from the south and the scent of pine trees hung in the air. Some walked, some rode horses, and many of the painted ladies came in buckboards provided by the madams. Charlie's men had rummaged chairs from town and set them up outside. He had two of his men in nice looking white and black plaid shirts directing the seating.

Charlie and Calamity Jane sat in the front row. Charlie's arms were folded and he stared ahead in silence. Calamity Jane was silent too. Mr. Hickok's pine casket lay directly in front of them on a table Charlie's men had constructed that morning. The casket was closed, as directed by Charlie. A bouquet of wildflowers rested on the casket. Steel had the feeling that it was Calamity Jane who had made that thoughtful gesture.

Steel, Cattie and Lucy sat in the third row. Steel held his hat in his hand and his gun was strapped on his hip. He'd given some thought to wearing his gun to the service and decided that from now on the prudent thing was to have his Colt with him at all times. Other than a few whispered greetings, things were quiet, people most likely reflecting on Mr. Hickok's life and their own mortality.

When all were seated, Charlie rose from his chair. He took two small steps, turned, and faced the gathering.

"I couldn't have asked for a better friend than Bill Hickok," he began with a quiver in his voice. He gave a brief history and told of some of Wild Bill's famous doings, his remarks garnering both tears and laughter. He paused numerous times when his emotions overwhelmed him. When he finished, he asked for additional testimonials from anyone who felt so inclined. Calamity was the first to come up followed by three other card-playing friends.

When testimonials were concluded, one of Mollie's painted ladies, sang *Meet Me in Heaven.*

Even though Steel wasn't religious like his father, he had the feeling Mr. Hickok was looking down on the service with gratitude and approval of his friend Charlie's earnest and touching words.

While the mourners stood in silence, contemplating the heartfelt service, Charlie announced that he was taking the casket to the cemetery. Five assistances helped him load the casket on the buckboard pulled by two black horses. Charlie, himself took the reins and departed toward the cemetery, no more than ten minutes away.

The gathering broke up and most attendees started to make their way back to town. Steel, Cattie, and her mother, along with a fair number of other folks went on foot.

When they neared the edge of town, Cattie gripped Steel's arm. "Steel there's Rusty!" she cried.

"I see him." With a wary eye, Steel watched Rusty walk toward them. "He could be liquored up."

"The saloons are closed," Lucy said.

"He could have a bottle stashed away. He's looking for trouble. Cattie, Lucy, walk over by those pines."

Rusty stopped in the middle of the street, spread his legs, and pointed his finger at Steel "Hickok ain't around to protect you!" he hollered. "I told you I was gonna kill you. That day has arrived! They'll soon be carting you off to the cemetery to be with your pa and Hickok, and I ain't afraid none of Mr. Charlie Utter, damn his soul!" He spit on the ground.

People started to skitter out of the way, sensing another Deadwood killing was about to take place.

"I see you're wearing a hawg leg," Rusty shouted. "Never seen you with a gun before. I was going to kill you even if you didn't have a gun 'cause I don't like you. This way it's a fair fight if you know what I mean. People can't say I killed an unarmed man." Rusty snickered.

"Rusty, I don't have a quarrel with you, and you've had a little too much to drink. Why don't you go home and sleep it off."

"I do my best shootin' when I've had a little firewater. Yes sir, I do. That's why I'm going to kill you now."

Steel figured he was about two hundred feet away. *My chance of hitting him from a hip shoot is probably not great.*

Rusty started waving his hands. "I see all these folks looking on," he said, "and your pretty girl and her ma. I sure wouldn't want word to get back to Mr. Utter that you weren't killed in a fair fight, so I'm gonna give you to the count of three to draw, and then I'm drawin'. Well, maybe I lied. If you don't draw, I'm drawin' anyway. I told you I'm going to kill you this very day."

Steel's nerves turned cold. *Relax the arm and shoulder and aim small.*

"One… two… three! Rusty shouted. His hand moved toward his holstered pistol.

Steel drew his pistol and dropped to one knee.

A shot rang out and whizzed by Steel's head.

Steel raised the gun to eye level and squeezed the trigger.

Rusty's knees crumpled. He stared wide-eyed straight ahead and then he toppled to the ground, landing facedown in the dirt.

Several men ran up to Rusty and turned him over. After a moment, they looked up, one of them cried out, "Shot in the heart! He's dead!"

Steel stood up and looked at the body lying in the dirt. Cattie ran up to him and put her hand on his shoulder.

Steel holstered his gun. "Let's go back to town and let the undertaker do his job," he said coldly, feeling neither elation nor remorse. He had no problem leaving Rusty in the dirt. As far as he was concerned, if his friends, or someone didn't come and get the body, the buzzards could pick his bones clean.

Steel walked Cattie and Lucy home.

"Are you okay, Cattie?" Steel asked.

"The question is, are you okay? There's just so much killing in Deadwood," she said with a heavy sigh. "You've got to try and get out of this town as soon as you can. I know you think you owe Charlie... It's just too dangerous."

"I'll be leaving Deadwood as soon as I think I can. That's a promise." He took Cattie's hand and gave a light squeeze.

Cattie looked up into his eyes "A little over two weeks and my mother and I will be back in Denver. I'll be waiting for you," she said.

"I'll come for you just as soon as I can. I think I'll get Paint and ride out south of town. I need to be alone and do some soul searching. I just killed a man. Killed him in self-defense, but I did kill a man."

Cattie gave a slight nod.

"Steel, he was a bad man trying to kill you," Lucy said. "You really had no choice. You could have been the one who was shot."

"Under the same circumstances, I'd do the same thing again. What's bothering me, I didn't have to think twice about shooting him." Steel frowned, feeling like he was in a bad dream.

"To stay alive, I suspect that's how a gunfighter thinks," Lucy said.

He thought of Mr. Marks' words: *Becoming good with a gun could be both good and bad.* "I'll be back at six or a little before."

"You're going to have dinner with us?" Cattie questioned, as she again took hold of his arm.

"I'll be at your place for dinner."

The thought of his father interjected into his thinking. He knew his father's killer was out there, most likely at French Creek panning for gold, and feeling he'd gotten away with murder. *I need to deal with his killer before I leave Deadwood,* he thought, feeling a newfound confidence now that he had a Colt pistol on his hip.

27

Lucy, Cattie, and Steel were seated around the small dining table when they heard a knock on the door.

"I don't know who that could be," Lucy said, getting up from the table. She opened the door. "Why, Charlie, come in."

Cattie and Steel's eyes turned toward the door.

Charlie walked in and took off his hat. "Good evening to you all. I don't mean to be a bother. I just learned about the afternoon's shooting. Red gave me a little bit of the story, he got it second hand. Said he thought you'd be here, Steel. So I came to find you and get the lowdown. Sounds like your lesson with Bill didn't come any too soon."

"Charlie, let me fix you up a plate," Lucy said. "We've got plenty and we just sat down at the table. Steel can tell you what happened while you're eating."

"You know, that fried chicken does looks mighty tasty. Lucy, if you could wrap up a few pieces, I'll take them back to my place."

"Charlie, put your hat on that hook and sit down, I'm insisting. I've got mashed potatoes, gravy, and hot biscuits to go with the chicken. I'm not going to send you back to your tent with a couple of pieces of fried chicken to get cold. Get the chair in the corner and we'll all move in a bit and make room for you."

Charlie smiled and said, "Well, since you put it that way I can't refuse."

Charlie sat down, and within a minute Lucy had a plate dished up.

"There you go, Charlie," she said.

"Smells and looks mighty good. Thanks, Lucy." Charlie took a few bites.

"Charlie, I know it's been an emotional couple of days for you, and I want you to know we're glad to have you with us this evening. We consider it a real treat," Lucy said.

"Thank you, Lucy." Charlie set down his fork and looked at Steel. "Steel, do you want to tell me what happened this afternoon?"

"Rusty had been drinking some and drew on me as I was walking Lucy and Cattie back home. That was shortly after you left the service for the cemetery. I'm sure he wanted to wait and make certain you were out-of-sight before he confronted me. I shot him. That's pretty much it."

"That's what I heard. Well, I'm glad you weren't shot. I think that would have been too much for me to handle. I'm thinking more and more that I made a big mistake coming to Deadwood. Denver is a mining town, but I don't think it ever had the lawlessness that I've seen in Deadwood. Right now, I got my hand in so many cooking pots here… Got a mail-rider service just started between here and Laramie, so I've no choice but to stick things out for a year or so more. Lucy, Cattie, at least, in a couple of weeks, I'll get you back to Denver where I know you'll be better off."

"Charlie, finish your dinner before it gets cold," Lucy said.

"I knew Rusty would be coming after me," Steel said. "I just didn't think it would be so soon. I thought you did a splendid job at the funeral. I'm sure everyone that attended felt the same way. We all enjoyed the personal stories, Charlie. You need to write them down for posterity."

"I thank you, Steel, for those kind words. Means a lot to me. You're right, I should write them down. I'm planning on contacting Bill's wife after I drop Lucy and Cattie off in Denver. I believe she's in Cheyenne, and if need be, I'll make arrangements to move his body there or where ever, according to her liking. I'm sure she'll hear of his death before I see her. You'd be surprised how fast news like this travels."

"You're a good man," Lucy said.

"Steel, with everything going on, I wanted to remind you that the Swede will be coming by the shop tomorrow morning."

"I haven't forgotten. I'm looking forward to it."

"The last matter on my mind and then I'll finish up my dinner and vamoose. Steel, Mr. Marks told me you went out to the Lakota village, I assume to find Chatan?"

"I did go out there, and Chatan took me to the spot where my father was shot. The man who killed him was working a pan on French Creek like I thought he might be." Steel had an inkling that Charlie learning of his visit to the Lakota village was most likely the main reason he'd dropped by. Steel continued, "Chatan recognized the horse and the man. I've seen him in Nuttal's at the bar several times. Don't recall seeing him at a gaming table. My guess, he might be coming in tomorrow or Saturday night like a lot of the prospectors."

"When he comes back into town, what do you have in mind?" Charlie asked, narrowing his eyes and looking directly at Steel with his fork in his hand.

"I'm not going to shoot him in the back. I could have done that yesterday. I'm going to call him out."

Cattie and Lucy gave Steel a startled look.

"I don't think that's a good idea," Charlie said, coolly.

"That's a horrible idea! Do you want to get yourself killed?" Cattie retorted.

"They're right, Steel. You can't do that," Lucy chimed in.

"You see him, you come and get me," Charlie said. "Me and some of my boys, we'll take a clothesline and string him up by the neck."

"Thanks, Charlie, but I'm not making any promises."

"Bill told me you were the fastest learner he'd ever seen with a gun. Said you were a natural, but I don't think you want to chance going up against the likes of that yellow-belly. You don't know how good he is with a talking iron."

"I'll think on it," Steel said. Wanting to calm the emotions that were running high in the room. "Oh, that reminds me, Chatan said feelings aren't good with the Indians."

"That's what I've heard," Charlie said.

"He said to tell you he won't be coming into Deadwood anymore, and his village won't be open to trading with the white man."

"I suspected as much and I really can't blame them. What worries me is that if enough of them got together they could wipe us all out without giving it a second thought. I heard a rumor that Custer could be making another trip out this way soon. I've got an uneasy feeling about that. I'll let you be. It's been an emotional day and I'm going to head back to my tent. Lucy, Cattie, Steel, I hope you get some sleep. Steel, I'll see you tomorrow morning. Lucy, much obliged for that dinner. You're a mighty fine cook, Lucy."

"Thank you, Charlie."

28

Steel's hammer struck the horseshoe and sparks flew. He held up the curve iron bar with his tongs and eyed it. "Looks good."

Charlie walked through the open side of the workshop with a tall, lanky young man about Steel's age who wore a bowler, overalls, and shoes that were ankle high.

To Steel he looked like an immigrant who had just stepped off the boat at Ellis Island. Steel placed the hammer and tongs on the anvil, took off the glove of his right hand and extended his hand. "Lucas Johansson, my helper," he said, warmly.

"Yeah, yeah, and you're Steel. Glad to meet ya. Mr. Utter says ya need some help, and I'm excited about trying to help ya."

Lucas shook Steel's hand with a strong, firm grip.

"I'll let you two get acquainted," Charlie said. "I've got some business to take care of. I'll check on things a little later today. Steel, are you planning on being here all day?" Charlie asked.

"Except for lunch at Nuttal's around one. I'll be here. I've got a full day's work and then some."

"Did you get your shooting practice in this morning?"

"I did," Steel said with a firm nod.

"Good. I'll see you boys a little later. Steel, you remember what I said last night," Charlie said waiving his finger.

"I remember. Thanks, Charlie."

"Thank ya Mr. Utter," Lucas said.

"Let's go into the shop," Steel said, leading the way.

"Lucas, there's an apron hanging up over there. Why don't you put it on and we can get down to work."

"Yeah, I for sure can do that."

Lucas did as asked and quickly returned, tying the bow behind his back.

"Right now, most of our work is shoeing horses, so that's what I'm going to teach you first."

"Yeah, yeah," Lucas said with eagerness in his face that almost made Steel smile.

"I'm going to tell you the basic steps on how to shoe a horse. Then I'll actually show you… No, on second thought, I'll show you now with that little, grey mare waiting to be shoed."

"Yeah, that sounds fine."

"Folks that have horses to shoe will bring them by throughout the day. I give them a general time. I'll shoe horses until around three and then I'll work on wagon hitches and other things people might need until around six. Seems almost every day there's some emergency where someone needs something right away. Most of the time I'll try to oblige them. Have you been around horses very much?"

"Yeah, I have in Sweden. We had two work horses."

"Good. Here's Nellie. She's nice and gentle. Some horses, however, aren't so friendly. The first thing is getting acquainted with the horse." Steel stroked Nellie's mane and said, "Nellie, you're going to get some new shoes today."

Nellie tossed her head approvingly.

"Good. Now we're going to move so we can gently pat her rump. Our goal is to get her to lift her foot. Watch, I'm going to run my hand down her leg, easy like. Now I'm going to squeeze the tendon above the ankle and lift the hoof." Nellie shifted her weight onto her other three feet. "Good girl, Nellie. Always compliment her when she does something right."

"Yeah, you make it look so easy."

"Watch, I'm tucking my hip against her hock and using the inside of my knee to pull the foot out slightly and up between my legs so that the sole of the hoof faces up toward me. I'm supporting the horse's toe with one hand. You can see this locks her foot in place."

"Yeah, I can see good."

Steel spent the rest of the morning with Lucas at his side, and then he took him over to Nuttal's for lunch and introduced him to Cattie, Lucy, and Sam. Cattie made them up some sandwiches. They spent more time visiting than Steel had intended, but it was an enjoyable lunch, Lucas being a welcomed contributor to the conversation.

On returning to the shop, Lucas remarked, "Cattie is a very pretty girl. Is she your girl? 'Cause if she's not, I'd sure would, by golly, like to get to know her better."

"Yes, she's my girl," Steel said with a chuckle. He was caught off guard, but after some thought decided it was a perfectly normal question. *Lucas is good looking: blond hair, light blue eyes, good facial features. He could present some competition for Cattie's attention. I hope he doesn't know how to fly fish,* Steel thought with an inward smile.

Steel enjoyed teaching Lucas. It didn't slow down the work a great deal, and it was quickly evident that he was a fast learner. They worked until a little before dark and then cleaned up the shop and got things ready for the next day.

"I think we need to call it a day, Steel said. "I'm tuckered out, and I'm sure you are too. I'm heading over to Nuttal's for dinner. You're more than welcome to join me."

"No, I thank ya. Ya are a very good teacher. I hope ya are happy with my work. I want to please ya."

"I'm very happy with your work. Sure you don't want to come to dinner with me?"

"It's Friday evening and I don't care for all the drinking and shooting. I'm going back to my tent to read. I like to read. I'm reading a book about Mr. Washington."

"I'm impressed. He was an amazing man—one of my heroes. Charlie didn't make it back today, but I'm sure I'll see him this evening or tomorrow. I'll tell him I'm very pleased with your work. Oh, I do work on Saturdays but not on Sundays. My father was a religious man and didn't work Sundays, so I'm going to follow his example."

"Ya, I'm happy with that. I'll be here tomorrow, first thing. Ya, I could use a day of rest on Sunday."

"I've something I need to do in the mornings and won't be able to make it until around eight-thirty. We didn't talk about your pay today. Here's five dollars for today's work."

"That's too much, I'm just learning."

"That's fine. I insist you to take it."

"Thanks." Lucas put on his bowler. "Are ya sure ya are Cattie's boyfriend?" he asked with a smile. He turned, and walked away whistling a tune.

Steel smiled, shook his head and went to the back of the shop. He strapped on his gun and holster. He drew his gun with a quick motion and then returned it to his holster. He took his Stetson off a hook and put it on, running his hand across the edge of the soft mélange of furs. *I like Lucas. He's a fast learner and a pleasant fellow to be around. And he's got a sense of humor.*

Pleased with the day's work, he went outside, closed the flap door and then headed for Nuttal's.

For the first time, Steel felt that in a few months he could leave Deadwood with a good conscience. *Charlie will be pleased, Lucas is going to work out fine... just fine; and when Charlie can, he can get an experienced blacksmith in to work with Lucas... I think I can see a light at the end of the tunnel.*

Steel pushed the saloon doors open. There were only a few scattered empty chairs. Most folks either had cards or a whisky in their hand. Several painted ladies leaned on the upstairs railings, looking down on the gaming from the balcony. Steel glanced over at the table where Wild Bill generally sat. His heart hurt...

29

Saturday started out promising and continued to be a productive workday. Steel was up before sunrise and got in a good hour of shooting practice before heading to the shop. Lucas was there to greet him with a big grin and a morning hello. They worked without a stop until the noon hour, had lunch with Cattie, and then went back and shoed horses until a little after six that evening.

With the arrival of evening, the saloons started to fill up. After Steel closed up the shop and said goodnight to Lucas, he walked down the street eying the horses that were hitched to the railings. He knew the horse he was looking for. A small twister diverted his attention for a moment, kicking up a cloud of dust. He shut his eyes and held on to his hat until it passed.

Dancehall music and loud laughter resonated through the Deadwood air. He knew the hullabaloo would only increase, climaxing around two in the morning. Hopefully, he'd be sound asleep by then. His Saturday night activities would consist of eating dinner with Cattie, enjoying a piece of wild berry pie, and walking Cattie and her mother home around nine. That agenda suited him just fine. He continued eying the horses as he walked, but didn't see the horse he was looking for. *It's just a matter of time,* he thought and turned back toward Nuttal's.

Entering the saloon, he saw Charlie seated at his favorite table with a deck of cards in his hand ready to shuffle and deal.

Charlie looked up and motioned Steel over to his table. "Steel, how did things go today with Lucas?"

"Good, really good. He's going to work out well—learns fast and he's not afraid of work. I like him."

"Glad to hear that. I was over at the mercantile store just after lunch when my mail rider came in from Laramie. I've got a letter addressed to your pa. I thought I was going to get over to see you this afternoon, so I took it to give to you. Anyway, I knew you'd be here for dinner with Cattie." Charlie reached into his vest pocket, "Here it is."

"Thanks, Charlie." Steel took the letter and gave it a quick glance. *It's from my grandfather. Strange, never thought he'd write.* Steel put the letter into his pocket. "I'll let you gentlemen get back to your card game." The letter triggered the fact that he hadn't as yet written his mother of his father's death. *I'll write my mother tonight. I can't put it off any longer.*

"Nice shootin' the other day. I heard tell, you were trained by Mr. Hickok," one of the men remarked, lifting a glass of whiskey and breaking into his thoughts. "I drink to Mr. Hickok and the man he taught how to shoot—right through the heart!" He put the glass to his lips.

"That's right. He was trained by my dear friend Bill Hickok," Charlie chimed-in and started to choke up. He bit down on his lip. "Jim, cut the cards," he said.

"Gentlemen." Steel, unhappy with the fanfare over killing a man, tipped his hat and walked into the kitchen.

When Steel returned to his tent that evening, after seeing Cattie and her mother home and spending a little time with them, he lit the lantern beside his bunk, tossed his hat on his father's bunk, unbuckled his holster, and laid it on his father's bunk. Without taking off his boots, he flopped down on his bunk, shut his eyes, and started to relax, thinking he was going to get a solid night's sleep for a change.

With a start, he opened his eyes. *The letter from my grandfather!*

He swung his feet over the side of the bed and inched up close to the lantern. "I can't fathom why my grandfather would be writing," he mumbled. He reached into his front pocket and took out the letter. He opened it and read:

Dear Blain,

I hope this letter finds you and Steel well. I'm sorry to be the bearer of bad tidings. Elizabeth has suffered what the doctors have told us is a stroke. Her speech was impaired at first but has made some positive improvement. She is confined to her bed at home for the time being and we have employed a nurse to tend to her needs. The doctors think she'll be fine. However, she could suffer another stroke at any time, so we are praying for her and watching her closely.

I trust you and Steel will return home immediately. She has been asking for the both of you. The doctors feel it will be beneficial to have you both at her side.

It is my hope that you'll have a safe and speedy trip home.

Sincerely,
Donald S. Williams

Steel's whole body went numb. He stared at the letter. *My mother, my dear mother, a stroke… father dead… What am I going to do?* He didn't think his heart could hurt any more or sink lower than it had when his father and Mr. Hickok were killed, but this news, with everything else, caused his spirit to spiral to even greater depths. *There's no question, I'll return home immediately. I'll tell Charlie tomorrow morning, first thing. Cattie…*

After another night of turning and tossing, it wasn't until the early morning hours that Steel finally slept. When he woke up, he realized he'd slept in longer than he'd intended. He'd forgo his shooting practice; he needed to talk to Charlie. He dressed quickly and headed for the barbershop, hoping to catch him there.

"Pete, have you seen Charlie this morning?" Steel asked.

Pete was getting ready to throw a smock over a customer for a morning shave. He stopped and thought for a moment. "Charlie was in early. I think he left for the cemetery... maybe twenty minutes ago. I suspect that's where you'll find him. By the way, nice shooting. You're getting quite a reputation."

"Thanks." Steel did a quick turn and headed toward the cemetery at a fast pace.

Charlie was setting on the sole cemetery bench with his hat in his hands, looking out over the grave markers when Steel approached him. Steel hesitated for a moment, uncomfortable about disturbing his personal time.

Charlie looked his way. "Steel, come on over and join me."

"Sorry to bother you, Charlie."

"No bother at all. Just visiting my friend this Sunday morning. I know you like to visit your pa in the evenings. Mornings work best for me. I'm generally in a good card game in the evening. I know Bill wouldn't want me to forgo that pleasure."

"The letter you gave me last night addressed to my father, it was from my grandfather. My mother has suffered a stroke. I need to return home right away, Charlie. I don't mean to let you down..."

Charlie raised his hand. "Steel, you're not letting me down, none. I'm so sorry. Your pa and now your ma. You're right, you've got to get home, pronto."

"I'm not sure how or what's the fastest way."

"Let me think on that for a moment... Hm, you know, the pony riders I just set up, from here to Fort Laramie are running real well. The next rider is scheduled to leave tomorrow morning at dawn. You can leave with Zack, my rider. You can catch a train out of Laramie that will take you, with a few likely changes, to Philadelphia."

"That would be great, Charlie."

"Let me tell you a little about my riders and the operation. I've pretty much followed the Pony Express format, which lasted for a total of nineteen months. It was abandoned by the US government for their unwillingness to keep funding things." Charlie frowned and then continued, "I've got stations located from five to ten miles apart and a few twenty-five miles apart. Depending on how rough the terrain is, a horse can gallop only about ten miles or so. I've sufficient fresh horses, so that's not a worry. I figure you can ride about fifteen hours a day. You're a might heavier than my riders. None of them weigh over a hundred and twenty-five pounds. They carry a gun, water, and of course the mail. I generally don't like a horse to carry more than a hundred and sixty-five pounds. What do you weigh?"

"About one hundred and seventy pounds."

"That's about what I figured. You won't be taking any mail, but you'll need to take your gun and water. I'm afraid that's it."

"That's fine."

"I'll keep your things here for you and we can figure out how to get them to you later."

"There are only a small number of items of importance to me: My fishing rod and equipment I'll give to Cattie. Charlie, I'd like you to have the Winchester rifle that Mr. Hickok gave me. There's my father's Bible and his pocket watch that I'd like to take."

"I can't take your Winchester."

"I'll never use it, and your friend would want you to have it."

"Well, that's mighty nice of you. All right, I accept, and I thank you."

"Oh, I'm going to have to sell my horse. I'm going to give you the gold nuggets my father found. If you could sell them, and after I'm gone give the money to Cattie and her mother."

"You're a mighty good man, Steel. I'll do that. I saw your pa's Bible. It's not real big. I reckon it'd be fine if you took it with you. In my written instructions to my station keepers, I'll tell them to put you on the biggest and best horses. I'll give you a letter to show them."

"How long do you think it'll take me to get to Laramie?"

"Two, two and a half days, depending on conditions and how the horses hold up carrying the extra weight. And don't ask me how long it'll take you to get to Philadelphia on the train 'cause I don't rightly know."

"Tomorrow at dawn… Yes, I think I need to leave then. The shop—Lucas?"

"We'll just have to close the shop. I'll get another blacksmith from Denver or Cheyenne. I've got plenty of other work for Lucas.

I think I might have him work with Red. If you see him before I do, ask him if he wants to bring his things and put stakes down at my place. It's a whole lot better than the tent city. That whole place is worth less than a hill of beans. Tell him to come to my place at eight in the morning. I'll see him after I get you underway."

"I'll let him know."

"The equipment, I'll buy from you," Charlie said.

"No. I don't need the money. It'll be there for the new man. You've done plenty for me and I'm running out on you in a way, which I do feel bad about."

"Something you have to do. If I were in your spot, I'd do the same thing. It's not the end of the world. I've found you try and do what you can and things work out sooner or later. I'll put some extra money with what I get for the nuggets and give it to Lucy and Cattie."

"Good idea. I've second thoughts on selling my horse. I think I'm going to have Mr. Marks continue to board her for a while. My mother may want me to return to Deadwood and bring my father's body home. I'll write and let you know."

"You're right, you just might need to return to here. I didn't think about that. Again, I'm mighty sorry about your ma. I'm hoping she'll recover soon and maybe something good might come out of all this. What are you going to do about Cattie?"

"Right now, everything is pretty much up in the air. You'll be taking her to Denver soon. I'll contact her after she settles-in, and I suspect I'll make a trip to Denver as soon as I get things settled at home."

"I hope everything works out for the two of you, but don't let too much water go under the bridge before you go see her."

"I won't."

"I am planning on seeing you off tomorrow morning with my rider Zack. He's a good man. If you could talk to Lucas, I'd be much obliged."

"I'll head over to the tent city now and see if I can find him."

"Tell him what I said, and not to worry none about work. I'll keep him busy. Tell him I'll try and catch him later today."

30

Steel had passed the tent city a number of times, but never had the urge to visit the place. Now, he was half-mile away and the smell of burning pinewood ruffled his nose. As he approached, the aromas of bacon and black coffee teased his senses. He saw a sea of eclectic tents that provided only minimal shelter and very little privacy. There were a smattering of miners seated around small, cooking fires, some with cups of coffee and some filling their bellies with bacon and sourdough biscuits. Most had already left that morning for the streams of hope. Perhaps today would bring flakes of gold to their pans and maybe a nugget that would dispel any thoughts of discouragement.

The Tent city's description could be encapsulated as a smelly, appalling den of humanity, Steel thought. Red had mentioned that the place had two redeeming qualities: It provided a kinship in a lonely land, and more important, it provided protection of one's acquired assets. Amazingly, a man could leave his gold safe in his tent without worry. Any stealing would be met with quick and deadly justice. There would be no trial, only execution.

Steel meandered through the maze of tents asking anyone he could see for the location of Lucas's tent. Finally, a positive response: "Oh, the Swede. He's over yonder," a weighty, bearded, malodorous prospector said in a stern voice. He pointed his finger at a cluster of small canvas tops.

Steel quickly parted from the nauseous odor and continued his search. He walked toward the directed location, calling out, "Lucas! Lucas!"

A blond head poked out from behind the flap of a tent. Seeing Steel, Lucas stepped out with a look of surprise. He had a book in his hand.

"Sorry to bother you, Lucas. I need to talk to you. I won't be going to the shop tomorrow morning." Steel related the situation with his mother and the urgency for him to return home.

Lucas nodded with a disappointed air.

"Charlie's got plenty of work for you. Go to his tent compound around eight o'clock tomorrow morning and he'll get you started. I think he's going to have you work with Red. You'll like Red. He's one of Charlie's best men. Oh, if you'd like, Charlie said to bring your things to his camp and you can live there. It's much better than the tent village, I can assure you."

"Yeah, that would be nice." Lucas's face broke out in a smile.

"I've got to go now. Good luck to you, Lucas."

"I am unhappy I can't work with ya. I like ya a lot and wish ya well with your mother."

A bit of melancholy overcame Steel when he left Lucas. He'd only spent a little time with him, but he enjoyed his company and he'd enjoyed teaching him. Fortunately, Charlie would see that he'd be taken care of.

Steel left the tent city for Nuttal's, intending to talk to Cattie. His thoughts drifted back and forth trying to predict how she'd react to his imminent departure. On the one hand, she might feel relieved to have him out of the inherent dangers of Deadwood, and then on the other, they wouldn't have time to firm up their personal plans.

The ten o'clock Sunday hour brought out a crowd awakening from a rowdy Saturday night. The warm sunshine portended a beautiful day, resulting in a morning of significant street activity.

Steel made his way down Main Street toward Nuttal's when he came to an abrupt halt. Tied to the hitching post in front of the mercantile store stood a lathered up army horse—a horse that was indelibly etched in his mind.

"The man who killed my father is in the mercantile," he muttered. The reality of facing his father's killer jolted his senses, flushing out all other thoughts.

Trying to determine what course of action he should take, Steel stood still for a moment staring at the open door of the mercantile store. He waited and watched several people walk out. Then, stepping out onto the boardwalk was the man Steel was waiting for. He had what appeared to be an arm full of food goods. He was packing a gun with the holster leathered to his leg, looking more like a gunfighter than a prospector. Unlike most prospectors, he was clean-shaven. He had a dark tan. Steel was close enough to see his sinister eyes that looked out under a weathered wide-brim hat. His black, stringy hair fell well below his shoulders.

The man's eyes met Steel's emotionless stare. He took two steps and stopped. Methodically, he set down his purchases and with slow measured movements stepped off the boardwalk onto the street.

Steel kept his gaze fixed on his father's killer.

"Kid, you planning to meet your maker today?" The words rang out loud and clear. "I saw you and the Indian the other day at French Creek. Well, if you try and draw against me, you'll be in the happy hunting grounds. I don't want to kill ya, so why don't you just mosey on your merry way and I'll do my business."

"You're a cold blooded killer! You shot my father in the back! He didn't have a gun! He's never had a gun!" Steel shouted with all sense of reason and caution thrown to the wind.

"Well that's your story, Kid. He was in my panning area. A man's got to protect his livelihood."

People stopped on the street. A couple of painted ladies, curious at the shouting, hung their heads out of one of the boarding house's upstairs windows. Except for not wanting to get in the way of a bullet, folks were always looking forward to a gunfight. It added interest to the day and made for good talking in the evening with a whiskey in hand.

Steel glanced up the way and saw Charlie and Red riding into town. They approached Steel and reined in their horses with sober looks of concern. Folks came out of the woodwork, as if they had a sixth sense that a shooting showdown was about to take place.

Steel had a good view of Nuttal's down the way. He saw Cattie, Lucy, Sam, and three other men come out of the saloon. Pete stepped out of his barbershop; and his customer, masked with shaving cream, got out of the chair and stood behind him, peering over his shoulder.

Charlie nudged his horse forward. "Hold on there. No need for any killing today," he called out. "We've had enough killing in the last few days. Deadwood needs a little rest."

"Deadwood don't need any rest!" a man from the crowd yelled.

Charlie gave him a hard look. "Maybe you're right," he said, as he placed his hand on one of his guns.

The man looked down sheepishly.

Steel, now focused on his mark, without giving Charlie a sideward glanced. "He's the one who shot my father! Shot him in the back! Murdered him!" Steel hollered.

With Charlie in the mix, the man seemed to relax a little. He dropped his gun hand to his side. "Ain't so. Your pa was panning in my spot. We got in an argument. I thought he was going for a gun and shot him in what I thought was self-defense. The kid weren't there, so he don't know nothin'. I'm telling the truth. Mr. Utter, I don't have any quarrel with you."

"You're a liar!" Steel said.

"Kid, no one calls me a liar and lives!" The man's eyes went cold and focused on Steel. His expression hardened! All in a quick second, he took a quick step forward and raised his right hand to his belt.

Steel watched the killer's gun hand closely. He relaxed his right shoulder.

"Don't do any shootin'!'" Charlie yelled.

The man's hand stayed still for several seconds and then moved toward the gun handle.

Steel's gun cleared the holster.

A shot rang out.

The man's gun cleared his holster and then fell out of his hand without him having fired a shot. He took two staggered steps back and fell backward against the boardwalk.

Several men rushed forward.

"Shot, shot in the heart!" one of the men shouted.

"Shot by the man Bill Hickok taught how to shoot!" another man cried out.

Charlie dismounted and threw the reins of his horse over the hitching post in front of the mercantile. He walked over to Steel while Steel slowly holstered his revolver. Charlie put his hand on Steel's shoulder and let out a long breath. "You all right? That was fast, fast as I've ever seen. It's probably a good thing you're leaving town tomorrow morning. I never should have opened my big mouth and told people you were taught to shoot by Bill. Don't know what I was thinking. There'll be gunfighters now wanting to go against you just to enhance their reputations. It's a good thing you're returning to Philadelphia. If you stayed in the West there are those who would force you to become a gunfighter, whether you liked it or not. Being good with a gun is a two-edge saber—I see Cattie standing in front of Nuttal's with Lucy and Sam. You better go try and calm her down. I suspect she's pretty shaken up." Charlie took a long pause. "Steel you look as calm as a cucumber."

Steel nodded, not sure how Charlie was feeling toward him.

"There's the undertaker, busiest man in town. Steel, I'll catch up with you a little later," Charlie said, and gave Steel a pat on the back.

Steel turned and looked at the man lying on the ground. The only thing that bothered him was thinking that his father and his killer would be sharing the same cemetery. Last night, after reading his grandfather's letter, Steel knew it wouldn't do his mother any good if he'd gotten himself killed. He'd made the decision to leave town without seeking revenge for his father's death, but when he saw his father's killer walk out the door, the yearning for revenge immediately took precedence. Something had come over him, and he'd no intention of backing away. *My father's killer is dead and a small measure of justice has been satisfied.*

He looked at Cattie as he drew near. Their eyes met but she didn't greet him as she always did with a pleasant smile.

He stepped up onto the wooden walkway that fronted Nuttal's. "Cattie," he said, tenderly, knowing they'd soon part.

She put her arms around him and laid her head on his shoulder. He let her remain there for a long moment. She drew her head back and looked up at him with teary eyes.

"Let's go in the back," he said. "I've received some unpleasant news from home."

She made no response.

"Steel we're all glad you're safe," Lucy said. "You've sure been giving us a scare these last few days." She put her hand on his arm. "Sam and I need to go the mercantile. We'll see you and Cattie in a few minutes."

"That was some fancy shootin'," Sam said, giving Steel a pat on the back. "I declare, Bill Hickok sure enough taught you good."

Steel gave Sam a slight nod, and then he and Cattie turned and started to walk into the saloon.

A stranger approached, Steel as he was readying to push the door open. "Dag gum good shootin'. Two killings! You're gonna have to start notching your gun. I'm glad I wasn't bettin' on that fight. The man you just kilt didn't look any too friendly. And that holster tied to his leg, he weren't no tenderfoot. That was the fastest draw I've ever seen, and I've seen a few—he never got a shot off!"

Steel tipped his head slightly, acknowledging the man, but said nothing. He pushed open the saloon door.

When Steel and Cattie got to the kitchen, Cattie finally spoke up, "Steel, I don't care how bad Charlie needs a blacksmith, you've got to get out of Deadwood. I heard again this morning from some of the men who came in to do early card playing that Jake and his two brothers are planning on killing you as soon as Jake feels better. I don't think the killing today is going to scare them off. There are three of them and they'll shoot you at night or whenever they get the chance. They aren't going to go up against you one on one. Please, go back to your home where you're safe. I don't want you killed."

"You're right. I do need to go home and that's what I'm planning on doing. My grandfather wrote my father a letter that Charlie gave me last night. I didn't read it until I got back to my tent. My mother has had a stroke."

"Oh, Steel, I'm so sorry. Let me sit down at the table," Cattie said.

Steel pulled out a chair for her and then seated himself across from her.

"She's bedridden. She can't talk very well, but her speech has improved since the stroke. She's been asking for my father and me. I need to go home right away."

"Of course. Did you ever write and tell her of your father's death?"

"No. And maybe it's a good thing. Better that I'm there with her so I can tell her in person."

"When and how are you planning on leaving?"

"Tomorrow morning at dawn, a little before seven. I'll be riding out with one of Charlie's mail riders for Laramie."

"How are you going to do that? You're not going to ride straight through to Laramie?"

"There are stations for changing horses every five to twenty-five miles, depending on the terrain. I most likely won't ride more than seventy-five or eighty miles a day. Once I get to Laramie, I can catch a train the rest of the way home. Charlie is giving me a letter of instructions for his riders and station keepers. I'm not sure when I'll arrive in Philadelphia, but I'm fairly certain there's no faster way to get there."

"It's all so sudden, but I am relieved that you're getting out of Deadwood, truly I am. I'm so sorry about your mother. When will we see each other again?"

"I'll write once I get home, but right now I don't have the answer. A lot will depend on my mother's condition."

"Of course. Your priority is certainly your mother. Your dear mother, my prayers will be for her recovery and your safe journey home. What about the blacksmith shop?"

"I talked with Charlie and he's going to close the shop. He has no choice. He's going to try and bring someone in from Colorado or Wyoming. He's going to have Lucas work with Red, I believe. I was just out at the tent city telling Lucas what was happening. He'll be fine."

"I like Lucas."

"I like him too. He wanted to know if you were my girl. He's definitely interested in you. Can't blame him," Steel said with a smile. Oh, I'm giving you my fly rod and fishing gear. I can't take it with me."

"Oh!" Tears came to her eyes. She went to him and wound her arms around his neck. "Oh, I'm going to miss you so much. You know I love you," she sobbed.

"And I love you. I want to marry you, Cattie, and bring you and your mother to Philadelphia." He stroked her hair and held her close. "Somehow, I'll figure things out."

"I'll be waiting for you, I promise. Are you really going to leave your bamboo rod with me?" A quick smile broke through the tears.

"Yes."

"Are you taking your gun?"

"Yes. A gun, water and that's it. Oh, and my father's Bible and pocket watch. I have to travel light for the horse's sake."

Tears again began to flow.

They held each other for a long moment.

"I know you need to go. I'll see you tonight and I'll be there tomorrow morning to see you off."

"I'll be by tonight about seven. We can eat together and then walk up to the cemetery to say goodbye to my father and Mr. Hickok."

It was a hard conversation, but Cattie took things well, as Steel had hoped she would. He thought again of the man he'd just killed. He could have shot the gun out of his hand and held him for a hanging noose as Charlie had suggested, but he'd chosen to kill him, and for that he had no remorse… And with Rusty, he had no choice. He was starting to understand Mr. Hickok's comments about the men he'd killed. *Some you kill in self-defense and some just need to be killed.*

31

At a little before seven in the morning, Steel, Charlie, and Zack stood in front of the blacksmith shop. Cattie hadn't as yet arrived. There was little activity in town, only a few people were out and about at the early morning hour. Steel heard the melody of several meadowlarks, which he always listened for in the early morning hours. He hoped their song was a favorable omen for their ride to Laramie.

"Steel, this is the best horse we have," Charlie said. "His name is Alcatan."

"Alcatan is eager to go," Zack said, looking at the reddish-brown coat of the handsome gelding.

"Steel, you can see he's a might bigger than Zack's palomino. They're both real fast horses, and Alcatan should carry your weight just fine. I am a little concerned about some of the other horses you'll be riding. Take care, and if you see a horse starting to labor, slow up. You and my rider will just have to be a little late."

"Will do." Steel patted Alcatan's neck. "Good boy. I understand we're going to do some hard riding today, so I'm counting on you," Steel said.

"You've got the letter of instructions for my station keepers."

"I've got it." Steel patted his pocket.

"It's a mighty pretty morning. I love riding on days like today," Zack said. "I suspect we could run into some thundershowers later on. I'll watch and make sure we get to high ground if that happens. Them flash floods can come down on you like a hawk on a rabbit."

Steel guessed Zack was no more than sixteen or seventeen years of age. He was short, his head coming up a little above Steel's shoulder. He had a dark complexion, most likely from riding long hours in the sun. He carried a pistol on his hip, and road a pretty light colored palomino with a white patch running down his head. A mailbag was secured with rawhide straps behind the saddle.

"Zack is one of my best riders. He'll take good care of you. There's Cattie now, coming to say goodbye. You're a lucky man, Steel. She's a fine, fine young lady. Don't you forget her."

"I won't."

They watched her as she scurried their way.

"I'm sorry I wasn't here sooner," she said.

"Cattie, they're about ready to ride out," Charlie said. "You're here just right."

Steel stepped forward. He took Cattie in his arms and kissed her.

"Write me as soon as you get to Philadelphia, so I know you've made it safely," she said haltingly, fighting back tears.

"I will." He looked at her, wishing somehow, someway, he could take her with him. The thought of not knowing when he'd again see her stirred his feelings to a near breaking point. He kissed her again, turned, looked at Charlie and gave him a nod.

"Time to saddle up," Charlie said. "I hope you've got your pa's Bible, and I know you've got your gun and water. Steel, you best tighten down that Stetson. You don't want to lose your sombrero."

Steel turned and mounted Alcatan. Zack was already on the Palomino.

"Zack, why don't you briefly review what's going to happen over the next three days."

Zack held his eager mount still. "Steel, we'll start by taking the main road south out of town and then turn eastward. Our first swing station where we'll change horses is twenty miles out. Mr. Grey's the station keeper. We'll have to wait there and at each station for the first seventy-five miles until a fresh horse is saddled up for you. Seventy-five miles from here is a home station. A new rider will take the mail, but Mr. Utter wants me to stay with you all the way to Laramie. With resting four or five hours at each home station, I figure, we're three days out of Laramie. Oh, the riders ahead of us will let the station keepers know we're coming, and they'll have fresh mounts for us." Zack pulled back on the reins.

"I think Zack has summed things up right fine," Charlie said, giving Zack an affirmative nod.

"Thanks again, Charlie," Steel said, tipping his hat. He turned and gave Cattie a last look.

They turned their horses southward. Zack touched his spurs lightly to his horse, and his horse was off, knowing what the day was all about.

Alcatan instinctively knew his job, and with no coaxing from Steel, followed the Palomino. They caught up with them before they reached the edge of town, and Steel reined in Alcatan, letting him know that they wouldn't be taking the lead.

Charlie and Cattie watched the two horsemen until they were out of sight.

"He's a good man," Charlie said. "Cattie, he'll come to Denver for you as soon as he can. That I'm sure of."

Cattie nodded. "Thank you, Charlie. How many times have I thanked you?"

Charlie just smiled. "I've got something to tell you. I received some news yesterday evening from a friend who just came in from Denver. Your father got in a fight with an inmate and was stabbed to death—doesn't surprise me none. You and Lucy won't have to worry about him. I haven't told Lucy yet. I told Steel and I thought I'd tell you and Lucy this morning."

"Thank you for telling me, Charlie. That'll go a long way in easing my mother's mind. As you know, he's caused her a great deal of hurt, emotional and physical. I rarely saw him, Charlie. I pretty much grew up without him. I always had my mother and grandfather there for me. I have to tell you, Denver is looking mighty good."

"Are you and your mother going to like the East?"

"I've been there a number of times. I love the East and I'm sure my mother will too, if she decides to go with me. As you know, she has friends in Denver, so we'll just have to see. I'm more of a city girl than my mother."

"I know that. You're a lot more sophisticated than most folks, but the thing I like the most about you, Cattie, is you never act like you're better than anyone else. And you're a hard worker. You peel those spuds with no complaints."

"Thanks, Charlie." Cattie walked over to him and gave him a kiss on the cheek.

"I'll be over at Nuttal's around noon. Would you like to tell Lucy about your pa?"

"I'd prefer that news comes from you."

"Fine. I'll be happy to tell her."

I know my mother will be greatly relieved, knowing she won't have to worry about my father causing us trouble, she thought. She stood there with her emotions swinging between the sadness of not knowing when she'd see Steel again and relieved that she and her mother would soon be getting out of Deadwood without the worry of a threatening father.

"Speaking of potatoes, Charlie, I think I'll get an early start helping Sam this morning."

32

"WE'VE GOT A COUPLE of men close to death! One might be dead, can't tell!" the army sergeant hollered. His men carried two stretchers through the Laramie Hospital door.

"Doctor Northrup! Doctor Michaels! You're needed right away!" a nurse shouted as she hurried down the corridor.

An older grey-haired man appeared wearing spectacles and a white jacket with a stethoscope hanging around his neck. A much younger man in a similar white jacket rushed out into the hallway.

The older man took a quick look at the bodies lying face up on the stretchers. He saw no movement and their eyes were closed.

"Put them in the first two rooms on the left," the older doctor ordered. "John, I'll take the first one. We're going to transfer them to the beds. Sergeant, could your men give us hand?"

"Yes."

"Good. Easy now. Lift on three—one, two, three. Susan, let's get the bloody shirt off this kid. Wait, is he breathing? Doesn't look like he's breathing!" The doctor's fingers quickly went to the side of his patient's throat to check for a pulse.

"I'm getting nothing," the doctor said. "Susan, give me a towel." The doctor lifted the man's shirt and blotted some of the blood off his chest. "There's the bullet hole, not far from his heart," he announced in a dispirited tone. "This one looks to be what... sixteen or seventeen? He didn't make it. The doctor stepped back and looked at the boy lying before him. A pall of sorrow fell over the room.

The doctor took a long pause and then said, "Someone get a sheet and cover him up. Susan, let's go see if the other young man is alive."

"John, my young man didn't make it," the older doctor told his colleague in the next room. "I suspect, he died before he came through our doors. A kid, sixteen or seventeen, I'd venture to say. Nothing we could do. It appeared to be a severed artery next to the heart."

"I think we lost this one, too," the young doctor said, glancing up. "I can't get a pulse. He doesn't appear to have been shot. He's got a large lump on his head. Could have hit his head on a rock or something. Who knows?"

The sergeant stood by the open door with a restrained look.

The older doctor turned and looked his way. "Damn shame, two young men, both dead. Cut down in their youth," he said and shook his head.

"I've seen death many times. It doesn't get easier," the sergeant said. "Especially hurts when they're young like that."

The older doctor followed the sergeant out into the hall, joining him and four other solders. "I'm Doctor Jim Northrup. Indians?"

"A band of Crows. We were out on patrol when we heard shooting. The Crows have been causing trouble round about lately. They burned down a cabin north of town yesterday, so we were out in that area. The Indians took the mail rider's horse and shot the other horse from underneath the other rider. My guess is he got the knot on his head when he flew off after they shot his horse."

The doctor nodded.

"The younger kid was a mail rider working for a man by the name of Charlie Utter out of Deadwood. They just started carrying mail from Deadwood to Laramie and back."

"I heard about that," the doctor said.

"We recovered the mail pouch. Somehow the kid was able to untie the pouch. I'm sure he was trying to save the mail from the Indians destroying things. Got to give him credit for that. The other young man had a Bible, three hundred and fifty dollars, two letters with Philadelphia addresses, and a pocket watch in his pouch. I'm going to leave those items with you. Oh, he was also wearing a nice Colt pistol and holster. So there's money there to bury him. Kendal, go get those items and the younger kid's gun, and we'll leave 'm here at the hospital," the sergeant said.

"Yes, sir."

"Take those things up to the front desk and they'll take care of them," the doctor said, and then continued, "You said the letters have Philadelphia addresses... We'll see if we can use them to find the one's kinfolks."

"Even though it's the worst news one can get, I'm sure they'd like to know," the sergeant said. "We best be getting along. We're going back out to see if we can find that Indian party."

"Good luck to you, Sergeant. Those Crows are a mean bunch. You and your men take care. I don't want to see any of you in here."

Dr. Northrup accompanied the sergeant and his men to the front door and watched them mount and ride off. He waited at the door for a moment thinking about the unnecessary loss of two young lives.

"Doctor! Come here quick!" a nurse called out. "The young man's alive! His eyes are open!"

Both doctors and several nurses rushed into room.

The young man opened his eyes halfway and moaned. "My head." He shut his eyes and lapsed back into unconsciousness.

"Go to the ice box. Let's get some ice on that lump and see if we can bring the swelling down," Doctor Northrup ordered. Turning to Doctor Michaels, he said, "I've treated many wounded men in the war. Some lived and some died. You just never know what the good Lord has in mind for you. I could have sworn this boy was dead, too. No pulse, nothing, yet here he is a few minutes later opening his eyes. He's not out of the woods, but he's got more than a flicker of hope it looks like."

A day later, Steel fought to open his eyes, and every so slowly, his blurry vision cleared. He squinted at barren white walls surrounding him... a window bright with sunlight warmed his face... a painting of a coyote chasing something... A *rabbit.*

His sore body told him that he'd been injured. He raised his arm slowly and touched the lump on his head, then let his arm fall back onto the bed. His head ached and his left shoulder was sore. Making no more effort to move, he lay there staring at the ceiling. "Hello," he called out with all the strength he could muster.

A young woman wearing a blue dress and white apron came in, answering his call."

"Where am I?"

"You're at the Fort Laramie Hospital. You were riding here from Deadwood and met up with some Crow Indians. They shot your horse and our guess is that when the horse went down, you flew off and struck your head on a rock or something else hard. We put ice on the bump right after you were brought in and have continued intermittently. The swelling has gone down considerably."

"I felt the bump. My head hurts as well as my left shoulder and left side."

"You must have landed on that side. Miraculously, no broken bones. I suspect, you'll start feeling much better by tomorrow, but the doctor will be able to give you more information. Is your name Steel?"

"My name… I, I don't remember my name. Steel… I just don't know."

"You don't know who you are?" the nurse asked in a calm voice.

"No, I don't know my name… I can't remember."

"You had two letters in your belongings. One was addressed to Blain Madison and the other to Steel Madison. Both letters came from Philadelphia. We think Blain is your father and that you were on your way back to Philadelphia. Oh, and a Bible with the name Blain Madison written in it. Does any of this sound familiar?"

"No… Nothing sounds familiar. I don't know who I am or where I've been."

"You came from Deadwood in the Black Hills. That we do know. Does that ring a bell?"

"The Black Hills… I don't ever remember being in a place called Deadwood, but I know the name."

"Philadelphia?"

"Philadelphia... a city in the East. I know that name too, but I can't remember being there, or anything about it."

"Do you remember anyone? Do any family names come to your mind?"

"No. No—nothing." Steel started to shake his head, but the pain stopped him.

"You need to get some rest. I'm sure you'll start to remember things soon."

Doctor Northrup peeked his head in. "Venice, how's he doing?"

The nurse joined him at the door. "He woke up a few minutes ago. He's coherent, but he can't remember his name or the names of any family members. He knows the names of Deadwood and Philadelphia, but can't remember ever being there."

"Hm... well, all we can do is wait." Glancing at his patient, the doctor spoke quietly, "It looks like he's resting well and the swelling has gone down considerably. I'm thinking, he'll be well enough to get out of bed tomorrow, or even later today. I don't want him to stay bedridden too long. As for his memory, it's anybody's guess when that'll return. He may never regain what he's lost, but at least, he's alive, and hopefully, he'll be able to live a normal life."

"I was thinking that we might give him the letters."

"Let's not do that today. Tomorrow would be better."

33

Outside the Deadwood barbershop, a rider dismounted his lathered horse and hastily threw the reins over the hitching rail. He scampered up the wooden steps and entered the small barbershop through the open door.

Charlie leaned forward in the barber's chair when he saw his mail rider. "What are you doing here, Bobby? Looks like you've been running from a mountain lion. You ought to be in Laramie."

Bobby took off his hat and gave it a quick shake. He gave Charlie a sober look. "Mr. Utter, I've mighty bad news for you. A sergeant in the US Army came by our Laramie station three days ago and said Zack and Steel had been killed by Indians. They were attacked by a band of Crows. Apparently, the Crows have been causing a fair amount of trouble around Laramie."

"Killed! Zack and Steel killed!"

"Yes, sir."

Charlie sank into the barber's chair speechless for a moment, his throat tight. "We… we haven't had any problems with our riders. Zack and Steel killed by Crows," he said, stunned and shaken at the news. "You're sure? Did you see the bodies?"

"No. I'm just repeating what the sergeant said."

Charlie got up out of the barber's chair and looked out at the rolling white clouds for a long moment "Do you know what's happening with their bodies?"

"Mr. Stevens, your Laramie station manager, said you'd most likely want Zack's body to be brought back to Deadwood so you—his family—could give him a proper burial and all that. I think they're trying to notify Steel's kinfolks. He had two letters with addresses."

Charlie nodded. "Stevens is a good man. We'll get Zack back here and take care of things. Steel's body… I want to follow up on that and make sure his kinfolks get the proper notification. What am I going to tell Cattie? Her heart is going to break in two."

Shaking his head, Bobby said, "Sorry, Mr. Utter."

"Bobby, you go get yourself something to eat and some shut-eye. Thanks for making that ride. I'll find Zack's brother right away and let him know what happened."

Charlie turned to Pete, who had been standing there listening with a pair of scissors in his hand. "I'm going to forgo my hair trim and wash this morning. I'd appreciate it if you didn't say anything just yet, at least for today."

"I understand. I won't say a thing. I'm sorry, Charlie, really sorry. I know how much you think of your riders and Steel. I didn't know Zack. He did his own shaving, cutting his hair, and such, but I'm sure he was a fine young man."

"He was… They both were." Charlie took his hat off the rack and left the barbershop. *I don't know how to tell Cattie… News is going to get out fast. I better find her and tell her now. I sure don't want the news to come from someone else.*

34

STEEL SAT ON THE side of his hospital bed, buttoning his shirt, when Doctor Northrup walked into the room. "It looks like our patient is feeling much better. How's the memory coming this morning?"

"Good morning, doctor. As to my name, family, friends, people, faces—nothing, nothing at all. I'm feeling much better, thanks to you and your people."

"Don't thank me. It just took a little time for your body to heal. The body is a marvelous thing. I understand you ate a good breakfast. Jennie's a fine cook. And I see you're getting dressed, so I assume you're feeling well enough to leave us?"

"Yes. I'm a little sore on the side of my chest, but that's about it. My head doesn't hurt anymore, and for that I'm grateful."

"As I told you, you've probably got some bruised ribs. They'll take a while to heal. May I ask what your plans are? I see you've been reading your letters."

Steel glanced at the two letters lying on the bed. "I've read them several times. There's nothing in them that has jogged my memory. I'm discouraged, but I've made some decisions."

"And they are?"

"To take the train to Philadelphia and go to the address of the person whom I believe to be my grandfather. I assume my name is Steel Madison and I was on my way there to see my ill mother."

"Yes, I'm sorry about your mother, and I can understand the urgency."

"Blain Madison would be my father. Why wasn't he with me? That's one of those things I can't remember."

"I read your letters and I agree that sounds logical. You're well spoken. I can tell you're well educated. Sounds like you've got a girl that's serious about you."

"Savannah. Yes, I read her letter, but again no memory of her. Well, if I'm not Blain Madison's son, hopefully I'll find out just who I am. Until I learn differently, I'll go by the name of Steel Madison."

"Have you thought about returning to Deadwood? I'm confident you'd be recognized there."

"I thought about it. If it's my mother who is ill, which I believe to be the case, I need to get home before I go anywhere else."

"I'd have to say your mind is working extremely well. I agree, you should take the first train out of Laramie to Philadelphia. You may need to change trains several times but that shouldn't be a problem. You have a Bible and a nice Colt pistol. Oh, and you have three hundred and fifty dollars, which you can pick up from Annie."

"I want to pay for my hospitalization and for the clothes."

"Your shirt wasn't in the best of condition so one of the nurses found or bought you a shirt. Annie O'Dell will take care of you. She's been here from the start of this hospital and handles all the financial affairs. She has an office close to the reception desk. So Steel, I wish you well. If you pass by our way in the future, please stop and let us know how you're doing."

"Thank you, Doctor Northrup. I'll do that."

The doctor turned to leave the room and then stopped and turned back to face Steel. "I think there are a couple of young nurses that will be sorry you're leaving so soon." He smiled before stepping out of the room.

Steel finished getting dressed then put the letters in his pocket and walked out to the hospital entrance.

"Well, look at you, getting ready to leave us," the short, plump, rosy cheeked receptionist said with a smile. "You know when they first brought you in, everyone thought you were dead—couldn't find a pulse. Good thing they didn't haul you off to the mortuary right then and there."

Steel returned her smile.

"Remember your name yet?"

"Not yet."

"Well that's a shame. I've heard of such a thing, but I've never known anyone to have it—amnesia, I think they call it—until you. Anyway, I sure hope you can remember soon. Now that I'm thinking about it, there are some things I wish I could forget."

"I owe you some money for my stay and the shirt."

"Annie will take care of you. She's in her office right over there. Just give the door a good knock. Her hearing isn't quite what it used to be."

"Thank you."

Steel walked across the entranceway and knocked on the door.

"Come in."

"Mrs. O'Dell, I'm leaving and need to settle up."

"Glad you're feeling well enough to go. I've got your things in my bottom desk drawer. As for charges, I think fifteen dollars should cover everything."

"That sounds more than reasonable. The shirt, too?"

"Yes, everything. They brought you in with three hundred and fifty dollars, less fifteen dollars… Here you are, three hundred and thirty-five dollars. And here's your Bible, pocket watch, and gun and holster. You could be a gun-traveling preacher."

Steel chuckled. I don't think so. I think the Bible belongs to my father, if Blain Madison is my father. Thank you." Steel looked at the gun and holster for a long moment before buckling it on, and then picked up the Bible. "Oh, where is the train station?"

"Just head toward town. The Laramie train station, you can't miss it. It was one of the first buildings in town. It's not only a station, but it's also a hotel and restaurant. Two weeks after the station opened in 1868, Laramie had over two thousand new residence, and most of those folks came by train. I was one of them. I never regretted coming."

"Annie, I detect a little Boston accent."

She looked at Steel incredulously. "Well, I'll be... You can't remember names but you picked up on my accent. I thought living out here so long, I'd lost it. Yes, my family is from Boston."

Steel smiled, surprised at his perceptiveness.

"If you get through this way again, stop by and let us know who you really are. You're a fine gentleman."

"I'll do that, Annie, and again thank you."

35

Knowing that the word would spread fast about Zack and Steel's deaths, Charlie went directly from the barbershop to Nuttal's, only slowing his stride for a moment as an ally cat made its way across his path.

"Little early for a game of poker, Charlie," the bartender drawled when Charlie entered the saloon.

Without saying a word, Charlie went straight to the kitchen, pushing open the swinging door.

"Morning, Lucy," he said solemnly.

"Morning, Charlie. You look like you're all in a huff. To what do I owe this unexpected visit? You're generally at Pete's getting a hair wash this hour of the day."

Charlie took off his hat and held it in his hands, looking down at the brim. "I don't know any easy way to tell you, Lucy... Steel, and my rider Zack were killed by a band of Crow Indians, just outside Laramie. While I was at the barber shop just now, one of my riders rode in with the news."

The plate Lucy was holding fell to the floor, shattering into a hundred pieces. Her face tightened. "It can't be... Steel and your rider killed. I don't know what to say... Cattie... How am I going to tell Cattie? She loves that boy so much. Charlie, I just can't bear to tell her."

"I'll go tell her. Is she at your place?"

Lucy put up her hand. "No, no, I'll tell her. I'm her mother. It's good we'll be leaving Deadwood soon. Getting her back to Denver and working will be the best thing for her. Oh, Charlie, I just don't want to believe you. You're sure?"

"That's what I was told."

Lucy's eyes brimmed with tears. "Why is life sometimes so cruel, Charlie?"

Sam walked in from the back. "Everything okay?" He looked down at the broken dish. "I'll clean that up," he said. "Lucy you're crying. What's goin' on?"

"Steel and my rider, Zack, were killed by some Crow Indians just outside Laramie," Charlie said.

"That's downright terrible news. I'm mighty sorry. I knew Zack too, a good young kid. Does Cattie know yet?"

Lucy wiped her eyes with a dishcloth and took a deep breath "I'm going to tell her now," she said.

"Don't you worry about coming back today," Sam said.

"Sam, I haven't told you, Charlie is taking some of his mules back to Denver in about a week, and Cattie and I will be going back with him."

"Well, I'm sure gonna miss you, Lucy. I'll miss Cattie too, but Denver is a whole lot better place than Deadwood for you two. For that reason, I'm glad you're going. It's just not safe around here for folks like yourselves, and most everybody else, for that matter. A young mining town without law."

"Lucy, I'm moving things up," Charlie said. "I think we can be out of here in three days. The sooner we can get you and Cattie out of Deadwood the better. How does that suit you?"

"Thank you, Charlie. Yes, that would be greatly appreciated."

"I'll stop by your place a little later and check on the both of you."

Lucy nodded.

"Lucy, Sam." Charlie put on his hat, turned and walked out of the kitchen. *I've got to go find Zack's brother and tell him.*

Charlie looked over at the bartender. "Walt, no poker today," he said and walked out the salon doors.

36

The horse carriage pulled up to an impressive Tudor home with a stone circular driveway. The house was painted light green with white window trimmings. White, pink and lavender azaleas adorned the center of the circle. A rose garden bloomed to the right of the house, while large trees in full leaf bordered the sides of the property.

Steel paid the driver and requested that he wait for a moment until he signaled him. Carrying his belongings in a small satchel he'd purchased in Laramie, he made his way up the front steps. His heart pounded. He took a deep breath, exhaled, and rang the small iron bell beside the oak door.

Within moments, a middle-aged colored lady opened the door. Her eyes widened with a look of disbelief. "Oh, land a Goshen, Steel! Steel, it's so good to see you. You come in! Come in! Your grandparents are in the parlor and your mama's up in her room. She's going to be so glad to see you. Where's your father?"

"I'll tell you later," Steel said awkwardly. *At least now I've confirmed my identity.* Relieved, he turned and motioned to the driver.

"Well, come in, come in. Don't just stand there. You're looking good, all nice and handsome. Your skin has got a little color like mine—not quite." She put her hands on her plump hips and laughed. "Oh, Steel, I must tell you that the pretty little, Southern lady you befriended, she comes over almost every day to visit your mama, and she takes her for a walk. I know she's going to nursing school. She sure is an angel. Just follow me."

"Mr. and Mrs. Williams, Steel has come home," she announced with a broad smile as he trailed after her into the parlor. "Don't he look just fine and handsome."

Steel's grandfather got up out of his easy chair. "Steel, you received my letter. I was worried you might not get it. Where's Blain?"

"I don't know I was injured on my way here. A Crow Indian shot my horse and I went down, hitting my head. I have amnesia. I can't remember names, faces, or being at places. I'm hopeful my memory will return soon. Right now, I'm at a great disadvantage."

"Oh, Steel, my poor grandson," Mrs. Williams said. "So, dear, you don't know where your father is?"

"No, I don't know. He wasn't with me when I was attacked. There was another young man. He was shot and killed. The people at the hospital in Laramie took care of me until I was fit to travel. I could have returned to Deadwood and most likely could have found out about my father, but I thought the most important thing was to come here and find out who I am and see my mother, assuming I'm Steel."

"Dear, you most certainly are our Steel!" his grandmother said. You need to go upstairs and see your mother. Hanna will show you to her room. She'll be so glad to see you. We can visit later. Oh, Steel, it's so good to have you home," his grandmother said.

His grandfather gave him a nod and a smile. "Yes, you go up and see your mother," he said.

"Waite a moment," his grandmother said. "I need to tell you she's doing much better. Her speech is back to normal and she can take short walks. Savannah comes and takes her for a walk almost every other day."

"I don't remember her—Savannah."

"Well, to forget the name of someone that pretty, you must have hit your head hard," his grandfather said.

"Hanna, please show Steel where his room will be," his grandmother said. "We'll have him stay in the one next to Elizabeth. It has a nice window view. Steel, this is your home now, so whatever you need, you let us know. I can see your grandfather will need to take you shopping tomorrow for some clothes."

"How would you like me to address you?" Steel asked.

"Well, Sara and Donald would be appropriate, or Grandfather and Grandmother. We'll leave it up to you," his grandmother said.

"Perhaps both, depending on the situation."

She gave him an approving smile.

"I'll go upstairs and see my mother."

When they reached his mother's room, Hanna knocked softly and said, "There's someone here to see you."

"Oh, is Savannah here?" a women's voice called within the room. "She's early. I'm still in bed."

"It's not Savannah," Hanna said.

"I'll take it from here, Hanna, thank you."

"I'll put your things on your bed," she whispered.

Steel handed her his satchel and then opened the door slowly. He poked his head in before walking in.

His mother bit down on her lip and tears started flowing down her cheeks. "Steel, my son. Oh, Steel, you've come home. Please come over next to me."

Steel walked over and held out his hand. She reached out and grabbed it and held it tightly. For the moment, she said nothing but just looked up at his face.

How Steel wished his memory would return. He said nothing waiting for her to start the conversation.

"Your father. Where's Blain?"

"I don't really know." Steel spent the next few minutes explaining what had happened to him.

"At least I have you back and for that I'm so grateful. I'm doing fine and hoping in another month I'll be as good as new. Did your grandparents tell you about Savannah?"

"Yes, they did. Sounds like they're quite taken with her."

"We all are. I've grown fond of her. She should be coming over fairly soon. So you can't remember at all about your father?"

"Nothing."

His mother's face turned sorrowful. "Steel, I know your father. If he were able to come back home he would have been with you."

"If we don't hear from him, I'll need to return to Deadwood."

"I don't want you to return to Deadwood! You need to stay right here and start working for your grandfather like you planned. I can't bear the thought of losing you. Your grandfather would like nothing more than for you to start learning the business. Your future is in your grandfather's business. He owns a chain of very successful merchandising stores. There's one here, one in New York, and one in Boston."

"I see. I'm not opposed to working for my grandfather."

"Good." She squeezed his hand.

"I'm going to put my things away and clean up a little, but I look forward to going on a walk with you."

He leaned over and kissed her on the forehead.

Steel stepped out of the room and went into the bedroom next door. He walked over to the window and looked out at the view. *Strange, me being here with people that love me and I have no recollection of them at all. I can't even recognize my own mother's face, but there's something in me that says I love her and that I care for her deeply.*

He walked over to the bed and opened his satchel. He took out his father's Bible and his gun and holster. He strapped the gun belt on, buckling it tight. His hand dropped to the gun. He felt the cold ivory handle and quickly drew the gun out and pointing it at the wall. His instinctive actions surprised himself. *I think I'm good with a gun. I need to ask my grandfather where I can find a place to shoot.*

He eased the gun back into the holster and tried to remember where he'd learned how to shoot, but the memories were dark and wouldn't come. He took the gun and holster off and returned them back into the satchel.

There was a soft knock on the door. "Steel, it's Hanna. Miss Savannah is downstairs with your grandparents. Your mother is just finishing getting ready for her walk, and she'll be down in a few minutes. Oh, your bathroom is directly across the hall."

"I'll be down in a minute or two. Thanks, Hanna."

Steel descended the carpeted stairs. He could hear voices coming from the parlor room. He entered the room with an interest in meeting the much-talked-about Savannah.

All eyes turned in his direction. He hesitated for a moment waiting for someone to say something. Savannah was lovely, with long, cascading blond hair, blue eyes, a fair complexion, and elegant features. Now, he could understand his grandfather's comment.

"Steel, I guess I need to introduce you to Savannah," his grandmother said.

"Savannah, I must apologize for not recognizing you. I understand we met before my father and I left for the Black Hills. I assume my grandparents have told you of my head injury. I'm certainly hoping I'll soon regain my memory of faces and places. Such a pretty face as yours underscores the severity of my injury. Oh, and I do have your letter to me."

Savannah blushed and then gave Steel a warm smile. "Your grandparents did in fact tell me. And I'm so sorry, but we'll do all we can to help you remember."

"You're from the South."

"That's one of the things you remarked on when we first met, my Southern accent. I understand you don't know what happened to your father."

"No, I don't."

"Well, I pray he'll return home safely," she said.

"Yes, thank you. I understand you take my mother for a walk most every day. That's very kind of you."

"I can assure you the pleasure is all mine. She's such a dear, fine lady. I always enjoy spending a few minutes visiting with your grandparents too, and I love Hanna."

"We enjoy Savannah," Steel's grandfather said. "She's always so pleasant and makes our day a little brighter. She's in nursing school right now."

Elizabeth entered the room.

"Here's Elizabeth. You're looking lovely, Elizabeth. That blue dress is very becoming on you," his grandmother said.

"Thank you. Hello, Savannah. It's wonderful to have Steel home. Father, you'll be happy to know we talked briefly of Steel starting to work for you."

"That's what I've always hoped for," his grandfather said.

"We can discuss all of that later. Steel, are you going to accompany your mother and Savannah on their walk?" his grandmother asked with a gleam in her eye.

"Yes, I'd like that."

"We'll have some tea, and I believe Hanna will have some fresh-baked cookies when you return. Oh, Savannah, would you like to join us for dinner this evening?"

"Thank you, Sara. I have a class tonight but some other time I'd be most pleased to accept your invitation."

37

Two covered wagons stood in the morning sun along with fifteen mules tethered together. With Lucy at his side, Red held the reins of the first wagon. Zack's brother Ivan held the reins of the second wagon with Cattie alongside. The horses seemed in no hurry to get started as they stood patiently waiting for a driver's signal, but the mules were eager to get underway, swishing their tales as a signal to Hank.

Sitting on Butter Cup, Hank looked over his shoulder at several of his mules kicking up the dust, fending off horseflies looking for a morning meal. "Wonder what's keepin' Charlie?" he hollered. "It's not like him to be late. I'm itchin' to get started, and so are my mules. Hold still, Butter Cup!"

"Charlie told me he was going to town to check on an incoming mail rider," Red said. "He's concerned about more trouble with the Crows. He'll be here shortly. You know, he's not one to be late. It must be important… There he is now! We'll be rollin' out in a few minutes."

Charlie rode up to Red's wagon and reined in his horse. "Red, Lucy, sorry, I'm a little late. One of my riders just got in from Laramie," he said, and then directed his palomino over to Pete and Cattie. "Cattie, I've got some news for you," he said eagerly. "Steel is alive!"

Cattie's jaw dropped. "He's really alive?"

"He is. I found out just a few minutes ago. Someone from the hospital went over to our station and said they thought we'd like to know that one of the riders survived. Said he had a concussion and couldn't remember names or places. He took the train headed for Philadelphia. I'm sure that was cause of a letter he had addressed to his pa from his grandfather."

"Oh, he's alive! Mother, Steel's alive!" Cattie called out.

"I'm sure like a mother bear that's lost her cubs, he'll come looking for you, Cattie, as soon as he gets his memory back. I know he's sure in love with you."

"What if his memory doesn't return?" Cattie asked knitting her eyebrows, and then said, "I don't want to think about that. Right now, I'm... I'm just so happy he's alive, even though he must have gone through a harrowing experience. Charlie, if your rider hadn't come in when he did, who knows when we would have heard that Steel's alive. Oh, thank you dear Lord, and thank you Charlie."

"Let's head out for Denver," Charlie said with a broad smile, feeling better than he'd felt since his good friend's death. He looked at Red and Lucy and gave a nod. "Move 'em out!"

38

Steel stood in a secluded area of cedar and white birch trees. Through the trees he could see a lazy flowing river not more than a hundred yards away. On another day, he'd ride along the river and explore its banks. He recalled his mother mentioning how much he liked to fish.

He glanced over at his grandfather's carriage horse with her reins tied to the stump of a tree. She munched contentedly on an ample supply of long grass. He walked over to one of the larger cedars and tacked up a target he'd made out of some canvas he'd found in his grandfather's shed.

Stepping back, he eyed the target. Satisfied with its position, he turned and walked over to the horse. "Easy there Dolly. I'm going to be making some noise." He patted Dolly on her neck and then opened the saddlebags. He took out his gun and holster and secured the holster around his waist.

As he walked away from his target, about twenty-five paces, a thought came out of seemingly nowhere. *Relax your arm and aim small.*

Like the strike of a rattler, his hand went for the ivory gun handle. A shot rang out. Dolly whinnied. Steel gave her a momentary glance and watched her return to her afternoon snack.

He looked at his target, not sure where the bullet had landed. He walked over to the cedar and examined the circles he'd drawn on the canvas. He stared, astonished at what he saw. *Almost in the center!* "Perhaps a lucky shot," he said to himself.

He spent the next hour shooting from various distances and angles. His target was filled with holes when he finally holstered the gun for the day. He decided to tell no one of his newly found skill.

The river called him to its banks that afternoon and he decided to answer the call. He sat in his saddle, watching the weaving and melding of the currents. An occasional fish would rise to the surface, piquing his interest.

I've lost so much of who I am, frustrated with not knowing the genesis of so many of my emotions. I have to find out what happened to my father… and that means a return to Deadwood… and hopefully, I can also find the missing part of myself. The question is when shall I go? Fall and winter are almost upon us. I think it makes the most sense, considering my mother's health, to remain in Philadelphia until the winter is over. Until I'm ready to leave, I'll keep my plans to myself… I can start working for my grandfather. That will please everyone, and then in the spring, I'll leave… I must answer the siren call.

"Come on Dolly, let's go home."

39

Cattie walked into the Denver office of the Colorado National Bank, hoping Mr. Kountze, the bank owner would be there.

Looking about, she searched for someone she recognized. Several people were waiting in line to do business at the three teller windows. The faces of the tellers looked unfamiliar.

Off to the side and sitting behind a dark walnut desk was a man grimacing at a stack of papers he held in his hand. He appeared to be in his late fifties. He had a short, well-trimmed beard and ruddy completion. Certain she hadn't seen him before, Cattie hesitated for a brief moment, before walking up to the desk. She read the copper nameplate: "Mr. Thomas."

He looked up with a practiced smile. "Yes, miss. May I be of help?"

"My name is Catherine Winthrop. A little while back, I interviewed with Mr. Kountze for a position with the bank. I was wondering if he is in this morning."

"He's been out of town. For the moment, we're not hiring. Why don't you check back with us in a month or two?" he said in a dismissive tone, and gave her a parting practiced smile.

"Thank you." Disheartened, Cattie turned to leave. Her eyes widened, Mr. Kountze was coming her way.

"Oh! Mr. Kountze. Back from his trip." Mr. Thomas said before Mr. Kountze was within hearing distance. He swallowed hard, pushed his chair back, and stood up straight.

Mr. Kountze was distinguished looking, well dressed in a banker's striped suit with wide lapels and a white handkerchief in his suit pocket. He was of medium height, and had a thick mustache and dark hair parted to one side.

"Mr. Kountze, it's so good to see you," Mr. Thomas said in a benevolent tone. "I trust you had a successful trip?"

"Yes, thank you, Martin. Ah, Miss Catherine Winthrop, I believe Mr. Winthrop's granddaughter. You were to start working for me and left for Deadwood with your mother, if I recall."

"Yes. We've returned to Denver. I was hoping a position with your bank was still open."

"Martin, Miss Winthrop has a Law degree from… I believe you said William and Mary Law School in Virginia. She's better educated than both of us," Mr. Kountze said straightforwardly.

Mr. Thomas raised his brows, speechless for the moment.

"I can certainly see your value, Miss Winthrop. Do you mind if I call you Catherine?" Mr. Kountze asked, giving Cattie his full attention.

"Most people call me Cattie, please."

"Then Cattie it is. You're here at an opportune time. Our silver deposits are again on the rise. I need someone who can deal with our East Coast bankers, and with your legal background, I think you're just the person we need. It will, of course, take some training as to the transfer procedures and so forth, but I'm certain you'll pick that up quickly. How does that sound?"

"Fine—yes, I'm excited."

"Good. Martin, I know we generally start people off as tellers but I want her to start learning the silver business side of our banking right off." Mr. Kountze turned to Cattie. "Can you start tomorrow morning at eight?"

"I can start today if you'd like."

"Well… Yes, let's get you started. Robert Reins is working in that area now, but he has other responsibilities I'd like him to spend more time on. Martin, is Robert in his office?"

"Yes, sir."

"I'll introduce you to him. We'll start your training immediately. Martin, I'm going to have her report to Robert."

Mr. Thomas nodded.

"Cattie, you'll like Robert. He's smart, comes from a good family." Mr. Kountze turned to Mr. Thomas. "Martin, in about an hour, I'd like to meet with you to review some financials."

"Whenever you're ready, Mr. Kountze."

"Cattie, come with me."

Mr. Kountze knocked on the office door.

"Come in."

"Cattie go ahead," Mr. Kountze said, allowing Cattie to precede him into the small office.

Mr. Reins put down his pen and stood up.

He's quite good looking, she thought. He was tall, at least six feet. He had chiseled cheekbones and a prominent, narrow nose. His brown eyes were warm and his wavy brown hair matched the color of his eyes. *He has a nice smile,* she thought.

"Robert, how are you, my boy?" Mr. Kountze asked.

"Well, thank you, sir. I hope your trip to Omaha went well."

After Mr. Kountze left, formalities were quickly dispensed with and Robert went to work instructing Cattie.

"It took me two days to get the hang of that. I can see why Mr. Kountze hired you," he said.

They exchanged smiles.

It was six o'clock when Cattie left the bank that late afternoon. "Good night, Robert, and thank you," she said. "You were very patient with me."

"It went well, really well. You're a fast learner. I'll see you tomorrow, Cattie."

Cattie left the bank feeling better than she'd felt in some time. *I love the work, and Robert is a good teacher—patient. I must admit I'm glad Mr. Thomas isn't training me. With my mother's little job and this income, I know we can survive. I so wonder how Steel is and if his memory has returned.* She sighed and then her spirits lifted as her thoughts turned to the events of the day.

40

THE PORCH SWING ROCKED back and forth with an easy motion. A soft, early evening breeze had helped bring the daytime temperature down to a comfortable level. Savannah, with a repetitive push of her foot, kept the wicker swing from coming to a stop.

Steel sat in his grandfather's cushioned porch chair, taking in the beauty of the twilight hour. A hungry nocturnal bat darted back and forth feeding on the evening hatch of tiny midges. The clatter of an occasional carriage and horses' hooves were the only sounds that disturbed the quiet of nightfall.

"Steel, you've been home a little over a week now. What are your thoughts?" Savannah asked.

"My thoughts? That's a good question. Savannah, I'm going to confide something to you that I was planning on keeping to myself. I feel strongly that I need to return to Deadwood in the spring. Only for a short time, maybe a couple of days."

"Oh, and why is that?"

"I need to find out what happened to my father. I can't leave that question unanswered. We've heard no word from him so I presume he's dead. And if it's my mother's wish, I'll make arrangements to have his body transferred here to Philadelphia for burial."

"Reluctantly, I agree with you. As much as I dislike seeing you go back, you need to find out what happened to your father, and perhaps it will help you remember the past, if your memory hasn't improved by then."

"I'm glad you agree. Please don't say anything right now in that regard."

"I won't mention a word. No, that information most certainly needs to come from you. I will tell you that your mother confided in me that she's worried you'll want to return Deadwood to find out what happened to your father—mother's intuition."

"Savannah, there are things—impressions, shadows—that are hanging in the back of my mind. It seems like they're dammed up waiting to come out. I don't know how to explain it. Our relationship... I feel, I can't move forward until I have answers, and I'm hopeful I'll find those answers in Deadwood."

"I'm considering returning to Georgia after I've completed school."

"Oh." Steel raised his brows caught by surprise with her comment.

"I'll remain here until the spring when the winter semester is over. I know I can get a good nursing job in Atlanta. Speaking of work, how are things progressing with your grandfather?"

"Fine, fine. My grandfather is an amazing individual. I've really grown to appreciate him. He's not easy on me, and I'm absolutely okay with that. Right now, I'm working the floor selling things. He wants me to learn all aspects of the business. He told me that he never wants me to have the attitude that one position is more important than another. It takes everyone working together to be successful. Respect everyone's job," he said. "He's very successful, as you know, and he treats all his employees with respect, and that I respect."

"That's an admirable quality, I do declare. You'll do well working with your grandfather. You know how to work hard. Working for your father as a blacksmith was no easy job. When I first met you I was so impressed with your patience and kindly manner. I could tell you were a good person by looking at your kindly, warm eyes."

"I don't know about that." Steel chuckled lightly. "I went over to the blacksmith shop across town. My father sold most of our tools and things to the owner before we left. He didn't recognize me, but of course he knew my father. He said if I needed a job he'd put me to work. I thought that was nice of him."

Savannah got up from the porch swing. "Time to hitch up Dolly and take me home." She walked over to Steel, leaned down, and kissed him.

"I'm sorry… No, I'm not," she said and smiled at him.

Steel's emotions were muddled. The kiss was nice, very nice. He liked Savannah. He liked her a lot.

41

Big Jake sat back in Pete's barber chair. He closed his eyes and leaned his head back. A white smock covered the front of him. Pete stood at his side with a cupful of lathered shaving cream in one hand and a shaving brush in the other.

"That kid was lucky to get out of town," Jake snarled. "I heard he was dead, now I hear he's alive. His pa's grave is here, and when and if he comes back, I'm gonna kill him."

"You're talking pretty big, Jake. Hold still if you want a shave. I need to daub you up. Mr. Utter hears you talkin' like that, you'll have him to deal with."

"Charlie Utter don't scare me none now that his friend Hickok is dead. I know he carries two fancy pistols in his belt, but I reckon it's more for show than anything else. I ain't never heard of him using those pistols. I'm mighty fast, and I've been practicing. I'll be ready to go at the kid face-to-face. I don't want anyone to say I shot him in the back. You know, I kilt two men, fair and square."

Pete raised his brows and looked over at Smiley, who was sitting in one of the two waiting chairs.

Smiley spoke up. "Steel took care of that gent who shot his pa and the one he had a run-in with on the wagon trip here. Shot 'em both in the heart."

"It weren't nothing more than two lucky shots," Jake said with sarcasm in his voice.

"Has Doc still got your lizard in his office?" Smiley asked with a smile and a snicker.

Before Jake could answer, Pete lathered up his face good. "No need to answer that, Jake. I got to get you done. Smiley is waiting for his shave, and I got another costumer coming in soon."

Pete looked at Smiley and gave his head a shake. Smiley was pushing things a bit too far with Jake, and Pete didn't want any trouble in his place.

All was quiet while Pete worked the straightedge over Jake's face.

"You're all done, Jake. Smiley, you're next."

Jake reached into his pocket and paid Pete. He grabbed his hat off the hat rack and stomped out without saying another word.

"Pete, that Jake is a no-good skunk," Smiley said. "It'd done everybody a whole lot of good if your razor had slipped right around his throat area."

"Mighty tempting, Smiley. Mighty tempting."

"You know, Jake's two brothers are ornery, mean cusses," Smiley said.

"Yeah, I know that. The three of them built a pretty nice cabin north of town, I'm told. They found some gold. Don't know how much. I do know that one of the painted ladies is living with them. I think the older brother actually married her. I believe it was Molly who told me. She said the painted lady insisted that the brother marry her. Probably thinking of some kind of an inheritance. Can't think of any other reason someone would want to marry one of them," Pete said.

"I heard the same thing. That wasn't more than a few months ago. We don't have a justice of the peace, so I don't know who would have hitched them up. I guess they could have gone to Laramie and gotten hitched," Smiley said.

"No matter, I feel sorry for the lady having to deal with the likes of those three. Well, let's get you shaved. Ben'll be coming in pretty soon, and he don't like to wait none."

42

Eight months later

STEEL LOOKED OUT THE train window at the open countryside where a herd of antelope fed leisurely on wild prairie grass. A few heads popped up from their late afternoon meal to give the locomotive a momentary glance. The winter snow still blanketed the peaks of the distant mountains. It had been a mild winter, but nonetheless spring was a welcomed sight. There was a plethora of yellow and white flowers that carpeted the landscape adding to the beauty of the decor.

Steel and Savannah saw each other almost weekly during the winter months. Savannah remained busy with her studies and Steel's time was occupied in learning the retail business. The family remained hopeful that they'd marry. Savannah did invite Steel to spend Christmas with her and her parents at her parent's Georgia residence. "We both could use some Georgia sun," she'd said. Steel accepted the invitation, but right before Christmas his mother turned ill with a fever and he decided it would be best to forgo the invitation.

More than once during the winter months, Steel's grandfather asked, "When are you going to propose to Savannah? She's not going to wait forever."

"I'm not ready yet. I still have some things to work out," he'd respond.

Working with his grandfather was a real pleasure. Besides tutoring Steel in the everyday running of the business, his grandfather had seen to it that he met the right people. Right before Steel left for Deadwood, he'd been at his grandfather's side most of the time. It was evident to everyone that he was being groomed to take over the reins of the business sooner or later, and the bets were on that it would be sooner.

Steel departed for Deadwood on a rainy morning with his mother giving him an anxious look and a few words of concern. "Steel, I hate so to see you go. Don't stay long. We'll all be looking for your quick and safe return. You know, I'll worry every day about you until I can again see that handsome face." She accompanied her words with a kiss on his cheek.

The night before leaving, Steel said good-by to Savannah. She knew he wasn't prepared to make any commitments. They parted with a kiss, but it lacked the heartfelt passion of two lovers. He had the feeling that she might return to Georgia and leave it up to him to pursue her after he returned home. He wished he could have offered her more, but for the time being it wasn't to be.

His grandfather drove him in the horse carriage to the train station. He could tell that his grandfather was downhearted, but kept a stiff upper lip.

I know I'm doing what I need to do... Oh, please, Lord, help me to find the peace I'm looking for in Deadwood. He looked at the steam, rolling out from the locomotive engine. Two sharp whistle blasts hung in the air.

"Time to go aboard," Steel said.

He shook hands with his grandfather and then boarded the train.

Steel opened his eyes at hearing the train steward's rhythmic calls: "One hour out of Laramie! One hour out of Laramie!" The steward passed him as he made his way down the aisles of the passenger cars.

Steel planned to stay at the Laramie Train Station's Hotel, remembering he'd enjoyed his dinner and especially the rhubarb pie the time he'd dinned there. *I want to stop by the hospital, and again thank the people who cared for me, good people.* He took the newspaper off his lap, thinking he was actually looking forward to trying to solve some of the mysteries of his forgotten past.

A fellow passenger, learning that Steel was headed for Deadwood, had informed him that with the coming of spring a stagecoach run had just started weekly between Laramie and Deadwood. "That's great news," Steel said. He'd been contemplating what he'd need to work out to get from Laramie to Deadwood; and with that information, his problem was solved.

"A man out of Deadwood named Charlie Utter started the stagecoach run," the passenger had said.

The name Charlie Utter wasn't totally unfamiliar to Steel. The name had first come up at the hospital. Steel recalled that he was the one who owned the mail-rider business from Deadwood to Laramie. His mother had also mentioned Mr. Utter. "Mr. Utter telegraphed your father encouraging him to come to Deadwood. I know your father intended on doing some blacksmithing there while the two of you were looking for gold. You need look him up," she'd said in a resigning tone.

43

A FULL MOON LIT up the nighttime sky. Cattie stood on the porch and was about to say goodnight when Robert leaned down and kissed her. She didn't resist, but neither did she let her lips linger on his. The kiss catching her by surprise, she pulled back, uncertainty flooding her emotions. She took a deep breath and glanced up at the moon—*a hunter's moon.* Her thoughts turned to Steel. *Was that an eternity ago?*

"Cattie, you know I'm in love with you." Robert gave her a searching look.

Over the past eight months, Robert Reins, Cattie's mentor at the bank, had been courting her. She knew this first kiss took their relationship to a different level. She couldn't deny that she'd grown fond of him. They had a good working relationship. Of late, he had invited her to several social events, and then a week ago when he invited her to dine with his family, she knew his intentions were becoming more serious. Now with the kiss, she had the feeling a marriage proposal was on his mind.

There wasn't a day that went by that she didn't think of Steel. Over eight months had passed since he'd left Deadwood and she hadn't heard a word from him… not a letter… not a note. *In all probability, he doesn't even know I exist,* she concluded. The last few months these words had been a reoccurring theme in her mind.

"Robert, I'm not ready to make any commitments," she said.

"It's been almost a year," Robert said with a strained face and harshness in his voice that she hadn't heard before.

"Eight months," Cattie corrected.

"Eight months then, and you haven't heard one word from this Steel fellow. You've got to get on with your life, Cattie. If he hasn't regained his memory by now, most likely it's not going to happen. I suspect he doesn't even know you exist."

Hearing Robert say those words that echoed her own thoughts only added to her pain. "You're probably right, but I'm not ready to move on," she said resolutely.

"I'm a patient man, but my patience has its limits. Cattie, I'll see you tomorrow morning at work."

The frustration in his voice didn't escape her. She remained on the porch and watched him march off. *Robert is so nice, and he has a wonderful family. I do like him... I like him a lot, but I don't love him. I love Steel.*

She shut her office door. Robert had walked passed her that morning without responding to her "Good morning, Robert." It hurt to realize that, at least for the moment, he couldn't even be civil. He was right though: *Steel may never know that there's a girl who loves him so very, very much.* Tears welled in her eyes with the thought. She quickly took a deep breath and sat down at her desk. Quickly she turned her attention to the things she needed to accomplish for the day.

She and Robert spoke several times on business matters that morning, but made no reference to the night before. At a little after eleven, a knock on her office door interrupted her train of thought.

"Please come in," she said, looking up from a transfer order for silver she was reviewing.

"Charlie!" She got up from her desk and gave Charlie a heartfelt hug. "Oh, Charlie, it's so good to see you!"

"It's been too long, Cattie," he said with a warm smile. "Look at you, your own office. I ran into Mr. Kountze in Laramie. I'm doin' some business with him. He said one of the best things he ever did was to hire you. Said you deal with those Eastern bankers better than anyone else in his company. Said he wanted you to go to Omaha but you turned him down. I should have hired you to help me run my businesses. I missed out, but it's mighty good to see you, Cattie. You're looking as pretty as ever."

"Have you seen my mother yet?"

"I'm going to visit her first thing after I leave here. I'm hoping the two of you will have lunch with me."

"We'd love to. I'm sure she's free for lunch. She's at home now."

"How about the Western Steak House at twelve-thirty?"

"I'll be there."

"And I'll bring your mother," Charlie said with a warm smile.

"Charlie, have you heard anything about Steel?"

"I knew you were going to ask me that. The winter has kept me pretty much penned in other than a couple of trips to Laramie and one to Omaha. To answer your question, I'm afraid not." Charlie hesitated for a moment, "I haven't heard anything more than what we knew when you left Deadwood. I was hoping you'd have heard something. One thing I'm sure of is that if his memory returns he's going to come looking for you."

"Charlie, the fact is, his memory may never return." There was a momentary silence. "Oh, Charlie, it's so good to see you! You know you're like family."

"We are family, Cattie. I love you and your ma. Always will. I'm going to let you get back to work and call on your mother. I'm thinking more and more about returning to Denver—I'm excited to tell you about my plans at lunch. I know I need to let you get back to work."

"Mother and I would love to have you back in Denver." Cattie smiled and watched the door close. Then her smile quickly faded. Seeing Charlie had lifted her spirits, but there was still no word from Steel.

44

STEEL STROLLED UP TO the door of the mail-rider station. It was a small, wooden building that looked like it could only accommodate a desk and a few chairs. Behind the building was a corral with eight or nine horses standing lazily in the shade of several overhanging trees. Several horses trotted over to size-up. *They're most likely looking for something to eat,* he thought, wishing he had an apple or two. Steel couldn't help but notice a lathered up horse with his head in the drinking trough. A saddle, saddle blanket, and bridal hung on the log corral fence.

Steel rapped his knuckles on the station door.

"Come on in if you think you can find room," a voice within croaked.

"Steel pushed the door open and took a small step inside. An older man wearing a visor and spectacles was sitting at a small desk talking to a cowboy leaning against the wall with a cigarette hanging from his lip. The cowboy held a dust-covered hat in his hand.

The cowboy turned and looked at Steel. He grabbed the cigarette from his mouth as his jaw dropped. "Steel! What in tarnation are you doing here? We thought you were in Philadelphia or someplace like that. Got your memory back?"

"I haven't. I'm sorry, but I don't recognize you."

"I'm Red! I first talked to you and your pa at your blacksmith shop in Philadelphia. I've got family there. You and your pa shoed a horse for me. Are you sure you don't remember me? I work for Mr. Utter. You and your pa went with us from Colorado to Deadwood.

You don't remember any of that?" Red looked at Steel with an air of disbelief.

Steel shook his head dispiritedly. "I don't even remember my father."

"Hell, if that ain't a piece of bad luck. Do you remember anything about Deadwood?"

Steel shook his head again. "No, nothing."

"You two want to do some jawing, step outside so I can work," the older man grumbled.

"Let's go outside," Red said. "He gets a little crotchety at times—most of the time."

They stepped outside.

Red threw his cigarette down and stamped it out. "Damn shame you lost your memory. Must be mighty hard not remembering important things." Red said shaking his head. "Hell, you're looking good, though. I've never seen you in a suit before. If you're headed for Deadwood, I most strongly suggest that you don't go lookin' like that. You're gonna want to change those fine britches unless you wanna be taken for one of those gun tottin' gamblers."

Steel smiled. "I'll take your advice. I've got other clothes."

"What's taken you back to Deadwood? Cattie ain't there anymore—your pa's grave?" Red asked.

"To learn what happened to my father. You said his grave?"

"You don't know?"

"No."

"He was kilt. Shot in the back. Sorry to be the one to tell you."

"I surmised—thought he was dead, but I just didn't know the circumstances."

"He was shot while panning for gold on French Creek. Chatan, an Indian friend of yours brought his body back to town. That's about all I know."

Steel nodded with a puckered brow.

"You don't remember Cattie Winthrop? Prettiest girl I ever did see, long dark hair, deep blue-green eyes the color of a mountain lake at midday. You two were mighty sweet on each other."

"No, I don't remember her."

"Damn! Well, you saved her from Big Jake one afternoon. He was trying to have his way with her behind Nuttal's Saloon. I see you're not wearin' your silver-tip boot. That boot is famous. Anyway, you fixed him so he won't be having kids any more. You can go see the souvenir in Doc's office and it'll explain things." Red grinned and then continued, "Jake keeps telling people that if you come back to Deadwood, he's gonna kill you. You best find someone to point him out real fast. He and his two brothers come into town most every Saturday night, so it's best you watch out for 'em."

"Can you tell me any more about my father?"

"Not a whole lot. You buried him in the Deadwood cemetery. I can tell you that you shot the man who killed your pa in a fair gun-fight. I hope you brought that Colt pistol of yours and remember how to shoot it, 'cause I've got a feeling you're gonna to be needing it."

"I brought it," Steel said, not sure what to think of this new information.

"Once you step foot in Deadwood, the word that you're back in town is gonna travel quicker than a hen runnin' from a fox. And as I said, you make sure you've got that Colt on your hip, 'cause it's gonna be your best friend. I'll tell you something: You were taught how to shoot by none other than Bill Hickok. He was considered one of the best men with a gun that ever lived. He was kilt, shot in the back while you were in Deadwood. Did you know you kilt two men? Shot 'em both dead through the heart."

"I killed two men?" Steel asked with a disbelieving scowl.

"You sure enough did. One of the men was the man who shot your pa in the back and the other was a bad skunk you had a run-in with on the wagon train trip from Colorado to Deadwood. Steel, you don't know it, but you got yourself a hell of a reputation with a gun. There may be some young gunfighter trying to up his reputation and challenge you out. I think your main problem though is going to be Big Jake and his two brothers."

"You mentioned Cattie Winthrop and I were an item. What happened to her?"

"Mr. Utter took Cattie and her ma, Lucy, back to Denver right after you left town. He said he heard that Cattie got a fine job at one of the banks there. Her ma, Lucy, wrote a letter to Mr. Utter and said, under the circumstances, they were doing real well. Mr. Utter was sure glad to see them get out of Deadwood for their safety. Took a lot of worry off his mind."

"I see. Mr. Utter sounds like a good man."

"He is indeed. Mr. Utter has his hands in more businesses than a pig has piglets. He helped you and your pa set up your blacksmith shop in Deadwood. By the way, when you left, he brought in another blacksmith from Denver, a Mr. George Nopal, and there's the Swede that works with him. I do believe you started to train the Swede. Anyway, I know Mr. Utter thought a lot of you and your pa. He's in Denver right now and I don't think he'll be back for a couple of weeks."

"I'm thinking I need to go to Denver and meet Miss Cattie Winthrop."

"You sure as shootin' should! Like I said, you were mighty sweet on each other. Mr. Utter told me he thought the two of you were gonna get hitched."

"Hm, get married you say?"

"I don't think you asked her. He just thought you were planning, or something. I know the two of you would go fishing out on French Creek, and you ate dinner together at Nuttal's most every night."

"Hm… I understand there's a stage now from Deadwood to Denver."

"That's right. Leaves Deadwood every Monday morning. It just started several weeks ago. That's all Mr. Utter's doin'. That's one of the reasons I'm in Laramie. Checking on the horses."

"I thought you might be a mail rider."

"Hell no. I'm too big and wouldn't want the job anyway. What are you going to do now?"

"I'm going to go over to the hospital and say hello to the good folks who took care of me. Maybe do a little shopping for some clothes." Steel smiled. "To be honest with you, I'll be glad to get out of this suit."

Red chuckled. "Yeah, you need to get rid of that choke strap."

"You don't like my tie?" Steel smiled.

"The more I'm thinking about it, the thing that concerns me the most is Mr. Utter is out of town. Don't know if that would stop Big Jake anyway from comin' after you. You may want to go outside town somewhere and tune up your shootin'."

"Are you staying over or heading back to Deadwood?" Steel asked.

"Oh, you betcha I'm staying over. I'm tuckered out. A hot bath and a good meal is all I want right now. I'll be gettin' back to Deadwood before you. When you get in, you ask for the directions to Mr. Utter's camp. I stay in one of his bunkhouses. There's always a couple of extra bunks. I know Mr. Utter would want you to stay there. Damn shame he's out of town."

"Red, I'd like to have you join me for dinner tonight at the Laramie Station Restaurant. Dinner's on me."

"I'd enjoy that, Steel."

"What's a good time for you?"

"I'm thinking six o'clock."

"Red, I'll see you at six."

45

Steel sat in the stagecoach, his arms folded and his eyes closed. Thoughts of his dinner conversation with Red ran through his mind. For some reason the possibility of dealing with Big Jake and his two brothers didn't frighten him, but it did cause him concern. *I sure don't want to get involved in any gunfights. I've killed two people. I can't imagine that, but I'm sure Red wasn't making up a tale.* Red had assured him the killings were justified. But Steel was uncomfortable with the idea of killing anyone, no matter the reason. Right now, the foremost question was how to handle Jake and his two brothers. If they intended on killing him, it befitted Steel to meet them face-to-face before they had a chance to shoot him in the back. "Bushwhack him," Red had said.

Little by little, Steel was finding out more about Charlie Utter, the man who apparently had shepherded him and his father during much of their Deadwood experience. Steel's first priority would be to visit his father's grave, but he also wanted to learn more about Cattie Winthrop and the extent of their relationship… and yes, that meant a visit to Denver.

"Whoa! Whoa!" the stagecoach driver shouted. He tugged back on the reins, bringing the stagecoach to an abrupt halt.

Steel opened his eyes and stuck his head out the window. "Ben, everything okay up there?"

Ben set the brake and jumped down from the driver's seat. "We're about to enter a narrow pass, and there's a tree limb blockin' the way. I don't like the looks of things since there's not trees close to the pass." He put his hands on his hips, contemplating the situation.

Steel got out of the coach. "You're going to need a hand moving that limb," he said.

The sound of horses' hooves redirected their attention. Two masked men wearing black hats, with dark bandanas covering their faces galloped up, leaving a cloud of dust. They reined in their horses as they neared the stagecoach. Each brandished a firearm.

"Looks like your road is blocked up ahead," the larger man grunted. "Well, we came passing-by to lighten your load, and I'd appreciate it if you two would raise your hands nice and high. We don't want them near those pistols you're wearing."

"We're not carrying any gold or silver. Don't have no strong-box," Ben hollered. "Just taking four passengers to Deadwood. You can see I have no one riding shotgun. This man is just a passenger who got out to help me move the tree limb blockin' our way."

"Well, we're interested in one passenger in particular. Oh, we're going to include you all, so don't you fret none about being left out. The one we're the most interested in is an older gent, wearing a nice suit with a gold pocket watch chain hanging out of his watch pocket. We'd like to invite the other three out of the coach right now. Come on out!" the bandit yelled, "So we don't have to waste any bullets shootin' at the coach. I mean now, pronto like, out!"

Three men reluctantly climbed out of the coach and joined Ben and Steel.

"What makes you think I've any money?" the older man asked, and then took in a deep breath.

"Oh, we know you got money. We just happened to do our banking at the same bank in Laramie yesterday. You made a sizable withdrawal, and we're willin' to bet you've got all that cash tucked away in a nice, fat money belt or something. If you'd be kind enough to take off that fancy suit coat and just hand us the belt, we'd be obliged. Oh, and the gold watch and anything else that you might have, let's say of value for poor folks like us. And the rest of you, empty your pockets.

My partner will collect everything and go through your baggage while I keep an eye on you. We like to be thorough at our job; you can understand that. And that means shootin' you if need be."

"I'm not giving you road agents my money!" the elderly man spoke up with a tone of resolve that surprised Steel.

Directing their attention at the defiant gentleman, the bandits pointed both guns in his direction. Their looks turned vicious. "Well, I guess we'll just have to kill you, old man. You don't have too many more years anyway."

Steel, seeing the bandits' attention focused on the defiant man, dropped his arms. His gun was out of his holster and two shots fired before the bandits knew what was happening.

Pistols flew out of their hands and landed in the dirt. Their horses jumped. Eyes over dark bandanas widened as they stared for a moment at the smoking barrel of Steel's gun. "He shot my hand!" one of the bandits cried.

They turned their horses with a jerk, spurred them hard, and rode off in the direction of Laramie.

"That's about as fancy shootin' as I ever dern seen," the driver said, breathing a heavy sigh of relief. Those two hombres aren't going to be bothering us anymore. And the one, he's not going to be shootin' with that hand for a spell."

"I want to thank you kindly young man—Steel, I believe," the older gentleman said. "Like our driver said, that was mighty fine shooting. I'm investing in a small lumber mill in Deadwood and I'm carrying most of my savings. I acted foolishly by my words, but I've worked hard for my money. Again, I thank you."

The other two men patted Steel on the back.

"Mighty fine shooting."

"Sure glad you were here," the other man added. "I'm carrying a fair amount of cash, myself. Thank you. You said your name is Steel Madison. I won't forget that name. Are you staying long in Deadwood?"

"Just a few days."

"Well, I'd be happy to buy you a drink or two when we get there."

Steel turned to the driver. “Let’s get that log moved. Ben, do you mind if I join you up top for a while?”

“Mighty glad to have you. Dag gum, that was fine shootin!” Ben said as he and Steel walked over to the log.

46

Savannah and Elizabeth sat on a newly painted white park bench. The park was a short walk from Elizabeth's home. A pair of mallard ducks seemed to be enjoying the warmth of the afternoon sun as they made their way around the lily pond. The occasional bellowing of a bullfrog could be heard. A variety of azaleas under mature leafy trees provided a palette of colors for the park visitors. Visits to the park were the highlights of Elizabeth's days, especially when Savannah accompanied her.

"Savannah, I haven't said it out loud to you before but I know Blain is dead. I've accepted that. I know he would have returned with Steel if he'd been alive. I think I should have done all I could to have stopped Steel from returning to Deadwood. I'm truly fearful for his safety."

"I think we need to be positive. In talking with Steel, this is something he had to do for himself. Not only learning what had happened to his father; but hopefully, there'll be something in Deadwood that'll trigger his memory. He's so frustrated not being able to remember so many important aspects of his life."

"Savannah, do you know he has a gun, a pistol, and that he'd go out shooting for an hour or so, three or four times a week?"

"Yes, I know that, even in the winter. He took me with him once. He's very, very good at shooting, I do declare."

"I looked in his room, and I know he took the gun with him to Deadwood. I'm not sure if that's a good thing or a bad thing."

"I'm sure he knows what he's doing. Perhaps he took his gun so he could practice, nothing more," Savannah said. "Elizabeth, to lose a good part of one's memory must be extremely difficult. You know, we were all strangers to him and in a sense we still are. He's had to reshape his life with no memory of the past." Savannah paused and looked directly at Elizabeth. "I'm not sure if he loves me. If I'm honest with myself, I don't know if our relationship has made any progress… We're good friends, just good friends. I've made the decision to move back to Georgia. I have a full-time nursing job waiting for me there. I did tell him before he left that I was thinking about returning to Georgia. If I'm the right person for him, he'll come and find me… and I need to go before he returns."

"Oh, Savannah, Savannah. Are you sure this is what you want to do? Can't you wait until he comes back?"

"Now that my schooling is finished, I need to get on with my life. Frankly, I miss Georgia. I have lots of lasting friendships there and that's where I grew up. That's my home. No, I need to go home."

"Oh, Savannah, you know how much I want you as a daughter-in-law. We've grown so close. I'm going to miss you something terrible."

"I'll miss you too. I promise I'll write."

"I hope you do, no matter what the outcome is between you and Steel. What you're saying is true, and I'm only thinking selfishly wanting you to stay here, Savannah. You do need to get on with your life, I can see that."

Two mallard ducks took flight off the water. They flew against a backdrop of dark thunderclouds approaching from the north. "Elizabeth, we'd better leave. It looks like an angry spring shower is coming our way." A gust of wind tossed the blond tresses of Savannah's hair. She looked at Elizabeth and forced a smile.

47

"PETE, GUESS WHO JUST rode in on the stagecoach, sittin' by the driver?" the smart-dressed gambler asked. He took off his wide-brim hat and tossed it on the barbershop hat rack and then continued, "The Madison boy, he's back in town. Sure wonder if he's got his memory back."

"Steel Madison... I'll be a son-of-a-gun. It's been almost a year since he left Deadwood. Jesse, sit down in the chair. I suppose you're wantin' a shave."

"That's right. When are you going to get a decent barber chair?"

"I've ordered one, and it's comin' in from Denver next week."

Pete got his razor strap out and started warming up the straight-edge with long practiced strokes. "I'm thinking, Jesse. Too bad Charlie is still in Denver. He might have been able to stop Jake and his brothers from going after Madison. I like the Madison kid, don't want to see him get kilt."

"Jake will either waylay him or bring his brothers along to help him. Three against one. Jake isn't faster than Madison, that I'm sure of. The other thing I'm sure of, it ain't gonna be a fair fight," Jesse said.

Pete put a white smock around Jesse, fastening it at the neck. "Sure you want just a shave this morning? Them locks are gettin' kinda long. I can trim 'em up a bit for you."

"A shave'll do me just fine. I'm going to grab me a bite to eat after you're finished with me, and then I've got an early afternoon poker game."

"I suspect someone will go out to Jake's place and let 'em know Madison is back." Pete said, stopping what he was doing for a moment in thought.

"I don't know anyone in town that would tell 'm. All three are no-good scamps."

"I guess you're right about that, but you know how this town likes a shootin'."

"Well, I'm going to be in town tonight, that's for damn sure, and we'll see how the cat jumps," Jesse said.

"I want you to be quiet now. Don't want to cut you up too bad." Pete took the badger brush and painted Jesse's lower face white. With the straightedge in his hand, he stepped back. "If Jake and the boys kill Madison, dimes to dollars, Charlie and his boys are goin' after them."

"I think you're right about that. We could have a real war on. Now get that straightedge working, I don't want to be late for my card game."

Steel stood by the stagecoach and shook hands with the three other passengers. "Don't forget that drink," one of the men said before leaving with his baggage.

Steel turned and looked up at Ben who had a tight rein on four lathered horses that were eager to get to the barn.

"Steel, I want to thank you again for saving our hides. If there's anything I can do for you, let me know," Ben said.

"Ben, I meant to ask you, do you know Red?"

"Yeah. We both work for Charlie."

"I met up with Red in Laramie. He said I could stay at Mr. Utter's camp and bunk there. Could you tell me where the camp is located?"

"Hell, I'll do more than tell you, I'll take you there. That's where I bunk. If you'll go over to Mr. Mark's livery stable with me cause I got to take care of these horses and all that first. Hop back up."

Steel climbed up onto the stagecoach driver's seat. He looked down the street and saw an open-sided building that caught his eye. "That looks like the blacksmith shop," he said.

"Sure enough is. Nice young man, a Swede, works there with an older man. They call him Shorty. Don't rightly remember the Swede's name. Most people just call him Swede."

Ben gave a shake of the reins and the horses were off, knowing they were heading for the *barn.*

The coach pulled up at the livery stable and Ben gave a tug on the reins. "Whoa boys, whoa," he said.

Mr. Marks was out in front waiting to greet them.

"Heard you comin' in... Why Steel! You're a rip-roaring sight to see." Mr. Marks said. "Heard you lost your memory. You got it back?"

"Afraid not," Steel said, jumping down from the stagecoach.

"That's an awful shame. I'm Frank Marks, and I've been taking care of your Indian pony. I'd let Catherine, the pretty young lady you took a likin' to ride her, but no one else. Then she and her ma went back to Colorado, so your horse hasn't been ridden for a long spell. What would you like me to do with her?"

"I'm sure I owe you boarding money. I want to settle-up."

"Well, yes, I guess that's right."

"I'll think on the Indian pony and get back to you before I leave town."

"I'll be more than happy to buy her from you. I'll pay you a fair price."

"I'll think on it. Thanks for the offer."

"Are you long in Deadwood?"

"I'll be leaving on the Monday morning stage for Denver."

"I heard Charlie Utter is in Denver, so it'd be good if you saw him."

"I'm hoping to meet him there."

Mr. Marks turned his attention to Ben. "Ben, I'm sorry, just so surprised to see Steel. How'd your trip go?"

"We arrived here safely thanks to Steel. We were held-up by two bandits just a few hours out of Laramie."

"That for sure ain't good news," Mr. Marks said. "First holdup I've heard about. Course you just started. I know Charlie is not gonna be happy about that."

"Steel shot the guns plumb out of their hands. Fanciest shootin' I've ever seen. Those two turned their horses and lit off like scared jackrabbits. I've got their pistols right here in the coach. Guess, I'll just sell 'em."

"Cody, get your hide over here," Mr. Marks shouted at his young helper. "Take the stage around back and unhitch them horses and take care of 'em."

"Yes, Mr. Marks," Cody said. The teenage boy ran over to the stagecoach, climbed up onto the driver's seat and took the reins from Ben.

"Cody, give us a minute to grab our things," Ben said as he climbed down. "I set the brake, so you need to unset it when we've finished."

"After you unhitch the horses and give them water and feed," Mr. Marks said, "put them in the second pen. I don't want 'm with the mustangs we just got in. I'm gonna take Ben and Steel in the buckboard over to Charlie's camp. I'll be back in about twenty minutes or so."

"I'll get right on things, Mr. Marks."

"Ben, Steel, throw your gear into my buckboard."

"Much obliged," Ben said. "I know we could walk, but my old bones are tired."

"Happy to take you both—Steel, it's a real pleasure. I've got a feeling that someday you may come close to Mr. Hickok's reputation."

"No, that's not going to happen, I can assure you," Steel said, wondering why Mr. Marks would make such a ridiculous remark.

48

Except for the parade of stars across the sky, it was a dark night. The crescent moon wouldn't make its appearance for another two hours. Only the flickering lights from the saloon windows shed a dash of illumination on Main Street. Red and Steel stood outside the doors of Nuttal's Saloon, mulling things over.

"I'll go in first and spot where Jake and his brothers are sittin'," Red said. "You sure you wanna do it this way?" Red asked with an unsteady voice. "I hope you're not out of your mind. I may be out of my mind for going along with you."

"Just tell me where they're at. And Red, you stay out of it. This is my fight."

Red gave a nod. His boot echoed on the wooden plank floor as he walked through the saloon doors.

Steel took in a deep breath and slowly exhaled. *Red could be right, but I really don't want to kill Jake or his brothers.*

Moments later, Red darted back out of the saloon.

"Jake and his brothers are sittin' at a card table with two other gents at the far back corner. Jake's got his back to the wall. He's the biggest of the bunch, not much hair on the top, and has one of them Indian necklaces with a big turquoise piece in the middle. His brothers are sittin' next to him. You won't have any worry about spotting them, the three of them look like peas in a pod."

"Thanks, Red. Again, stay out of it. This is my fight. I'm going to try and talk them out of it. I'll let 'em know I'm leaving town on the Monday stage."

"Damn! That ain't gonna work!" Red said with a scowl at hearing Steel's head snapping remark.

Steel pushed the doors open before Red could make any further comments. For a split second an image flashed through his mind of a gunfighter with silver spurs entering the saloon and then it was gone.

Standing just inside the saloon doors, he located Jake and his brothers. He took two steps forward and stopped. A surprising calmness came over him.

A gambler looked up at Steel and his jaw dropped. He pushed his chair back, got up and moved out of the line of fire. Others followed, leaving an empty line between Steel and Big Jake's table.

Jake, attracted by the commotion, saw Steel looking his way. His eyes widened. Slowly he stood up and pushed his chair back against the wall and stared at Steel with dark, beady eyes.

"I understand you've been doing a lot of talking about killing me. Here I am, Jake. I'm calling you out. From what I hear you're a coward that likes to hurt women, or at least you did before you got your just deserts."

Red walked in behind Steel with his gun out. "This is between Steel and Jake. Anyone try and interfere, I'll gun 'em down."

"That's the way I want it," Jake hollered, inflamed by Steel's words. "I've been looking forward to this moment for some time. Yeah, I'm gonna kill you right now!"

You could have heard a pin drop. Everyone in the room froze.

Jake's hand went for his gun.

Two shots rang out. The gun flew out of Jake's hand and tumbled to the floor. A red bloodstain appeared on the shirtsleeve of Jake's right arm. He looked at his arm with disbelieving eyes.

Jake wasn't able to get a shot off before Steel's second bullet struck his shooting shoulder.

"I don't want to kill you, Jake, so be glad you're still alive. You come after me, and I will kill you. I'm leaving town Monday morning on the stage, and you won't ever see me again. I don't think you'll be using that gun arm for a spell." Steel turned to Red and said, "Let's go."

The two of them with guns raised slowly backed out the saloon door.

"Thanks, Red," Steel said.

"Hell! You should have kilt him! What were you thinkin'? He's a sidewinder that's gonna be back. He's going to try and ambush you for sure—and his brothers'll help him! I know it's comin'."

"I'll be careful."

Shaking his head, Red looked down. "I just hope you live until that Monday morning stage takes you out of here. Hell, Charlie's gonna be a heap mad at me if you're kilt. So is Cattie! "Let's get back to the bunkhouse and play checkers. I need a good game of checkers to calm my nerves," Red said.

"I owe you, Red. Playing checkers with you is a pretty high price to pay," Steel said with a grin.

About eleven o'clock that evening, one of the working hands came in from Nuttal's. He put his hat on the hat rack, took off his gun belt, and sat down on his bunk.

"Don't want to interrupt your game of checkers, but you're the talk of the town, Steel. The town is not only talkin' how you took care of Jake this evening, one of the men on the incoming stage is telling how you shot the guns out of the hands of two highway men trying to rob the stage and its passengers. Even though you got a hell of a reputation with a gun, they're wagering ten to two odds against you not making the Monday morning stage to Denver alive. I'd have stayed longer to see if the odds changed but got to get up real early tomorrow mornin'. Everyone I talked to said you should have kilt Jake and his two brothers—they're all weasels. Red, didn't you tell him anything?"

Red looked up from the checkerboard. "Hell! Sure, I told him. Told him a half-dozen times. He's stubborn as Hank's damn mule Butter Cup. Right now he's beatin' me in checkers, and I ain't too happy about that either."

49

Steel slept in and finally woke up groggy a little after nine. He looked over at Red's bunk and saw it was empty. "Is Red around?" Steel asked the lone working hand left in the bunkhouse.

"He left about an hour ago. You can find him at the corral. He's breaking horses this morning. He told us not to wake you up. There's coffee and some biscuits that were cooked yesterday over on the iron potbelly stove. If you want something good to eat, you'll have to go into town."

"Is Ben around?"

"Nope. He's gone too. Hell of a good shootin' last night, I hear."

"A cup of coffee and a biscuit or two will do me fine. Thanks."

"Don't thank me yet. The coffee is probably a little cold by now and the biscuits ain't that chewable."

Steel dressed quickly, downed a cup of coffee, wrapped up a couple of biscuits in his handkerchief, put them in a jacket pocket, and headed over to the corral.

Red didn't notice him when he approached the corral fencing. Steel leaned against a post and watched him with the utmost interest. He was both surprised and impressed to see how patient and soft-spoken Red was with the mustang he was breaking.

Red finally looked his way but he kept working for several more minutes. Steel watched him slowly ease a saddle onto the mustang's back. Then leading him with a hackamore, he walked him easy-like around the corral.

"Morning, Steel. I'm just about ready to tighten the cinch and climb aboard this little old mustang. She's gonna be a real fine horse. I can tell she's got a good temperament."

"Red, you certainly know what you're doing. I'm impressed. I wanted to let you know that I'm going over to the livery stable and saddle up my horse and ride out to French Creek for a spell. That is if Mr. Marks is there this morning. I guess he can tell me which way to head my horse."

"He's most likely there. It he's not, his helper will be there. I don't think you need to worry about Jake or his brothers this morning. You know rattlesnakes don't come out while it's cool. It's the warmth that brings them out, coldblooded creatures that they are. You be careful as the day warms up."

"I'll do that. Thanks, Red."

"I'm going to be breaking horses most all day today. I think I'll go into town around one. I'm planning on eating lunch at Millie's. That's a new little eatin' place, just opened up a week ago. Love to have you join me."

"I'll see you around one. If for some reason I'm not back by then, don't wait for me."

The ride out to French Creek was pleasant and relaxing. The snow had melted at the lower elevations, and the spring showers had summoned lush grasses and a variety of wildflowers. It came to Steel's mind's-eye the vast number of flowers he saw on his train ride to Laramie. *It's certainly a pretty time of the year.*

He tied up his horse and found a log to sit on where he could watch and listen to the fast-moving water that for the moment, because of the snowmelt, crested the stream bank's edge.

The screech of a red-tail hawk caught his attention. He strained his neck for a moment to watch the bird maneuver overhead. *I'm sure he's searching for a field mouse or a rabbit.* For those few moments, his cares of late melted away. It wasn't long, however, until the feelings that kept dogging his mind returned.

Cattie Winthrop… As hard as I try to remember, I don't have any recollection of her. Perhaps there's a shadow of a memory and that's what's keeping me from moving forward with Savannah. The decision to go to

Denver and meet Miss Winthrop is the right one that I'm sure of. It's too important of a blank chapter in my life to leave empty… And I'm looking forward to meeting Mr. Charlie Utter.

Steel spent a good hour at the water's edge. He thought of his father, and try as he may, the memories still remained hidden. *I'll head back and have lunch with Red, and then head up to the cemetery and say a last goodbye to my father. It looked like the blacksmith shop is closed on Sundays. My father, apparently a God-fearing man, would be happy about that.*

Millie's was a quaint little place. The sign in the window read "Breakfast or Lunch / Opens at 7:00 closes at 3:00." Red was seated at a small window table. Deadwood activity had come alive now that the afternoon hours had arrived. The mercantile store looked like it was doing a healthy business. *Probably prospectors packing up supplies for the week,* Steel thought. The warm sunshine on his face reminded him of Red's rattlesnake warning. He needed to keep a watchful eye out for Jake and his brothers.

"Sorry I'm a little late, Red," Steel said.

"No matter, I'm just glad to see you're alive and healthy. Sit down. They got the menu on the blackboard. I think it's all good."

Red spent most of their lunchtime continuing to fill in blank spaces about Mr. Utter and what he knew of Steel's life in Deadwood. "He's a pretty amazing man," Steel said.

"Yeah, he is. I better be getting back to breakin' mustangs or he won't be happy. I told him I'd have 'em all broken in by the time he returned to Deadwood."

"Do you like living in Deadwood?" Steel asked, thinking that the only reason anyone would be serious about living in a mining town like Deadwood would be for some kind of financial gain—gold or gambling winnings. Of course, there were a few enterprising people like Charlie Utter who made their money by providing services to the gold-seekers and such. Other than that, Steel couldn't fathom why anyone would want to live here.

"Most everyone is here for the gold or money they can make off people looking for gold. I like breaking horses, and Mr. Utter pays me good. I'm saving up to buy a little spread of my own in Wyoming.

I've got kinfolk there. Another three or four years. I've talked to Mr. Utter. He's not happy with Deadwood like he thought he'd be. I suspect he'll be heading back to Denver in a year or two. Right now, he's got a lot invested in this town, and this town is damn lucky to have him."

"I understand. As always, I enjoy your company, Red."

"Likewise. Hell, I know I talk too much though. You don't chew tobacco anymore."

"Did I chew tobacco?"

"Only for a very short time. I think you started after your pa was killed. I don't think you chewed more than a week or so. Bad habit, good you quit."

"Well, I'm heading up to the cemetery for an hour, and then I thought I'd come back and watch you break horses. I really do enjoy seeing how you handle them."

"Yeah, I love them horses. They're my life, and I try and communicate that to them. Except for a few people like yourself and Mr. Utter, I'd rather spend my time with a horse, and that includes talkin'. I talk to horses more than people. I'm like Hank in that regard. You don't remember, but he talks to his mules, especially Butter Cup. I'll see you at the corral a little later. Dinner this evening and a couple of checker games after?"

"That's fine," Steel said.

Steel sat down on the lone bench, knowing this was likely the last time he'd visit his father's gravesite. His gaze focused on his father's grave marker. Like the rest of the markers, it wasn't anything fancy, just a couple pieces of boards with writing on them. His heart pined, not only because his father was dead, but also because the memories of him were gone, perhaps lost forever. There was no doubt in his mind though that he loved his father.

He watched a blue jay land on his father's marker. It rested for a moment and then took flight, landing in a nearby pine tree. *Why, why can't I remember anything about him?* Steel looked at the grave marker labeled Wild Bill J. B. Hickok and remembered Red saying that he was the person who taught him how to use his Colt pistol. A couple of Deadwood folks had made similar comments. He glanced down at his holstered gun and felt a desire to learn more about Mr. Hickok.

Deep in thought, he jerked his head around when the sound of horses' hooves caught him by surprise. Two riders were almost upon him with lariats in the air.

He ducked without success. The rope burned his shoulders as it tightened. A second loop found its mark. Then with a sudden jerk, his body was pulled up off the bench. He landed on the ground with a resounding and punishing thud.

"We're taking you on a little ride and you won't need no damn horse," one of the men shouted.

Jake's brothers yelled, digging their spurs into their horses' sides as they rode side by side. Steel trailed behind them, his body twirling like a twister and bouncing like a rag doll over the uneven terrain.

I'm going to die!

Pain rippled through his whole body. All went black.

50

Steel fought to open his eyes. He tried to move his head from side to side, but bursts of pain prevented him. A woman's voice teased his brain. Consciousness only brought discomfort.

Little by little, his vision cleared until he recognized the top of an Indian teepee. After several minutes he became aware of two people standing and looking down at him. Steel squinted up at a recognizable face.

"Chatan… Chatan, what… what am I doing here? What happened to me? I don't… don't even want to try moving." His words sputtered in labored tones.

Chatan smiled. "Steel, good, you know me. I and my brothers hunted yesterday. We followed wounded elk and heard loud shouts. Saw you behind two horses with men. When they saw us they go and leave you."

"Chatan, I had a bad accident—long time ago—many moons ago. I lost my memory—Charlie, my father, I couldn't remember anyone. My memory has returned… I remember!" he exclaimed, drawing strength from this realization. "I remember! I remember you, Chatan, Charlie, my father… and Cattie! I remember Cattie! Oh, my whole body aches." His chest pained him with each breath he drew in as he struggled to express his joy. "My memory has returned, and I'm alive! I'm alive!"

"You need sleep. A few days you be fine. No broken bones, you only badly beat up. If we not come you be dead. Great Spirit likes you, Steel." Chatan smiled. "My wife, Winona, she take good care of you. When you well, you return to Deadwood. Now, sleep."

Fearful of sleep and afraid his memories might slide back into oblivion, Steel fought to keep his eyes open. Hurt and fatigue finally overcame his fear. He closed his eyes and slept.

On the third day of his stay, with bearable aches and pains, Steel walked out among the villagers. It was evident that Chatan was well respected by his people. Steel knew he was the beneficiary of that respect. Winona had been caring for and watching over him with a kind tenderness that he knew he'd never be able to repay.

Recalling the animosity between the Indians and the white man, he was surprised by the friendliness and hospitality shown him. He encountered no threats or even unkind looks while walking about the village. He had no doubt that they were aware of the white man's intrusions into their lives, yet he truly felt welcomed. He recalled the attack by the Crows on his way to Laramie and the killing of the young mail rider. *I'm fortunate to be alive and be among friendly people.*

Now that his memory had returned, Cattie was at the forefront of his thoughts. *After eight months, she surely must be asking herself if she's ever going to hear from me.* Red did say that Charlie had told him she had a good job at one of the local banks and was doing well. Going to Denver was the right thing, but he needed to keep an open mind: *There is certainly the possibility that she's moved on. And I do remember thinking that in Deadwood, I was the only frog in the pond. One thing I am certain of: I'm very much in love with Cattie.*

On the morning of Steel's departure from the Indian village, Winona placed a pair of buckskin pants and a white man's cotton shirt beside the buffalo blanket he had slept on. He took his time dressing. Even though he was much improved, the soreness was still ever-present.

Chatan brought in Steel's pistol and holster. "You need this. It is loaded," he said soberly.

"The white man's shirt?" Steel asked, wondering where that came from.

"Trade buffalo hides for some of white man's things. We make good trades. Have other good things—pots, pans, knives, good knives."

"Okay," Steel said with a nod, recalling Charlie had visited the village sometime ago and was one of the traders.

Steel strapped on his gun belt, and in doing so, that brought to mind Jake and his two brothers. *I know the stage leaves for Denver on Monday mornings. I don't know what I'll do if I meet up with them before that time, hopefully I won't. I suspect everyone thinks I'm dead. Red will be glad to see me alive. He'll have someone to play a few more games of checkers with.*

"You wait here. I go get horses. I go with you to town," Chatan said, interrupting Steel's thoughts. Chatan opened the tent flap, ducked his head, and walked out before Steel could respond.

Steel wasn't eager about Chatan accompanying him to town. He certainly didn't want to involve him with Jake and his brothers. *Hopefully, they won't be in town and I can avoid trouble. Chatan can turn around and leave as soon as he gets me to town.* He looked out over the Indian village and tried to divine what the next few days would hold. He quickly abandoned his efforts.

It wasn't long before Chatan came up the embankment riding a dark brown and white pinto. He had a buckskin pony at his side.

Chatan dismounted. Winona left a group of women and walked over to join them.

Steel turned to Winona. "Thank you, Winona, thank you, *kola,* friend," Steel said using the only Lakota word he knew. He wanted to somehow show his gratitude. An idea of how he could partially repay their kindness came to mind.

Winona smiled and nodded. "*Kola* friend," she said.

Chatan moved over to the side of the buckskin pony. He cupped his hands and motioned to Steel.

Steel put his left foot in Chatan's cupped hands and with a deep breath he shifted his weight to his left foot and threw his right leg over the horse. He winced when he landed bareback.

The buckskin shuffled its hooves. Chatan quickly calmed the horse down and handed Steel the reins.

"You all right?" Chatan asked.

"I'm all right. Riding bareback isn't going to be as easy as sitting on a nice saddle with a saddle horn to grab onto," Steel said with a smile.

Winona looked at him and smiled.

With the ease of an acrobat, Chatan threw his leg over his horse and drew himself upright. Turning to Winona, he said something in his native tongue that Steel didn't understand, and then he redirected his attention to Steel. "We go. Not fast. You follow."

As they rode out of the village, a woman, who was scraping the hairs off a stretched hide, stopped her labors and gave Steel a courtesy smile.

Steel returned the smile. *Chatan's people are good people.*

Chatan turned around. "Steel, elk we chased when found you," he said, motioning his head in the direction of the stretched out hide.

"I'm grateful for that elk running my way," Steel said, not sure if Chatan heard him. For some strange reason, he recalled his studies of George Washington and his numerous close calls with death. *Divine providence*, he thought.

It was a little after noon on a Saturday when Steel and Chatan rode their horses into Deadwood. The town was buzzing with activity. Most of the hitching rails were full and a number of buckboards were parked on the sides of the street. People meandered in and out of the mercantile store. Steel recalled that the storeowner, Mr. Nance, usually put on a couple of additional people to help handle Saturday's increased activity.

A man walking out of the store carrying an armload of goods gave Steel a startled look. Hurriedly, he put his goods in the back of his buckboard and rushed to the closest saloon, disappearing through its doors. Within moments, several men came out and gasped at Steel. Others on the street began to stop and look his way.

Chatan and Steel slowed their horses to a steady walk.

A man called out, "Steel, you're alive! Jake and his brothers are in the Bella Union Saloon right now. They rode into town about half an hour ago. Doing a little drinking and card playing, I suspect.

They've been mouthin' off about your death the last few days. Said they kilt you and fed you to the coyotes and the buzzards."

One of Charlie's hired hands approached Steel and Chatan. He put his hand up for them to stop. They reined in their horses.

"Mighty glad to see you alive, Steel. Red especially has been fretting something terrible. The whole town has been hummin' about what happened to you. Like that man said, most everyone was sure Jake and is brothers did you in. Anyway, the three of them are in the Bella. Big Jake's arm is in a sling, but he's wearin' a gun on the left side. Thought I'd best warn you."

"Thanks," Steel said and dismounted. He turned to Chatan. "I'm fine, Chatan. Go over to the livery stable and tell Mr. Marks you're to have my Indian pony. I want you to have it. Then you need to return to your village. I don't want you to get caught up in any more of my troubles. I'm going to end this thing with Jake and his brothers right now, one way or another."

Again, as in times past, Steel abandoned reason and common sense. His only thoughts were of revenge and a measure of justice. He'd given them a chance to back down, but knew his words of not wanting trouble had been for naught... His sore body confirmed as much.

At that moment, Jake and his brothers walked out of the Bella.

"I heard you were out here waiting for me," Jake yelled.

"What kind of lies have you been telling people, Jake?" Steel hollered. He glanced at Chatan. "Chatan, this is not your fight. You've only got a rifle in your scabbard and they'd kill you before you touched it. You need to go. Please, Chatan, go now!" Steel said.

"I not leave."

Steel, out of necessity, turned his full attention to Jake and his brothers.

"Looks like you're beat up pretty bad. I just bet you can't draw as fast as you used to," one of the brothers yelled.

"Well, you're going to find out," Steel said.

Jake and his brothers moved out into the middle of the street. Steel could see that Jake was in fact wearing a gun and holster on his left hip. He grinned at Steel, "I can draw from either side. Ambidextrous they call it."

"Jake, that's a mighty big word to be using for someone with such a little brain," Steel said.

People started chuckling.

Jake's face turned beet red.

Steel gingerly slipped off the Indian pony and grimaced as his feet hit the ground. He let the reins drop.

"We can see you're hurtin'. I am certainly going to kill you today," Jake yelled.

"Jake, I don't want a shootout with you and your bothers. I'm leaving on the Monday stage. So why don't the three of you just pack up and go to your place."

Jake snickered. "That ain't gonna happen."

"Steel's gonna send you to hell," an old prospector shouted.

Steel felt a familiar excitement rush through his body. He squared off against the three men. He felt no fear and the hurt disappeared. His eyes narrowed. He focused on the brothers. *Relax my right arm and aim small. One, two, three targets.*

A sizable crowd had gathered on both sides of the street, waiting to see who would live to see the sunset. Jake stood at the left of his two brothers. Steel watched him spread his feet and steady himself. His brothers looked at Steel with hard stares. *Three rattlesnakes in warm weather waiting to strike . . .*

"For the last time, Jake, walk away now. If you don't, I'm going to kill you first, Jake, and then your two brothers. I'm asking you to keep your guns holstered and go home. I don't want to kill any of you."

For a moment, Steel thought Jake would turn and leave. A nervous look crossed his face, and the bravado seemed to slip away when Steel announced that he'd be the first to die.

Jake gave a quick edgy look at his brothers.

"We'll get him before he gets you, Jake," one of the brothers said reassuringly. "And you might get him too. You're getting pretty good with that left hand."

"Let's get on with it!" Jake yelled and went for his gun.

Four shots rang out in rapid succession.

The legs of the brother closest to Jake buckled and he fell to the dirt. The next brother stood for a moment. His gun hand dropped to his side, then his grip loosened, and the gun fell onto the road. He sank slowly to the ground.

Jake stood staring at Steel, his eyes wide. He didn't utter a sound. His gun hadn't even cleared the holster. Jake's legs wobbled, and then he toppled face forward into the dirt.

Only one of his brothers had gotten off a shot, but that bullet had hit the dirt a few feet in front of him.

Three men ran forward and examined the bodies. After a moment, one looked up and yelled in astonishment, "Three dead, and it looks like they were all shot in the heart!"

A gambler standing in front of one of the saloons with a whiskey in his hand said, "I had a feeling I should have bet on Steel killing those three." He turned around and went back into the saloon.

"Chatan, it's over." Steel picked up the reins of his horse and turned his back to the three men lying in the dirt. "Let's go to the livery stable. One thing this town is good at is picking up dead bodies. I'll walk," Steel said, thinking he didn't want to get up on a horse for a while. The aches, though bearable, had returned.

Mr. Marks was out in front of the livery stable, trying to find out what all the commotion was about. He heard the shots and assumed there had been a killing. "Steel, you're alive. Most of us thought you were dead."

"And I have my memory back."

"We'll, I'll be... That is sure enough a good thing. Mighty glad to hear it," Mr. Marks said." What's all the shootin' about?"

"I'm sure the town's people will fill you in. I'm going to take my Indian pony. I just need the bridle. Mr. Marks, I'm giving you the saddle to sell, and you can keep the money. I appreciate you taking care of my horse."

"I sure would have liked that pony. What are you going to do with her?"

"Chatan saved my life. I'm giving him the pony."

"Well, I can understand that. If a man saved my life… Yes, I can understand. You know where your pony is. The bridle is hanging by the stall. Thanks for the saddle. Good luck to you Steel."

Steel looked at his pony. A momentary wish passed through his thoughts: *It would be nice to take her back to Philadelphia.* Of all the horses he'd shoed, he'd never seen one as well marked as Paint. Knowing that was impossible and glad he could do something for Chatan, he handed him the bridled. "Chatan, she's yours. She's a nice little mare and was bred by the Nez Perce Indians. She should give you some fine colts. I know you'll take good care of her. I wish you well my friend—*kola.*"

"Kola," Chatan said.

51

The stagecoach driver cracked his whip over the horses' heads. Steel glanced out the coach window as the wheels rolled out of Deadwood. He had no love for the town, and felt that if he never saw the place again, that would suit him just fine. For some strange reason, he felt that someday he'd return to Deadwood. An apparition of him standing in front of Nuttal's with a smoking gun barrel came into his mind, an image he quickly dismissed.

The shooting of Jake and his brothers had been the talk of the town. To Steel's discontent, his reputation with a gun was now legendary in Deadwood. He thought about the time, just after his father was killed, when he'd romanticized about being a gunfighter. That was no longer the case.

Before leaving town he'd given the undertaker money to make a better grave marker for his father. "One like Mr. Utter had you make for Mr. Hickok," he'd instructed.

Red had seen him off that morning. Steel had the feeling Red was breathing a sigh of relief as he watched the dust from the stagecoach settle. Red had told him that Charlie was staying at the Stanton Hotel in Denver and thought he'd be there for at least another week attending to business. "Charlie will be right glad to see you. So will Cattie and Lucy. Hell, it'll be a little like a homecomin'," Red had said. Steel didn't think homecoming was an applicable description, but that was okay.

When the stage arrived in Denver early Wednesday afternoon, Steel grabbed his satchel and went directly to the Stanton Hotel. He walked up to the desk clerk, an older man, wearing a teller's eyeshade and said, "I'm Steel Madison and would like a single room, please."

"Yes, we can certainly accommodate you, Mr. Madison. Let's see… room twenty-eight. It has a lovely window view and is one of our nicer rooms. Would you like someone to take your luggage up?"

"No thank you, I'm fine. I believe Mr. Charlie Utter is staying with you," Steel said, as he signed the hotel register.

"Yes. Mr. Utter… He's just down from you in room twenty-six."

"If he comes to the desk, please tell him that Steel Madison checked in. And if he could leave me a note as to a good time to meet him?"

"I'll be happy to do that, Mr. Madison. Here's the key to your room."

"Thanks." Steel picked up his satchel, turned and walked to the hotel stairs, thinking he was glad Charlie was still in town.

Steel stood at his bedroom window, looking down at the street but not focusing on the activities below. *Has Cattie moved on to a new relationship, thinking that because of my loss of memory that I'd never contact her? Eight months isn't a long time… but it may be an eternity to her, especially if she thinks I have no recollection of her. I don't know, I just don't know.* His thoughts swirled with hopeful optimism waning.

Physically, he felt much better now that he didn't have to endure the bumps of the stagecoach ride. A shave and a hot bath hopefully would assuage his frame of mind. After that, he needed to visit the train station and check the eastern departure schedules. His time spent in Denver would depend on how things went with Cattie—it was as simple as that.

After a bath and a shave, he returned to the hotel lobby. It was getting near the four o'clock hour and he hoped the desk clerk would have a note from Charlie.

"No, Mr. Madison, not yet. He should make an appearance any time now. It's about this time of day that I see him," the desk clerk said.

"I think I'll wait in the lobby for a spell and read your paper."

Steel walked over to a white, marble table by the window and picked up a copy of the *Rocky Mountain News*. He sat down in a large, comfortable armchair next to the window and tried to relax. The headlines, immediately caught his eye:

Jack McCall the Murderer of Wild Bill Executed.

The paper had excerpts from the *Dakotan Newspaper*. Steel's gaze went down the full-page article.

At precisely fifteen minutes after ten o'clock the trap was sprung, and with a single chocking expression "Oh God" uttered while the drop fell the body of John McCall was dangling between heaven and earth. The drop was four feet and everything having been carefully arranged there was but a brief struggle with the King of Terrors.

"Steel!"

He spun around to see Charlie standing at the front desk.

"Charlie." Steel got up quickly, newspaper in hand.

"I declare, it's great to see you. How's the memory? You recognized me! That's good." Charlie was dressed in his buckskins, his pearl-handle guns sticking out of his belt. *He's still looking like the front cover of a Western magazine,* Steel thought.

"It's back—pretty much everything."

"Glad to hear that. Hope you don't have plans for dinner. You haven't seen Cattie yet, have you?"

"Not yet. I arrived on the afternoon stage, and I have no plans for dinner."

"Good. I'm going to take you to the Western Steakhouse, the best restaurant in Denver. They have an elk steak that can't be beat. We can have dinner together and catch each other up on things. Did you come in from Deadwood?"

"Yes."

"Well, that makes sense. Any trouble there? I know Jake and his no-good brothers said some time ago that they were comin' after you if you ever showed your face in town."

"They're dead. I didn't want any trouble, and was hoping to get out of town without seeing them, but word got out. You know Deadwood. All three brothers faced me down in front of the Bella."

"You shot all three of them yellow bellies?"

"I did." Steel nodded with a grimace. "Nothing I'm proud of. I truly wanted to have avoided the gunfight. I told them in so many words I was leaving on the Monday morning stage and I didn't want any trouble."

"You shot all three..." Charlie shook his head. "Well, you did the town a service. All three were no-good hell-raisers. Anyway, I don't think you have a mind to talk about that. I suspect you're here to see Cattie."

"I am, and to say hello to you."

"Well, she is as pretty as ever and has a good position at one of the local banks."

"Red told me that. I'm glad things are going well for her."

"She and her ma are living in a charming little place close to town. You're showing up not any too soon. Lucy said a young man at the bank Cattie works at has been courtin' her with a most keen interest."

"Oh." Steel frowned, thinking his negative thoughts might be coming to fruition.

"It's been a spell now since she last saw you in Deadwood. It was when you left to tend to your ma. How's your mother doing?"

"She's fine. Pretty much completely recovered. Thanks for asking."

"Steel, I don't mean to put a damper on your thoughts, but I think you need to be prepared if things don't go as you're hoping. We were first told that Indians killed you and my mail rider. So she thought you were dead. And then later, we got word you were alive but you couldn't remember anybody—names faces, that sort of thing. So that day brought both good and bad news. I honestly don't know where her thoughts are right now. When I first arrived in Denver, she did ask about you right away. I, of course, had to tell her that I hadn't heard a word."

"I understand, and I'm in agreement with what you just said."

"Speaking of memory, I've got the rifle of Bill Hickok's you gave to me. I know you wanted me to have it."

"It's yours."

"Are you sure you want me to keep it? Give me your address in Philadelphia, and I'll have it boxed up and sent to you."

"No. I want you to keep it. I have no need for it. You were his good friend, I know Mr. Hickok would want you to have it."

"That's mighty nice of you, Steel. It does mean a lot to me. I thank you, again. Just wanted to make sure you didn't have second thoughts. You must still have that Colt pistol you fancied."

"I have it in my baggage. I still plan on shooting, a little target practice now and then. I enjoy shooting."

"Well, you're darn good at it. Killing Jake and his brothers, I'm certain your reputation in Deadwood is the gunfighter to beat."

"Gunfighter," Steel said. He looked at the floor and shook his head. "I'm finished with that, and I don't plan on returning to Deadwood. I sure don't have a desire to be a gunfighter. I suspect my mother is fine with leaving my father buried in Deadwood, so unless she wants his body returned, I have no reason to go back. Returning once was enough."

"Well, it's a dang good thing, 'cause I'm certain there'd be those coming to Deadwood just to draw against you. I've got a couple of things I need to tend to. You know, I've been thinkin' I made a mistake going to Deadwood. I believe I mentioned that before. More and more, it's been on my mind. I'll tell you about it at dinner, and I'd like your thoughts on the matter."

"Fine. Charlie, I'm looking forward to dining with you."

"I'll meet you here in the hotel lobby say at five-thirty. That's comin' up soon. We'll meet and have an early dinner, and I'll give you directions to Cattie's. It's not far from the restaurant I'm taking you to. You can go over there tonight."

"Oh, Charlie, did you read the news about the hanging of Jack McCall?" Steel asked, holding up the newspaper.

"I did, and the California collar is most welcomed news. Not a day goes by that I don't think about my good and dear friend. And Jack McCall can burn in hell!"

It was good to see Charlie… really good. Steel knew he couldn't refuse his dinner invitation even though he was anxious to see Cattie. A few more hours wouldn't make any difference, and Cattie and Lucy would most likely be eating dinner soon anyway. After he said goodbye to Charlie, he sat back down in the chair and tried to concentrate on reading the newspaper.

52

Seated at a table made of knotty pine, Steel and Charlie were surrounded by a variety of the local wildlife mounted on the restaurant's log-cabin walls. Deer, elk, moose, bobcats, and longhorn mountain sheep looked down at them with glassy eyes. A large, stuffed black bear gave unaware guests a fright as they walked through the entrance door that featured two hand-carved elk with snow-capped mountains in the background. Above the restaurant's long, highly polished wood bar hung a variety of guns, mostly rifles of various makes. The grill was open to the eating area. Two short-bearded men with handlebar mustaches, each holding a long pronged fork, were busy tending a variety of sizzling steaks and chicken breasts. The aroma of the steaks wafted through the air.

"It was right fine havin' dinner together," Charlie said after swallowing the last of the coffee from his mug. "I can see you're chompin' at the bit to see Cattie. Can't blame you, and I apologize for gabbin' so much of your time. I'm not going to keep you a minute longer, except to tell you how to get to Cattie's. Oh, I'm lookin' forward to breakfast with you tomorrow mornin' to hear how you fared. Say eight-thirty? I'll meet you in the lobby."

"I'll look forward to it, and you were right, that was a mighty fine steak. Thanks for dinner." Steel stood and pushed his chair in. "I enjoyed the food and the company."

"Likewise." Charlie tipped his head and then gave Steel directions to Cattie's house.

Steel left him smiling with a sizable piece of blackberry pie in front of him. He'd enjoyed having dinner with Charlie, but the man did like to gab and Steel was anxious to see Cattie. He would have left a half-hour earlier, but leaving a little later than he wanted wasn't the end of the world, and he wasn't about to be rude to Charlie.

Cattie and Lucy's little place was no more than a fast fifteen-minute walk from the restaurant. As Steel drew near, his footsteps slowed with an uneasiness he was unaccustomed to. The moon was just rising out of the east and was at his back. He felt a soft breeze on the nape of his neck. He turned the corner around a grouping of pine trees and stopped in his tracks.

The moon spotlighted Cattie standing on the front porch of a small cottage with a man facing her. Steel slipped behind the trunk of a large pine tree. The man reached out and took hold of her hand.

Steel's thoughts started to spin: *I'm not about to interrupt them—I assume he's the person at the bank that Charlie mentioned—maybe he's getting ready to leave… I'll wait and watch for a moment, feeling like an interloper.* A shroud of forlorn came over him.

The man leaned down, drew Cattie close and kissed her. It wasn't a long passionate kiss, but it wasn't a chaste kiss on the cheek either. Cattie took a small step back and they continued to converse. Steel wasn't able to hear their words, nor did he want to, feeling that would be an unwarranted intrusion into their privacy.

She's moved on, and I'm not about to cause her any more hurt than I have. I'll always love her… but I've lost her! Even knowing he'd lectured himself about this very possibility, this reality was so much harsher than supposition.

He stood there for several moments more, confirming in his mind that she had in fact moved on with her life. *I'll leave for Philadelphia first thing tomorrow morning… Perhaps I should become a gun fighter, my world without her is meaningless.* He dismissed his foolish thought born of frustration and hurt, turned toward town, and took his time walking dejectedly back to the hotel.

53

Steel was up early, feeling the agony of last night's revelation. He dressed quickly and went downstairs to the hotel lobby. The sooner he was on the train leaving Denver the better he felt he'd like it.

Steel surmised that Charlie had gotten up early that morning, getting a start on the day with a shave and his ritual hair wash. The way Steel was feeling, he preferred not talking to Charlie or anyone else for that matter… He just wanted to leave town.

"Do you know if Mr. Utter has left yet this morning?" Steel asked the desk clerk.

"He left about half an hour ago. Always leaves at that time. I can set my watch by him," the desk clerk said.

In order to catch the early morning train out of Denver, Steel needed to forgo breakfast with Charlie. He left him a note thanking him for everything, and asked him to look him up if he were ever in Philadelphia, noting his address. Then Steel added a PS: "*Please, don't tell Cattie I was in town. She's happy, and it's the best for the both of us that she doesn't know I stopped by her place. She's found someone else, and I don't want to cause her anymore hurt. Thank you for respecting my wishes in this matter.*"

The train trip back to Philadelphia was a forlorn journey, to say the least; it did however provide Steel with sole searching time to try and settle down his emotions and put in order some plans for the future.

He knew it wouldn't be fair to Savannah to ask her to marry him, and he didn't want her to hold false hopes in that regard.

Accordingly, one of his first priorities when he got home would be to sit down with her and explain what took place in Deadwood. *I'm hopeful that we can remain friends as I do care for her and value her friendship.*

He needed to tell his mother about Cattie, which would help her understand why things wouldn't work out with Savannah. Even though she had a fondness for Savannah, he was hopeful she'd understand and not try to push their relationship any further.

He'd continue to work for his grandfather. He enjoyed the work, and he knew it meant a great deal to him having him close by learning the business. And if he felt like a little blacksmith work, he had a standing invitation to help out at the blacksmith shop across town.

He'd certainly continue to hone his abilities with his Colt pistol. Would he ever again face a life and death situation that would call on his expertize with the Colt? He thought not.

Perhaps someday he would return to Deadwood to bring back his father's body. He'd discuss that again with his mother at an appropriate time, as she could come to want his body returned to Philadelphia so she could be interred near him.

Steel looked out the passenger car window as the train approached the outskirts of Philadelphia. A shrill, train whistle announced the soon to be arrival. He reached for the satchel by his side and put in a newspaper he'd purchased on the train. He recalled that Cattie had his bamboo fly rod. *Perhaps she'll think of me now and then if she goes fishing… I need to find a fine piece of bamboo and make myself another fly rod. And I need to write Mr. Orvis and purchase a fishing reel.*

The train pulled into the station mid-afternoon. Steel hired a carriage driver to take him to his grandparents' home.

"Thirty-two Baldwin Heights."

Steel walked up the steps and rang the bell, thinking the positive of the trip was regaining his memory. He knew his mother, his grandparents, and Hanna would be happy to know his memories had returned.

"Why Mr. Steel, you're lookin' so fine and handsome. You don't need to ring the doorbell. This is your home," Hanna said. "Your mama, grandfather and grandma are gonna be so glad to see you're back home safe and sound. Your mama, she's upstairs taking her afternoon nap. She's doing real fine. I do declare, you're looking as handsome as ever."

"Thanks Hanna. It's good to see you, and it's good to be home. I've got my memory back."

"Goodness gracious, that sure is a fine thing. We'll all be happy for that, especially your mama. I do have to tell you Miss Savannah left for Georgia not long after you left. We sure do miss her something terrible."

"Before I left, she mentioned she might return to Georgia while I was away. I'm going upstairs to wake up my mother."

"Just leave your traveling bag, and I'll take it to your room."

"Thanks, Hanna, but I'll take it up," Steel said with a warm smile.

Hanna returned the smile. "You get upstairs now."

Steel knocked lightly on his mother's bedroom door, opened it slowly and entered the room.

Elizabeth peeked out over the bedcover opening her eyes wide. "Why, Steel, you're home! I've been worrying about you. Savannah left for Georgia. You need to go after her. We all miss her."

Steel went over and kissed his mother's forehead.

"I've got my memory back."

"Oh, Steel, I'm so glad, if for nothing else you know I'm your mother. Come, sit on the bed and tell me about your trip. What did you find out about your father?" she asked the joy in her voice fading.

"I'm sorry, Mother, but he was killed while he was panning for gold. He was shot in the back. There's a lot of killing in Deadwood. It's a lawless town."

"My gracious. I've had the strongest feeling for some time now that something bad happened to him. Did they find out who did it?"

"Yes, and he's dead. He was shot too," Steel said, wanting to keep it at that.

"And you buried your father?"

"Yes. I wanted to talk to you about that. If you want, I can return to Deadwood and bring his body back."

"No! I don't want you going back to that Godforsaken place. I loved your father dearly. He was a good man, provided a good living for us and brought you up right. You know, he always wanted to go out West, and I think he'd be happy to be buried in Deadwood."

Steel thought, it was a good thing his mother had no idea what Deadwood was really like. His father, being a religious man, wanted no part of Deadwood except panning for gold.

"Well, let's talk about more pleasant things. You've got your memory back. How did that happen?"

"I was in an accident. Hit my head a second time. An Indian by the name of Chatan and his wife, Winona, took care of me. It had to have been the blow on the head that did it. I remember the doctor in Laramie said my memory could come back at any time or it might be gone forever. Anyway, it's back."

"What are your plans now?"

"To continue to work with Grandfather. I really do enjoy working for him. Oh, I do need to find a place of my own."

"No need to get in a rush in that regard. Your grandfather missed you a great deal. I know that he'll be happy to see you."

"I missed him, I missed all of you." He looked at his mother tenderly.

"What about Savannah?"

"While I was first in Deadwood, I met a girl. Her name is Cattie. Actually, she and her mother were on the wagon train with us when we left Denver for Deadwood. I got to know her. She has a law degree from the South—William and Mary in Virginia. I'll tell you her story later. The short of it is, I fell in love with her."

"And?"

"She and her mother returned to Denver. She has a good job at a bank there and is seeing someone else. I'm still very much in love with her and that's why it wouldn't be fair to Savannah to pursue that relationship. I know how much everyone here loves Savannah, but I have to be honest with her and you."

"I'm so sorry, Steel," Elizabeth said, reaching out and taking his hand. "I want you to know that even though I'm very fond of Savannah and miss her, whomever you choose to be your wife I'll love. I wouldn't want you to marry someone because of me. You say Cattie has a law degree? Quite remarkable. Your grandfather would certainly be impressed."

"And she has my bamboo fly rod," Steel said with a chuckle. "She likes to fly fish. I need to make another fly rod."

"She likes to fly fish? That explains a lot. Steel, time will heal that wound and maybe you might want to reconsider Savannah a little later on. Only thing I know is she's at an age that she wants to marry; there's going to be someone coming along for her sooner or later, and as pretty as she is, I expect it to be sooner."

"I like Savannah and wish her nothing but the best, but right now…"

"I won't say any more about Savannah, except we did grow to love her, and she was sure good to me. I miss our walks to the park together. My heart goes out to you, Steel. The best thing now is to get busy and get your mind on other things."

"You're right. I'm not going to mope around." He picked up a picture of his mother and father off his mother's nightstand. He looked at it for a long moment and then set it back down. "I love you, and it's good to be back home."

"I love you, too. I'm going to get up now, and you can walk me to the park before it gets dark, and then we'll have dinner."

"I'd enjoy that."

That night Steel penned a letter to Savannah and wished her well. It was a hard letter to write because he knew it would be the end of their relationship. He did like Savannah a great deal, but he knew he was doing the right thing. On Saturday he'd find a nice piece of bamboo and start making another fly rod.

I can't help not thinking about Cattie. She became so much a part of my life… my hopes, my dreams…

He slept.

54

Steel's grandfather had a carriage pick them up at the house at eight-thirty sharp weekday mornings. Steel was dropped off at the William's Department Store, and his grandfather went to his office location not far from the store. This morning, his grandfather told the driver to go directly to his office. "You won't be leaving Steel off at the store anymore. From now on, he'll be working with me at my office."

Steel gave his grandfather a staggered look. His grandfather had told him he wanted him to learn all aspects of the business. Steel had done just about everything in the store from marking merchandise to selling it. He got along well with the other employees and never tried to use his position as the owner's grandson to his advantage. Everyone knew his grandfather was a fair-minded man, but they also knew the reality that someday, in the not too far future, they would be answering to Steel.

A large mahogany desk separated Steel and his grandfather.

"Steel, please sit down," his grandfather said as he seated himself. "You've done a good job, a very good job. You've worked hard. You're likable and willing to do any job without complaining. I must admit, your father trained you well. You've completed your college education with a business degree. Now I want you to work in the office with me. You'll have your own office next to mine. There's a nice desk there, ready for you. Effective today, I'm making you my vice president."

Steel looked at his grandfather, dumbfounded by his pronouncement.

"My health isn't what it used to be," he continued. "My doctor insists that I cut my work schedule, so I want our employees to start looking to you. It won't be easy, but you're used to hard work."

His grandfather had always seemed in the best of health. To Steel's knowledge, he'd rarely missed a day of work, so this news came as a disheartening surprise. "I don't know what to say. I'll do my best not to let you down."

"We never quite do our best, grandson. As we go along, we can always do a little better, but I appreciate your attitude. As I said, your father taught you well, and I regret now that I didn't treat him better. It is something I have to live with."

Knowing the unfavorable feelings that had existed between his father and grandfather, Steel said nothing, but it was comforting to know of his grandfather's penitent spirit.

"Another thing. We were all hopeful you'd marry Savannah. Your mother told me about the young lady you met while you were gone. Knowing you, I'm sure she's a special girl. I'm sorry things didn't work out. The only advice I can give in that regard is to be patient. Remember, patience is a virtue. Life has taught me that."

"I don't know what to say, except thank you, and I'll try not to disappoint you."

"You won't disappoint me, that I'm sure of. Take a look at your office, and then in about fifteen minutes, come back to my office. This morning, we'll review the monthly profit and loss statements for the three stores. One of our most important jobs is determining what's selling and what's not. Next week, I want to take you to the Boston and to the New York stores."

"I look forward to that," Steel said, getting up out of the chair.

55

After a productive day, Steel and his grandfather arrived home at a little after six that evening. His grandfather had kept him busy, but it was an enjoyable busy. Thoughts of Cattie seemed to always be in the back of his mind, and he thought about Charlie, Red, Hank, and his mules, and Lucy's good cooking. He realized all his memories of Deadwood weren't bad memories.

To his surprise, his mother met them at the door. She kissed his grandfather on the cheek.

"Hello, Father, I hope you and Steel had a good day at the office." She gave them both a hint of a smile.

"We had a fine day, Elizabeth. You can be proud of that boy of yours. He's learning faster than I expected."

She turned to Steel. He was expecting a kiss on the cheek. "Steel, I've just had a charming visit with a delightful young lady. She's waiting in the parlor to speak with you. I warn you, she's most unhappy with you." There was a twinkle in his mother's eye and a playful tone in her voice that puzzled him.

"Don't keep the young lady waiting," his grandfather said, placing his silver-handle cane by the door.

Steel looked at his mother with raised brows. "Savannah?" he whispered.

"Steel, don't keep the young lady waiting," his mother said, her tone turning serious.

Not knowing what to think, Steel looked at his grandfather and shrugged before proceeding to go the parlor room.

His curiosity at a peak, he entered the room. The young lady was sitting in a chair with her back to him. She appeared to be looking out the window. His heart almost stopped. Long black hair… It couldn't be… He was afraid to say her name.

She stood up and turned to face him.

"Cattie!" he exclaimed, not believing his eyes. "It's really you. Cattie, how… What are you doing here?"

"Steel." She frowned. "Charlie said you went to see me, but you didn't see me, and left him a note saying not to tell me you were in town! What was that all about?" she asked firmly, tightening her lips.

"Yes… yes, I came to see you… You were on the porch with a good-looking young man. He was holding your hand—kissing, I thought."

"You thought what? I was in love with him or something?"

"Yes, and I didn't…"

"I just happened to have told him that evening that I was still very much in love with someone else by the name of Steel. I'd told him about you before. He invited me to several social events and walked me home a few times, and that was a mistake on my part. I've never stopped loving you, Steel. I knew if you were alive and well, you'd return to Deadwood and find out where I was living. You did tell Charlie you loved me?"

Steel grinned. "Did I tell Charlie that?" He purposely let a moment pass and then asked, "Cattie, will you marry me?"

Steel's mother peeked her head around the corner and smiled at Cattie.

"Oh, yes, yes, Steel." She walked into his arms.

Returning to Deadwood was definitely the right decision… I've got Cattie back in my life!

The End

ABOUT THE AUTHOR

PAUL HENRY JOHNSON IS a corporate business transaction attorney. He resides in Southern California with his wife, daughter, and two grandchildren. He's paring down his legal practice, writing more. This is his second novel, switching from adventure *(Scrolls of Darkness)* to Western. He has always loved Western movies and has immensely enjoyed the time and historical research he's put into this novel.

CPSIA information can be obtained
at www.ICGtesting.com
Printed in the USA
FSHW01n0800160918
52321FS

9 781633 386594